NO TIME FOR SORROW

A DCI Will Blake Novel

J. E. Mayhew

Obolus Books

ISBN-13: 978-1-9998407-3-0

Cover design by:Meg Jolly
Cover photo by Dave Mort

To Julie Rees, avid fan and old friend!

Although the story is set on the Wirral, the names of some establishments and roads have been fictionalised to protect the unloved and godless...
but you can have fun guessing...

The busy bee has no time for sorrow.

Proverbs of Heaven and Hell
by William Blake

CHAPTER 1

It wasn't a rock, as Ella Rogers had first thought. Galloping along the beach at West Kirby was exhilarating; the thunder of hooves, the churned-up circles of wet sand behind; the sky, wide and blue, stretching out above her, but it required a level of vigilance, too; one pit in the ground or mud pool and it could be game over. So she'd noticed the object poking out of the sand from a fair distance away. The sky was clear blue and it was too early for anyone but the most dedicated dog-walkers to be about. Gulls wheeled above her and Ella revelled in the smell of the sea and the wind in her hair. It was going to be a beautiful summer day.

Or at least that's what Ella had hoped.

Hilbre Island stretched out to her right, a destination for many day-trippers when the tide was out but Ella was enjoying cantering in ever tightening circles. Soon, once she was happy the path ahead was just smooth sand, she'd give Bullseye his head again but she needed to check out that object. As she drew nearer, she thought it might be a half-deflated beach ball, but it had some kind of wispy material stuck to it.

She pulled Bullseye up and he snorted and

twitched, picking up on her nerves. Inching him forward, her heart thumping, she squinted hard at it. It looked like some kind of Hallowe'en mask, the skin red and raw, stuck in the sand. The tongue, swollen and blue poked from its blistered mouth and a small crab scuttled out. Its eyes were screwed up in eternal agony and strands of hair clung to the blotchy scalp.

Ella caught her breath. Slowly a horrible realisation dawned on her.

Bile rose in her throat, blocking a scream that surely would have come. That was no mask. It was a head. A human head.

Blind to the danger, not looking for pits in the sand or stray rocks, Ella urged Bullseye into a full gallop. Sand sprayed up from the horse's hooves as he powered across the sands, towards the shore and help. But in reality, Ella didn't care where she was headed. In that moment of blind panic, it didn't matter as long as she was far away from that hideous gargoyle face.

CHAPTER 2

DCI Will Blake couldn't decide if it was the fact that the woman was staring across his garden and into his living room that was disturbing or if it was her expression. There was an intensity to it that he didn't like. He could only see her head and shoulders above the hedge but that was enough. Her mouth was set in a thin line and her eyes seemed to bulge. The warm breeze that blew up off the River Mersey ruffled her lank brown hair. Her thin face looked pale and strained. Blake thought she was trying to make a decision of some kind.

It would have been odd enough if Blake had lived on any typical suburban street but he lived in Rock Park, a small pocket of large Victorian villas right on the banks of the Mersey and cut off from the rest of Rock Ferry by a busy dual carriageway. Strangers didn't just wander down here first thing in the morning, as a rule. They came here for a reason.

The long jetty that poked out into the Mersey not far from Blake's house sometimes drew desperate souls looking to end it all. Some succeeded, others found themselves trapped on the slimy structure and ended up crying out for help. Others misjudged the tides and found themselves looking down on grey mud with a look of betrayal in their eyes. But this woman wasn't a potential suicide as far as Blake could tell.

It was strange too because she just appeared from behind the hedge. Blake hadn't seen her walk past and stop there. She just stood up, as though she'd been squatting behind it. She must have been down there for a while because Blake had been staring absentmindedly out of the front room window for some time, shovelling porridge into his mouth and mapping out his day. Surely she hadn't crawled along the road.

Blake was just about to go to his front door and confront the woman, when Serafina, his Persian cat, burst out from the hedge and padded across the front lawn, her tail in the air. The woman noticed Blake standing at the window and walked on quickly. Serafina's plaintive meow filtered through the windows. She had spotted Blake and wanted to come in through the front door, even though there was a perfectly good cat flap at the back. Blake hurried to the front door and out into the garden, but the woman had gone. She looked familiar but Blake couldn't place her.

Serafina tangled herself around Blake's ankles and Charlie, his Jack Russell terrier scampered out to relieve himself on the grass. "It's time for breakfast, then, is it?" Charlie bounced around and yapped at Blake while Serafina gave him a disdainful blink, licked her lips and sauntered in through the open front door. "I'll take that as a 'yes' then."

As Blake reached the kitchen, his phone rang. "Sir?" DS Vikki Chinn said, she sounded breathless. "You better get over to West Kirby..."

"Bad one, Vikki?"

"Horrible, sir. Just horrible."

*****

West Kirby sat on the north-western corner of the Wirral Peninsula and looked out over the sands that swept out across the Dee Estuary. A magnet for yachtsmen, windsurfers and kayakers, the seaside town boasted a marina and a long promenade. Hilbre island drew visitors and walkers exploring the northern coast. The island was something of a novelty, being accessible by foot when the tide was out. It had a long history, involving smugglers, pirates and revenue men. Local storytellers loved regaling the public with tales of the Wirral's dark, criminal past.

Despite the ever-encroaching marsh grass, there was still plenty of sand for families and gangs of youths to play on. The variety in landscapes within the peninsula never ceased to amaze Blake. Blake's view where he lived on the banks of the Mersey was so different and urban to the one he drove into at West Kirby. The gulls still screamed as they did on his side of the Wirral but here, the sky stretched on forever over the distant Welsh coast and the Clwydian hills.

Blake drove to the end of the South Parade where the road and the seawall curved right to avoid the sands. On this corner, a number of police vans huddled together. He tucked himself beside one of the CSI vehicles. They had cordoned off the steps down to the beach and blocked the road. Way in the distance across the sands, almost lost on the horizon, he could just see a group of small figures dressed in white moving about. The smell of the sea was so strong here, too. It was clear and bright, a sure sign of a lovely day ahead but Blake shuddered in the cool breeze that played across the estuary as he got out of the car. "Shit," Blake muttered to himself looking over at Hilbre Island. This part of the Wirral brought back too many bad memories.

"Morning, Will," Malachy O'Hare said, appearing beside him from one of the vans and startling Blake out of his dark thoughts. Malachy was a Senior Crime Scene Investigator and often oversaw his team, especially at serious incidents. He was a dour-looking man with a white beard and bushy eyebrows.

"Jeez, Malachy, you almost gave me a heart attack. What's going on?"

"It's the annual CSI trip to the seaside, Will, fancy an ice cream?" O'Hare said, grinning. "Last one in the water is a rotten egg."

"Very funny, Malachy, I'll have a ninety-nine once you've told me what we're dealing with. Your treat."

Malachy patted the sides of his white coveralls. "Sorry, mate, no pockets on this. Left my wallet at home. Pity, I could do with a cool down; I'm sweating like a pig at a hog roast. They should have a summer version of these. Shorts maybe..."

"Malachy..."

"Okay, okay. We've got a body out there."

"Suspicious?"

"Buried up to his neck in mud, feet bound together with rope. So no, probably a total accident, Will," Malachy said, giving Blake a sidelong glance.

"Jeez. Any ID?"

"Not that we know of..."

"Who found the body?"

"Some poor girl on a horse out for an early morning ride."

"Gives the dog-walkers a rest, I suppose," Blake muttered.

"We've got guys from the RNLI helping us retrieve the body and we'll know more, hopefully. Everyone will be over here soon..."

Blake frowned. "What about preserving the crime scene, Malachy? There must be footprints or…"

"Well, the tide's coming in fast, Will and as clever as us CSIs are, we can't do a King Canute and hold the sea back. Besides, there's a lot of paperwork when one of us drowns."

"Ah," Blake said. "Right. Yes. I'll head over quickly, then."

Malachy pointed to a dark-haired, suntanned character leaning against an RNLI Land Rover. He looked like a male model, posing for a casual beachwear advertisement. "You could ask Don Juan there to give you a lift in his Landy. To be honest, he's been posing like something out of Baywatch since we arrived and hasn't lifted a finger."

Blake nodded and approached the character and flashed his warrant card. "Excuse me, I wonder if you could run me over to the crime scene."

The man's smooth brow and perfectly plucked eyebrows puckered in confusion for a second and then he broke into a broad, white smile. "Sí," he said, the Spanish taking Blake unawares for a second. "I can take you over. Let's go."

As the ramp down onto the beach was back along the promenade, they had to drive through the growing crowds that gathered on the sands. Blake gripped the door handle with white knuckles as the man roared along the road and down the ramp, beeping his horn to move people. "Can you slow down, please?" Blake said. "I don't want a member of the public ending up crushed. I didn't catch your name, anyway."

The young man gave Blake another pearly grin and looked at Blake. "My name is Rio Pecina."

"Just look where you're going, Rio," Blake said, wincing as the Land Rover hurtled across the sands. "You been with the lifeboats long?"

"I've just started. Normally, I'm a personal trainer but I like the variety. It's great fun. Did you know they have a hovercraft?"

"Yeah," Blake muttered glancing at Hilbre Island as it came closer. "Yeah, I did." He wished he was on it now, the way Rio careened across the sands.

"This is a bad business," Rio said, his brow puckering slightly once again. "Do you know who the man is?"

Blake shook his head. "I don't, and anything you hear at the crime scene should not be repeated anywhere else, do you understand?"

"Oh, Sí, Sí. I understand," Rio said. He slammed on the brakes as they rounded behind the islands, sending spray and silt everywhere. Blake slapped his hand on the dash in front of him and felt his seatbelt snag his shoulder. "Here we are," Rio said, grinning.

"Right," Blake said, not disguising the relief in

his voice as he climbed out. “Thanks, Rio. Can you wait here to bring any of my team back?”

Rio gave Blake an enthusiastic thumbs up.

The ground beneath his feet was soft and wet and Blake wished he'd worn the boots he always carried in his car. Out here, West Kirby seemed miles away and gulls swooped over them, checking for any scraps of food that might be on offer. He could hear the waves swishing across the sand, drawing ever nearer.

A group of men in orange waterproofs and white helmets pulled a stretcher towards their waiting Land Rover. Blake could see a bagged body on the stretcher. Two crime scene investigators dressed in white followed alongside. A deep hole where the body had been was already filling with water. A couple of police officers stood holding blue and white tape, looking a little lost against the vast backdrop of the beach, the Welsh coast and the ever encroaching Irish Sea.

Detective Sergeant Vikki Chinn hurried over to Blake, pulling her face mask down. She looked pale. “Vikki, you okay?” Blake asked.

“Yes, sir. Just not the kind of thing you want to see first thing,” she said, leading him over to the hole. Blake could feel the mud shifting under his feet. “Male, possibly in his fifties or sixties. He was up to his neck in that mud, sir, ankles bound and left for the tide to wash over him. Who would do that to another human being?"

"I dunno, Vikki," Blake said. "Not a nice way to go, that's for sure. Can I see the body?"

"We need to get off the sands," Vikki said. "The tide's coming in quickly, sir."

"Fair enough" Blake said. "I've got my own transport. Fancy a lift?"

Rio gave Vikki a wave and a dazzling smile. "I might take you up on that, sir," Vikki said. "Bagsy I sit in the front."

Blake rolled his eyes and held the door open for her. Rio said something in Spanish that Blake didn't catch but was surprised to hear Vikki reply in kind. With a snort, he climbed into the back.

"You speak Spanish?" Rio said.

"A little," Vikki said.

"How about Galician?"

Vikki laughed. "No, sorry. How long have you lived on the Wirral?"

"Two or three years," Rio said, smiling at her. "It's the climate that I love most…"

Vikki giggled and Blake found himself rolling his eyes again.

"Any clues at all, Vikki?" Blake said.

"Oh," Vikki said, pulling her attention away

from Rio. "Not really, sir. The sand was clean of tracks, so we're assuming the victim was drowned last night in the last high tide. The only real evidence we have will be on the body itself and the rope around the ankles."

They thundered across the beach again, Blake wincing as they approached the crowds of people rubbernecking around the ramp. "Do you have a photo of the victim, Vikki?"

"Yes, sir," she said, passing the camera over.

Blake clicked it on and stared at the images. The face was mottled by the seawater, but it hadn't been in there long enough for it to begin to decay. Grey hair plastered the scalp; some had dried in the breeze and stood up in curly wisps. His mouth hung open, crusted with sea salt and sand, but Blake knew the face straight away. "My God, Vikki, that's Harry Thorpe."

CHAPTER 3

The Major Incident Room buzzed with the news of Harry Thorpe's death. Given that the crime scene was underwater and all possible evidence from it had been extracted, Blake decided to work from Liverpool HQ. Now he sat in the room, staring grimly at a photograph of Harry Thorpe. DS Vikki Chinn and DC Alex Manikas sat alongside DI Kath Cryer and DC Andrew Kinnear. A number of uniformed officers sat behind them. Everyone was glad of the air-conditioning as Liverpool baked in the hot sun.

"Okay, people," Blake said, deciding not to clap his hands as he often caught himself doing. Despite his years of experience, he always felt self-conscious addressing his peers. The clapping had always been an unconscious way of getting attention but he was aware it made him seem like a primary school teacher. "The body hasn't been officially identified yet but, unless he has a twin, it's Harry Thorpe," Blake said, pinning up a photograph of a stocky man with white, slicked back hair and tanned skin. He looked every inch the self-made man: confident, cocky even as he stared into the camera. But his eyes were hard and steely, offering no quarter. "Businessman and entrepreneur involved in some very dubious ventures. If you recall, we investigated his son's involvement in an alleged murder last year."

"Didn't his son change his name to Thor Magnussen, sir?" Kinnear said. "He ran the biker gang, The Sons of Sol."

"Yes," Blake said. "I think his original name was Fabian. Alex investigated our friend Thor, as I recall."

Alex shifted in his seat. "Yeah," he said, reddening. "He was working in one of his father's betting shops, giving out illegal loans to desperate punters as I recall. Never proved it, though. Thorpe and Magnussen walked away from the lot."

"Harry Thorpe was a nasty piece of work, though," DI Kath Cryer said. "He was suspected of all kinds of wickedness, wasn't he? Money laundering, drug trafficking, extortion, even murder."

"He was, Kath," Blake said. "So there's probably a long list of people who would be happy to make a sandcastle out of him."

"But only a small list of people brave or stupid enough to attempt it, sir," Vikki added.

Blake nodded. "That's true, Vikki. You'd have to have balls of steel to have a go at Harry Thorpe. But someone did." He pinned up the photograph of Thorpe after he'd been dragged from the mud, wet and dead. "And they went to a huge amount of effort, too."

"What are you thinking, sir?" Kath Cryer said. "Underworld rivals?"

"It's possible, Kath," Blake said. "I mean, whoever did this knew he'd be found. It seems like a statement."

Vikki looked thoughtful. "Somebody must have seen whoever it was that planted him in the sand. Plus, you'd need time and maybe even equipment to bury him like that..."

"And probably another person to carry Thorpe?" Kath Cryer said.

"A knowledge of the tides, too," Kinnear said. "You'd have to get him there as close to when the tide comes in as possible to minimise the chances of him being rescued."

"Fair point, Andrew," Blake said. "Can you check the tides for the last forty-eight hours? That'll give us some kind of timeframe for the murder. The rope around Thorpe's feet might give us some idea of who did this. As soon as anything comes from forensics on the rope, let me know."

"I'll organise a door to door, sir," Vikki Chinn said

"Thanks, Vikki? And maybe a request for witnesses," Blake said. "There must have been someone out on the beach, whatever the time. Is night fishing a thing round there? I dunno."

"Did Thorpe have a mobile on him, sir? Want me to chase that up?" Kath said.

"It wasn't on his person, sir," Vikki said.

"I need to go and see Mrs Thorpe, so I'll ask her about it. If we can get a number, maybe we can locate it. Could you look into Thorpe's business dealings?" Blake said. "He had a couple of betting shops and rented out a few properties. See if that throws anything up." Blake looked over at Alex Manikas, who stared out of the window. "Are you okay, Alex?"

Alex almost leapt to his feet. "Sorry, sir, miles away. What d'you want me to do?"

"Pay attention for a kick-off," Blake said. "Any thoughts on the actual case before I allocate you a task?"

Manikas looked thoughtful. "Wasn't there a DI who was accused of planting evidence on Thorpe a few years back? Or did I imagine that?"

"Glad to have you back in the room, Alex," Blake said, smiling. "Good point. DI Nigel Clements. He was investigating Thorpe about three or four years ago. Thorpe successfully sued Merseyside Police because of Clements. He was dismissed."

"Would he murder Thorpe for that, though, sir?" Kath Cryer said, folding her arms. "I mean, it seems a bit farfetched."

Blake shrugged. "It's very unlikely, Kath, I'll grant you, but Clements was never as pure as the driven snow, and we all know he had something of a vendetta against Thorpe. Off the top of my head, I can think of three occasions when Clements reported Thorpe for illegal parking alone."

"PC Robertson told me that Clements had spoken to him about Thorpe dropping litter in Heswall car park last week, sir," Kinnear said. "It's a wonder Thorpe didn't make a complaint about low-level harassment; Clements must have been following him around."

"True, Andrew. I'm sure Clements will have an alibi but we need to explore every avenue. Alex, you go and have a word with him, okay?"

"Will do, sir," Alex said, looking decidedly relieved for some reason.

"I doubt he'll come here to chat with us, so take Kinnear with you. I'm not sure how friendly Clements will be," Blake said. "I'll go and meet Tasha Cook at the Thorpes'."

*****

The journey over to Nigel Clements' house was quiet. Kinnear had found the disgraced inspector's address and was interested to learn that he only lived down the road from the crime scene in Heswall. Manikas followed Kinnear like a robot, sliding into the passenger seat of the police car without even objecting. Normally he would insist on taking the wheel. They set off, sinking into the cool twilight of the Mersey Tunnel.

“You okay, Alex?” Kinnear said as they emerged in Birkenhead. “You’ve been so quiet. Is something up?”

Alex shrugged. “It’s nothing. Just the case, that’s all.”

“Yeah. It’s a bit grim, isn’t it? Imagine being buried like that. What a way to go.”

“Buried?” Alex said, his voice shaky. “What do you mean by that?”

“Thorpe, of course. He was buried up to his neck, wasn’t he? You’re away with the fairies, mate. You sure nothing’s wrong?”

“Everything’s fine,” Manikas said, staring out of the window at the passing buildings. “I’m fine.”

Kinnear glanced at him but only saw the back of his head and couldn’t gauge his expression. “Good, because we need to be on our toes for this Clements character,” Kinnear said. “I don’t suppose he has any love for his old employer. Couldn’t expect him to, though. Imagine the disgrace…”

“Fuck’s sake,” Alex hissed and put his face in his hands.

Kinnear pulled the car into a bus stop lay-by, causing a car behind to blare its horn. “What is your problem, Alex?" he snapped. "You've been like this all day..."

"Like what?"

"Surly, snappy and distracted. What's going on?"

"Nothing," Alex muttered. "I'm sorry, mate. I'm just feeling a bit off, I suppose..."

"Are you ill?"

Alex shrugged. "I dunno. Just a bit down, I guess. I'll buck up. Just don't go on about Thorpe that's all."

"Okay, then, but it'll be a bit hard, given that's why we're going to interview Clements," Kinnear said and started the car again, pulling out into the traffic again. He wasn't convinced by Alex's explanation. It was too vague. Maybe the sight of Thorpe's body had upset him. Kinnear wondered what that said about his own reaction to the drowned man. He felt detached from it. Thorpe was a criminal anyway. In all likelihood, he brought it on himself. Not that he deserved to die but rather that than an innocent member of the public. There was no time to feel sorry for Thorpe but Kinnear couldn't help wondering why Alex had reacted so strangely to the news of Thorpe's death.

*****

DI Kath Cryer had hung back when the others

had scurried off to start the investigation. When she was certain that they had all gone, she sidled up to Blake who stood with his hands in his pockets, deep in thought. “You okay, sir?” she said.

Blake blinked at her. “Yeah, Kath, I’m fine. Why do you ask?”

“It’s just that, I couldn’t help thinking of the obvious suspect if we’re talking about Thorpe’s rivals, sir.”

“I know, Kath. It had crossed my mind,” Blake sighed.

“Kyle Quinlan stole a lot of money from Harry Thorpe. He wouldn’t let that lie, especially when Quinlan returned to the Wirral with such a fanfare. I mean, he’s been rubbing Thorpe’s nose in it, hasn’t he?”

“He has, Kath, but I wonder if Quinlan would be so obvious about it…”

“Like you said, sir, maybe he’s making a statement. Showing others what happens to anyone who challenges him. I know DCI Cavanagh’s team is looking at another body found in the docks. Another rival of Quinlan’s apparently.”

“Has Cavanagh linked it to Quinlan at all?” Blake said.

“Not yet, sir but we’ve got to consider that possibility, sir and…”

Blake nodded. He knew what she was going to say next. "And because of my involvement with Laura Vexley, Quinlan's current partner, I'm compromised. Is that what you're getting at, Kath?"

"Sir, I'm sorry. I didn't mean to overstep..."

Blake had loved Laura. She had helped him tame Serafina, his psychotic cat to a degree, but, what she had done was bring Blake back to life. After his mother had wandered out of the house some years before, Blake had existed in a limbo world. He lived in his parents' house, unchanged since their deaths, working and sleeping but doing little else. Laura had changed all that but then her own past caught up with her in the form of Kyle Quinlan, a violent criminal and her ex-husband. She had fled from Quinlan at first but then she returned and threw her lot in with him. Blake didn't know what hold Quinlan had over Laura, but now there was no way Blake could approach Quinlan without being accused of harassing him because of Laura. Personally, it was a dagger in his heart, professionally, it was a pain in the arse.

"It's okay, Kath," Blake said at last. "You're right. We need to investigate Quinlan but I'm going to have to keep my distance on that one or it might jeopardise the whole case."

CHAPTER 4

The Thorpe family home was a converted farm near Thurstaston on the Dee side of the Wirral Peninsula. A neat farmhouse sat in the corner of a cobbled yard surrounded by converted barns. Blake had visited it before and knew that some of them housed offices and even accommodation for Thorpe's son, Thor Magnusson. In the bright sunshine, it had a quaint, picture postcard quality. A white Range Rover sat in the yard. The family liaison officer, DC Tasha Cook, had parked her car beside it.

"Morning, sir," DC Cook said as she opened the door. She looked uncomfortable, as though she'd been given a hard time. Blake wouldn't be surprised, family members reacted in a variety of ways to news of bereavement. The nature of Thorpe's death might provoke an unpleasant reaction.

"You okay, Tasha?"

Cook ran her fingers through her bubbly, honey-coloured hair. "Bit of a tough one, sir. Mrs Thorpe is pretty cut up but obviously, she has no fondness for us..."

"Right," Blake said, stepping into the house. He looked around the hall. "Nobody else here?"

"No, sir, just Mrs Thorpe. Why?"

Blake shrugged. "This place normally has a few of Thorpe's heavies hanging around. Seems strangely empty. What about Mr Magnussen? Is he in his flat?"

"Nope," Tasha said. "Just Mrs Thorpe, sir."

"Oh, well, lead on," Blake said.

Tasha paused. "You will be careful, sir, won't you? I know she's a criminal's wife but..."

"You don't need to tell me that, Tasha," Blake said. "I'm not a monster, you know..."

"No, sir," Tasha said, biting her lip.

"Don't worry," Blake said. "I know I can be a bull in a china shop, sometimes. I'll take it steady with her."

"Thanks, sir," Tasha said, breathing an audible sigh of relief. Blake honestly didn't know where he'd got this reputation from. Admittedly, he wasn't always the most diplomatic man in the room, especially when he thought family members were hiding something, but he always tried to tread carefully. He could see what Tasha was getting at, though; she was more than just the friendly face of the force. Tasha's job was to harvest information about relationships in the household and feed it back to the team as much as it was to offer support. It was unlikely that Mrs Thorpe would want Tasha hovering around the house if Blake alienated the widow. This was a tricky one.

Tasha led Blake into the house. In the past, he had not got past the entrance hall and was surprised at how small the building was. The hall was panelled wood and parquet flooring. The last time Blake had seen Thorpe alive, he had been on the stairs that ran from the hall.

Mrs Thorpe sat in a flowery living room. Everything was patterned with blooms, from the swirling, thick carpet, the heavy curtains to the wallpaper. The effect was quite dizzying, and Blake felt the urge to slump into the one remaining leather armchair. Shirley Thorpe was younger than her husband but hard to age. She was slim and it was clear she spent a lot of time, effort, and money on battling the advancing years. From her make-up and dyed blonde hair to her designer jeans and sloppy cashmere jumper, Mrs Thorpe oozed expense and artifice. She looked up when Blake entered the room. "What? More coppers? I thought you said I wouldn't be troubled with loads of questions, Tasha."

"I'm DCI Will Blake, Mrs Thorpe..."

"I know who you are. You're that copper off the telly, aren't you? What was the programme called?"

"Searchlight," Blake said, through clenched teeth. As a young constable, he'd been pushed into the limelight by his senior officers at the time and volunteered for the TV crime programme. Its aim was to engage the help of the public to solve different unsolved or current crimes by showing reconstructions or interviewing investigating officers. Blake had a role introducing CCTV footage of minor crimes such as corner shop robberies, traffic offences and burglaries. His good looks had garnered him something of a following in the short time that the programme ran and people still remembered him. The trouble was, it had been an albatross around his neck ever since, a stick with which senior officers regularly beat him. His own boss, Superintendent Martin, often brought up Blake's TV past as though it was an impediment.

"Searchlight, yeah, that was it. Never really watched it myself but Harry loved it," Shirley Thorpe stared at the wall behind Blake and then gave a long sniff. Her nose was red and her eyes glittered with tears. "He always joked about turning up on it one day."

"I'm sorry for your loss and want to assure you that we'll do our level best to find out who did this to your husband, Mrs Thorpe."

"Are you really? Sorry, I mean. Do you care? Harry wasn't exactly a saint, was he? I'd have thought you lot would be glad to see the back of him."

Blake settled himself in the chair opposite Shirley Thorpe and leaned forward. "I am sorry, yes. Whatever your husband may or may not have done in the past, I don't believe he deserved to die. I also believe that whoever did this to him should be brought to justice."

"Doesn't bring him back, though, does it?" Shirley Thorpe said, wiping her nose with a soggy tissue.

"No," Blake agreed, his voice soft, "but someone who has committed murder shouldn't be allowed to wander free, either."

"God. I've lived with him for so long, I don't know what's right and what's wrong anymore," Shirley Thorpe hissed, burying her face in her hands. She sobbed for a while, then looked up. "He wasn't an honest man, Mr Blake. He bent every rule he could and justified every wrongdoing to me until I believed him. To listen to him, you'd think the whole world was against him. He was always fighting someone. Looks like he finally lost."

"Have you any idea who might have done this to your husband?"

Shirley Thorpe shook her head. "No. I had my own life and kept away from Harry's circle of friends as much as I could."

"But you must have had some idea of what he was doing, who he was dealing with..."

"Absolutely not. I said from the day I married him that I'd have nothing to do with his business dealings. That way, I couldn't get into trouble even if he did."

"You just said that he thought the world was against him. He must have said who was against him..."

"Yeah but there were so many and it was all just bluster with Harry." Shirley Thorpe narrowed her eyes and stared across the room at nothing. "I tell you one person you could have a word with, though, that Nigel Clements," she said. "He's been stalking us for weeks..."

"Stalking you?"

"Yeah, following us, taking photos. He thought we hadn't clocked him but we knew he was there all right. It's a wonder Harry didn't have him kneecapped but then, Clements would have gone to you lot and got Harry banged up."

"So, just to be clear. Nigel Clements was following you and spying on you in the run up to Mr Thorpe's death..."

"That's what I just said, didn't I? You must have known; Clements was always bleating on to local bobbies about anything and everything. Harry was taking me for a doctor's appointment once and pulled into a disabled space just to let me out. Clements popped up from nowhere and took a bloody picture."

"We are aware that Mr Clements had made some complaints, but we hadn't quite realised the extent to which he was making a nuisance of himself. We'll look into that, rest assured. Did Mr Thorpe mention anyone else who might have wished him ill?"

Shirley Thorpe shook her head. "Nobody in particular. It was always a vague reference, never a name. Or it was you lot out to get him, or the taxman, or some housing charity..."

"Housing charity?" Blake repeated, looking puzzled.

"We... Harry... owned a number of properties, shops, gambling arcades, houses."

"Did he have a difficult time with tenants?"

Shirley rolled her eyes. "The usual nonsense. People on benefits not paying their rent or complaining because there wasn't a rooftop pool. I mean what do these people expect?"

"Is there anyone who stands out amongst those tenants. Someone who might bear a grudge against Harry?"

"Yeah," Shirley said, her voice laden with revelation. "I hadn't thought of it before but there was one. Doug Noonan. Come to think of it, I remember Harry going on about him *a lot*. Noonan was always complaining to Harry, to the council, to anyone who would listen."

"What about?"

Shirley pulled a face. "He said the house he rented was damp, I think and he said the drains were leaking. It was all nonsense. He threatened Harry. Can you imagine that? Harry was about to evict him."

"In what way did he threaten your husband?"

"Threatened to kill him. Said he and his mates would catch Harry on his own one day and that would be it."

"And your husband didn't think to mention this to the police?" Blake said, feeling foolish the moment the words fell from his mouth.

"My husband was no fan of you lot after what that mate of yours, Clements tried to do to him. Besides, he wasn't afraid of a gobby little shit like Noonan."

"Okay," Blake said. "That's very useful. We can talk to Mr Noonan as a matter of urgency. Tell me, when did you last see Mr Thorpe?"

"About seven o'clock last night. He just said he was going out. Didn't say where."

"Is that normal?"

"Like I said, I never asked questions about Harry's dealings. I went to my Pilates class at the health club then came back home. He often stayed out late, too, so when he didn't come in, I just went to bed."

"And what time was that?"

"About eleven. And no, I wasn't alarmed when he wasn't beside me in bed this morning. That happens, too."

"He went out in his car, then," Blake said, scribbling down a few notes.

"Yes, a black Jaguar... XE, I think was the model. He had a personalised number plate: HTHT 1."

"Thanks," Blake murmured. "We can put a search out for that. Was your son here last night?"

"Fabian? Or should I say Thor?" Shirley said, rolling her eyes. "No. He left home a few months back after all that nonsense over that paranormal investigator. I think it was you who accused him of murdering the loser, wasn't it, Inspector Blake?"

"Your son was questioned. I don't think we ever charged him with anything."

"Well, something went on there because soon after, he had a big row with Harry and packed his bags. He lives in one of my holiday cottages in North Wales, now. Not far from Prestatyn."

"You have some business interests of your own, then."

"A few holiday lets. Harry wanted to buy all kinds of businesses in my name but I wouldn't allow that. I'd end up holding the shitty end of the stick if it all went sour, wouldn't I? So I bought a few little cottages. My insurance if you want. Anyway, I had coffee with my son last week. He's fine but still sulking."

"Angry enough to harm his father?"

Shirley Thorpe bridled. "No, he wouldn't harm a fly. You've met him, Inspector."

"He's a big lad, as I recall and a bit too fond of axes and drugs."

"He isn't a killer," Shirley's eyes narrowed. "Whatever their differences, Fabian loved his dad and would never hurt him."

"Nevertheless, we'll need to talk to him. If you could supply us with an address or phone number, I'd be very grateful."

"So you can fit him up again? Fat chance. You'd like that wouldn't you? A nice easy case, pin it on the estranged son and move on..."

"I can assure you, Mrs Thorpe, that isn't what happens..."

"I want you to leave now," Shirley Thorpe said, standing up. "Both of you. I want you to go. You're just upsetting me."

"Mrs Thorpe, if I could just..."

"No. No. Just get out of my house. Now."

Out in the yard, Blake leaned on the side of his car. "Sorry Tasha, I tried my best."

"It wasn't your fault, sir," Tasha said, giving him a tight smile. "I think she's just angry at the world right now. Being married to a character like Harry Thorpe must have had its challenges, whatever you think of her."

Blake nodded. "Amen to that. We can come back when she's had a chance to calm down and process what's happened. In the meantime, I reckon we need to catch up with Thor Magnussen, as a matter of urgency."

CHAPTER 5

For an edgy ex-copper who took liberties with the law, Nigel Clements was something of a disappointment, Kinnear thought. He was older than he'd expected for a start, with a wrinkled face and lank hair plastered over an increasing bald spot. He wore thick glasses, a check shirt and baggy, tan chinos. He stood on the front step of his small bungalow, squinting angrily at Kinnear and Manikas as they showed him their warrant cards.

"What's all this about then? Fucking Harry Thorpe?" Clements snapped. "What does he want now? Blood? Hasn't he had enough?"

"Can we come in, Mr Clements?" Kinnear said, taking a step closer.

"If you must," Clements muttered and led them into the house. Kinnear shivered. It felt cold inside, despite the bright morning and this was made worse by the white anaglypta wallpaper that covered every wall. It was like walking into a fridge. A smell of fried food and body odour hung in the air. He and Alex followed Clements into a dining room with a table and chairs for four, a bookcase but little else. "Sit yourselves down."

They settled around the table and Alex took his

notebook out but said nothing.

"Early this morning, Harry Thorpe was found dead on West Kirby beach," Kinnear said. "We're treating the death as suspicious."

"Bloody hell!" Clements muttered. He paused and squinted at them. "Wait. You think I had something to do with it?"

"You said yourself, Thorpe ruined your life…"

"I was a hardworking copper, for Christ's sake! Thorpe came along and accused me of corruption. If I was going to top anyone, it'd be the senior officers who threw me under a bus just so they didn't get dragged in."

Kinnear glanced at Alex Manikas and back to Clements. "You're saying that you didn't plant evidence that would have convicted Thorpe?"

Clements blushed. "Well, no… but the bastard had it coming. He was up to all kinds of mischief. We could have nailed him, but top brass took his side, not mine. I lost everything." A sudden grin spread across his face. "So how did he die, then? Horribly, I hope."

"We aren't at liberty to say, I'm afraid, Mr Clements," Kinnear said. He didn't like this man. He seemed full of self-importance and self-pity. A dangerous combination, in Kinnear's book. "Can you tell me where you were last night?"

Clements licked his lips. "I was here, wasn't I?

Watching telly."

"What did you watch?" Kinnear said.

"I dunno. An antiques programme. Some shit music thing with people in disguise. Oh, and that programme about bent coppers, you know the one where they go after the organised crime group? That cracks me up."

Manikas shook his head. "That was on Saturday..."

"I watched it on demand, didn't I?" Clements said. "Oh and I went to the supermarket for some lager. Got to drown my sorrows somehow, haven't I? Seeing as someone else drowned Harry Thorpe."

Kinnear raised his eyebrows. "Nobody said anything about drowning anyone. We'll be checking that alibi, Mr Clements."

"Check away!" Clements said. "So he drowned did he?"

Kinnear felt himself colouring. "I never mentioned anything about how Mr Thorpe died. You did."

"Oh come on DC Kinnear, I was a detective inspector for years before I got thrown under a bus by your bosses. It was an educated guess. If you found Thorpe on the beach today, chances are he was dumped in the sea and washed up or something. Not sure the tide's back out yet, so it must have been early this morning. Who's your SIO? Is it Blakey?"

"Well, I..."

Clements gave a bark of laughter. "Don't start playing poker, DC Kinnear, you'll end up losing your shirt! So it *is* Blakey. I bet he's a bundle of fun. He never likes going near that beach."

Manikas and Kinnear shared another glance. "What are you on about?" Manikas said.

"He hasn't mentioned the Hilbre Island Affair, then?"

Kinnear pursed his lips. He'd heard that before, last year. Another old copper had mentioned it. Blake had been really uncomfortable then. "No he hasn't."

"You wanna ask him about that, lads. Not Blakey's finest hour. I should know, I was there."

Kinnear glanced at Manikas. "You made a number of complaints against Mr Thorpe recently..."

"Just being a responsible citizen," Clements said, holding up his hands. "I see a crime being committed, I'm duty-bound to report it."

"That would require you to be close to Thorpe," Manikas said. "And judging by the number of reports made, you must have been virtually stalking the man."

"Our paths crossed a lot, DC Manikas and if I'd

got evidence of something major, then I would have reported it. I admit I got off on being a bit of a nuisance; Thorpe ruined me, after all. I never killed him, though. I'm not that stupid. No, I'd have a word with some of his business associates, if I were you."

*****

PC Mark Robertson leaned on the railings of South Parade and stared out over the beach. The tide was slowly receding now and many of the day-trippers were packing up their beach towels and picnics and heading home. In a couple of months' time, he'd be able to join them at last when he retired. He was counting the days. His knees throbbed in time with his feet from walking around all day. The door-to-door hadn't yielded very much and he was ready to head home.

"You still looking for information about the fella you found out on the beach?" A voice said, startling Mark. A tall man dressed in waders and a grubby T-shirt stood holding a fishing rod and landing net. A creel hung at his hip, the strap stretched across his broad stomach. His red hair poked out in all directions.

"Yes, sir," Mark said, straightening up and trying not to wince as his knees cracked audibly. "Why, did you see anything?"

The man scratched his hammy, red face with a

big hand. "I was here last night and I saw a couple of people out on the sands where your police officers were this morning."

Mark pulled out his notepad. "That's great. How many people?"

"Hard to say. They were quite far away," the man said. "They had a Land Rover, I think, and a trailer with one of them mini-diggers."

Mark gave him a stern look. "A mini-digger?"

"Honest! They weren't out there long and I remember thinking that if they didn't do whatever they were doing quick, they'd be caught by the tide. I can't have been the only one to have seen them."

"What did they look to be doing?"

The man shrugged. "I dunno. I didn't stop to watch them for long. They had Hi-Vis jackets on and hard hats, so I thought it must be something official."

"I see," Mark said. "You didn't get a look at any registration numbers or anything like that, did you?"

"Sorry. Like I said, I didn't hang about."

"Would you be prepared to make a statement, sir?"

*****

From the security of his net curtains, Clements

watched the two Detective Constables climbing into their car and smiled. It would be a cold day in Hell when they got the better of him. He'd managed to queer the pitch for that prick, Blake, too, hopefully. He knew Blake wouldn't have forgotten Hilbre Island and maybe that would cloud his judgement a little further. Smiling, Clements picked up his phone and thumbed through the contacts.

"I've just heard the news. Well done," he said when it was answered. "I'm impressed you came through. To be honest, I didn't expect you to, but you've excelled yourself. Sit tight now. Weather the storm and you'll get your money."

*****

Winston's betting shop in Hoylake was small and faded, a brick cube with narrow, rectangular windows at the top of the walls. It reminded DI Kath Cryer of a public toilet. Clearly the competition from the big betting chains and online gambling sites had taken their toll. Inside, screens hung on the wall showing odds or footage from a race somewhere in the country. Faded posters displayed the odds for football matches and special offers on other ways to throw money down the toilet. Stubby pens and used betting slips littered the ledge that ran around the edge of the room. A couple of men leaned on the high tables that stood in the middle of the room and watched dogs racing on the screens. One of them glanced at her curiously as she entered but the pull of the hounds was greater.

A middle-aged woman with a hatchet face and dyed red hair tied back in a ponytail stood behind the sales counter by the door. She gave Kath a suspicious glance and her face hardened when she saw the warrant card. "I wonder if I can talk to Thor Magnussen," Kath said. Magnussen had worked at the betting shop last year, and nobody had notified Kath that Thor and his father had parted ways. She just assumed he would still be here.

"He's gone, hasn't he?" the woman said, with a sniff. "Left last year after he argued with his old man..."

"With Harry Thorpe?" Kath said. "What about?"

"I dunno, do I? He just didn't turn up for work one day. Lucky it wasn't his turn to open up shop or there'd have been hell to pay. Harry came in a few days later and told us that he wouldn't be coming back. Between you and me, he was a bit of a waste of space."

"So, did Harry come in more often after that? I mean, you'd be short-handed..."

The woman snorted. "Harry wasn't one to get behind the counter. He was more the come in, empty the till and tell you to stop lazing around type of boss."

"Was?" Kath was pretty sure that the news of Harry's death wasn't common knowledge, so the woman's use of the past tense puzzled her.

"Well, he isn't the boss anymore, is he?" the woman said, pointing at a poster that said: Under New Management. She leaned on the counter, her face softening. "The new boss is lovely."

"I see," Kath replied, glancing round at the scuffed paintwork and chipped surfaces. "He's not making big changes, then?"

The woman's faced snapped back to its pinched, meanness. "He hasn't had chance yet, he only took over last month but he said he was going to redecorate and get screens up for us. He even gave us a bonus. I'm tellin' yer, Mr Quinlan's gonna turn this place around."

CHAPTER 6

Although it was late, light still streamed in through the windows of the Major Incident Room. The core team sat around Blake, who stared at the board. Kinnear had updated it with a picture of Clements, the disgraced copper, an image of Harry Thorpe standing proudly beside his Jaguar XE with the personalised plates and new, rather picturesque, photographs of the crime scene.

"Where are we up to, then?" Blake said, massaging his temples. "I went to see Shirley Thorpe, Harry's wife. Apparently, he went out about seven last night and didn't return. It wasn't uncommon for him to stay out so she wasn't concerned."

"They were close, then?" Kath Cryer said, folding her arms.

"I don't know, really, Kath. She seemed upset. More angry than anything else but we all express our grief in different ways, I suppose. He went out in his car which has a distinctive plate, so I'm hoping we can locate that quickly."

"We have a number of members of the public who actually saw Thorpe being buried, sir," Vikki Chinn said. "It sounds like a highly organised job, with a Land Rover, trailer and a mini-digger. Accounts vary between two and three individuals."

"Any descriptions?"

Vikki shook her head. "No, sir. They all just said that they were wearing Hi-Vis jackets and white hard hats. Those that paid any attention were curious because the tide was well on the turn and they wondered if the workers were safe."

"Amazing that a bright yellow coat renders you all but invisible to the average member of the public," Blake muttered. "Did anyone get a reg for the Land Rover?"

"Sorry, sir, no. I've put a public request out for any information but the workwear was the only thing that people noticed. I'm checking CCTV on any roads, businesses or properties on the approach to the slipway down onto the beach."

"Good work, Vikki," Blake muttered, turning to Kinnear and Manikas. "How about Clements? Any joy?"

"Very flaky, sir," Kinnear said. "He still bears Thorpe a grudge and seemed very happy at the news. He also seemed to know that Thorpe had drowned when we said we found him on the beach. It could be an educated guess or maybe he has some knowledge. His alibi was pretty feeble, he claims he spent the night watching TV apart from a trip out to the supermarket to get some beer. I came away with the feeling that he was hiding something, but it's just that, nothing more."

Blake looked at Manikas. The young man still seemed as distracted as he did earlier in the day. "Anything to add, Alex?"

"No, boss," Manikas said, quickly bringing his attention to the discussion. "He seemed deliberately vague about his alibi, given that he'd been very shrewd to guess how Thorpe had died."

"Okay, we keep digging. It might be nothing, but Clements hasn't done himself any favours. See if he shows up on the supermarket CCTV. Kath, how about you, any luck?"

Kath grinned. Blake resisted the urge to roll his eyes. Cryer was a great detective but she was prone to the melodramatic and over-egged any discovery she made. "Some interesting developments, sir. I spent some time trying to track down Thorpe's businesses online, Companies House, any other references but came up with nothing. It was as if they'd all vanished. So I went round to one of his businesses, Winston's Betting Shop in Hoylake. It turns out Thorpe sold up a month or so, ago. A quick tour of his other business interests told me the same story. Three betting shops and two gambling machine arcades and a number of rental properties all told the same story. Sold off a month ago." She paused, like a judge on a TV talent show about to reveal this week's winner.

"Who to, Kath?" Blake sighed.

"Kyle Quinlan!"

"Jeez," Blake muttered. "Are you serious?"

Kath gave Blake a dubious look. "Do you think I'd joke about something like that, sir? The staff at each venue seemed more than happy with the arrangement. Apparently Quinlan's a bit of a charmer."

"Do you think it was Quinlan who killed Thorpe, then, sir?" Kinnear said. "I mean, it would take a bit of organisation to get a crew out onto the beach to dig a hole and bury Thorpe up to his neck. Manpower, too."

Blake chewed his lip for a moment. "But if Thorpe sold all his assets to Quinlan, why would Quinlan kill him?"

"Maybe Thorpe signed everything over to Quinlan under duress," Kinnear said. "Then Quinlan got rid of him."

"It's possible, of course," Blake said, with a shrug. "But a very risky thing for Quinlan to do. He could have let Thorpe stew in his own defeat for a while then finished him off."

"Or maybe it's a very public statement from Quinlan, sir," Kath Cryer said. "Publicly humiliating Thorpe by making him sell, then killing him. People are going to think twice before they cross

Kyle Quinlan after that, right?"

"But we don't know that Thorpe did cross Quinlan. Thorpe was a pragmatist; he might have seen Quinlan snapping at his heels and thought, 'you know what, mate? You can have it.' It doesn't follow that Thorpe would start a war."

"We have to investigate, though, sir," Kath said, biting her words back. Blake heard the unspoken second half of the sentence, though. Just because it might affect Laura Vexley, didn't mean Quinlan was off-limits.

"Let me think about the best way to do it, Kath. DCI Cavanagh is keeping an eye on Quinlan. Whatever we do, we have to keep him in the loop. And the Superintendent. Otherwise I'll have my arse served to me on a silver platter."

Kath smiled and nodded, reassured. "Okay, sir."

"The other line of enquiry we need to explore is Harry's son, Fabian Thorpe aka Thor Magnussen and his band of Viking-themed bikers. Apparently, Thor left the family home last year after an altercation with his father. Mrs Thorpe blamed us, saying we accused Thor of murder and tried to fit him up. Quite how that develops into an argument between father and son, I don't know but there was clearly bad blood between Thor and his dad so we need to find him and figure out where he was last night. He's living in one of her holiday lets near Prestatyn."

"That narrows things down a bit, sir," Vikki Chinn said, wryly.

"Tasha's going to have another go with Mrs Thorpe tomorrow, in the meantime, if we can try and get a firm address. I mean he's a big lad, quite striking and with a name like Thor, he's not going to blend in. Might be worth checking up with the police over in North Wales. Alex, can you do that?"

Alex stared at Blake as though he'd just been asked to wrestle a live alligator. "Me, sir?"

"What's up, Alex? It's a chance to polish up your Welsh," Kinnear said, giving a jab with his elbow. "Whose coat is that jacket?"

"Yeah," Blake said. "A little bit of cross-border liaison won't do you any harm, will it?"

Everyone jeered and Alex grinned, but Blake thought he looked a little sick, too.

"Another person of interest is Douglas Noonan," Blake said, posting up a picture of an angry-looking man with a red beard and glasses. "A resident in one of Thorpe's properties. Apparently, Noonan took Thorpe to task over substandard housing and even threatened to harm Thorpe. Thorpe was about to evict him."

"I've done a routine check on Noonan, sir, and he's known to us for assault and criminal damage," Vikki said. "He's been arrested on a number of demonstrations. He's an environmentalist, believes in direct action. Worth talking to, that's for sure."

"Okay, Vikki, can you have a chat with him? I know we're skirting around the elephant in the room that is Kyle Quinlan and a more organised outfit but I don't want to miss anything. No stone unturned, okay?"

Everyone nodded and murmured.

"Oh, sir," Kinnear said, raising his hand. "Clements said something odd when we were talking to him. He said something about the Hilbre Island Affair and said to ask you. He was there apparently."

Blake took a breath. It had been a while since that had been mentioned. "It's nothing, Andrew," Blake said. "Just something that happened a long time ago. Doesn't have anything to do with this investigation. I'd just forget it."

"Yes, sir," Kinnear said, but Blake could tell he wasn't satisfied.

"Right then," Blake said, clapping his hands before he could stop himself. "Alex and Andrew, you're tracking down Thor. Kath, more detail on these business transfers and Vikki, it's the post-mortem tomorrow. Seeing as you're the only one who doesn't come out of PMs looking like they've swallowed a mug full of frogspawn, you can come with me, if that's okay."

"Great, sir," Vikki said.

"Let's get some rest, everyone. Hit the ground running in the morning. I don't want anyone to think we're not working our hardest to find the killer just because the victim is a bastard like Harry Thorpe. Okay?"

*****

The woman was crouching by Blake's front gate when he pulled up outside his house. Even though it was nearly dark, he recognised her. It was the same woman who had been fussing with Serafina this morning. In the half-light, he didn't notice Serafina at first and wondered what she was doing. Stopping the car in the road, he wound the window down and looked out. "Can I help you?"

"She's a lovely cat," the woman said, standing up. "Where did you get her from?"

Blake frowned at the woman. "She was my mother's cat. I kept her on when my mother passed away," he said, trying to remain polite. "Is there a reason you're asking?"

"No," she said, breaking eye-contact with Blake. "No reason."

"You were here this morning," Blake said. "Fussing with the cat. Are you local? I haven't seen you around before."

"Just over the bridge," she said. "On the other

side of the by-pass. I've lived there for years. Just taken to walking out a little. It's good for my mental health. It's a long time since I've been this way. I just noticed the cat. Anyway, nice talking to you. Bye."

Blake watched her walk down the road as Serafina meowed at him. Somewhere in the house Charlie barked, having heard the voices. He would have been taken out for a walk by Ian Youde, Blake's neighbour but Blake thought he'd take him out again, as late as it was. He needed to think about Harry Thorpe, Kyle Quinlan... and Laura.

CHAPTER 7

The fact that the post-mortem theatre was air-conditioned was a bonus, Blake thought. Outside it was shaping up to be another hot day and the idea of sitting in a sweltering office didn't appeal to him. Whether it was worth having to sit and watch Jack Kenning, the pathologist, cut up Harry Thorpe, Blake wasn't sure.

On reflection, Blake decided that he'd rather be trapped at his desk with no blinds on the windows. Thorpe was never one of Blake's favourite people; the man was the cause of so much misery and he was as revolting inside as out. Kenning, the man cutting Thorpe open, wasn't one of Blake's favourite people, either. It wasn't that Kenning was inept or poor at his job; the man was sharp and astute, but he was so full of himself that he was constantly showing off. Or trying to. From his garish bowties to his inappropriate gallows humour, Kenning played the part of every pathologist he'd seen on TV shows but he did it really badly.

"So here we are, investigating Thorpe's corpse," Kenning said in a theatrical voice to his assistant. "Thorpe's corpse. You see what I did there?" The long-suffering assistant just hid behind her facemask and gave Kenning a deadpan, 'yes, I did."

Kenning beamed up at the viewing gallery where Blake and Vikki sat. Blake gave him a thumbs up and a pained smile.

"Jeez," Blake muttered under his breath. "I hope this doesn't take long."

Kenning assessed the body, talking into a Dictaphone and Blake wondered if that was entirely necessary. "Subject is one point seven metres, eighty kilos…." He chunnered on as the assistant took swabs from under Thorpe's fingernails and then he tucked his Dictaphone into a top pocket and began feeling the corpse's neck and joints.

"What the hell is he doing now? Thorpe didn't die of arthritis," Blake muttered.

"I think we just have to let it take its course, sir," Vikki said, making notes as Kenning's voice drifted through the intercom.

Blake watched as Kenning opened up the body and removed various organs weighing them and noting down various measurements. Vikki continued to make notes and Blake watched as Thorpe was taken apart. "Interesting," Kenning muttered, every now and then but Blake wasn't sure what he was referring to.

Finally, Kenning called Blake down.

"Well?" Blake said. "Any idea? I'm assuming he drowned but…"

"It's actually very hard to establish whether or not someone drowned, Blake," Kenning said. "There was a lot of fluid in his lungs and foam in his larynx which is indicative of drowning but it's hard to be certain."

"I just assumed that, with Thorpe being tied up and planted in the mud, he'd been left for the tide," Blake said.

"The great Will Blake, assuming something? Whatever next? The man's legs were tied but there's no sign of any kind of frenzied attempt to escape. No cuts or abrasion on the skin or rope burn. Of course the sand compacted around him might pin his arms but..."

"If you knew you were going to be drowned, you'd fight tooth and nail to get free, wouldn't you?"

Kenning shrugged. "There are no signs of trauma on any part of the body. Not even the slightest bruise to suggest he put up any resistance."

"Could he have been drugged?"

"That's a possibility," Kenning said, looking slightly deflated. Blake realised that the pathologist had been building up to that.

"So you'll check his blood for any toxins, Jack," Blake said.

"Yes," Kenning said, fiddling with his bowtie.

"He had a hearty meal before he died, that's for certain. What happened to him after that, we will have wait for the blood tests."

"Great," Blake muttered, trying not to make it sound like he felt he'd wasted his time.

"I know someone who might be able to help you with the rope, though," Kenning said, with a grin, realising he had regained the initiative.

"Really? Malachy O'Hare's team contacted us this morning," Blake said. "They thought it was pretty inconclusive; white nylon boat rope, common. You can buy it online by the kilometre..."

"What about the knot that was used?"

Blake shrugged, feeling his face redden. Kenning had caught him out. "What about it?"

"The type of knot and the loops used can reveal a lot about whoever tied it. If you know what you're looking for, of course. I happen to know a man who is an expert in such matters and he's local. I could arrange for us to meet him."

"What have we got to lose? Let me know when you hear back from him."

"Okay," Kenning said. He paused for a beat. "Must be strange for you, Will," he said, eyeing Blake up and measuring his words. "The body being so close to Hilbre Island."

Blake shrugged but felt himself blushing. "I'm not sure what you mean, Jack."

There was a mischievous gleam in Kenning's eye. "I mean wasn't it Hilbre Island where there was all that unpleasantness over that young man. What was his name again?"

"Just get the blood tests done as urgently as possible. I want this cleared up as quickly as possible," Blake said, turning on his heel and stalking out of the theatre.

"What was all that about, sir?" Vikki called after him, almost running to keep up as they hurried out of the hospital into the carpark.

Blake stopped at the car and drew a long breath. "Nothing, Vikki. Just Kenning getting his own back on me. It's a long story and not worth hearing. Have you managed to track down Doug Noonan?"

"Thorpe's troublesome resident? I called him first thing this morning. I was going to ask if you'd drop me off at his house so I could interview him."

"Do you mind if I join you? I could do with getting stuck into this case. I feel like we're tiptoeing around it."

"That's fine by me, sir," Vikki said, giving Blake a smile. "It'll be good to have you along, especially if Noonan is a bit uppity."

*****

Looking at the state of Doug Noonan's house,

Blake felt a certain sympathy with the man's constant objections to Thorpe about its condition. It was a standard semi-detached property in Thingwall but everything about it screamed out for a lick of paint or plaster or cement. The rooftiles were crooked and loose, the cladding on the outside of the house was grey and cracked and judging by the misted up double-glazing, the windows needed replacing. The overgrown front garden was cluttered with pots and containers with various plants and climbing canes. Blake could see tomatoes, a pumpkin plant, a rosemary bush, coriander, and mint. It had a pleasant scruffiness to it that the house lacked.

Doug Noonan matched his front garden. A big bushy red beard cascaded down his broad chest onto a potbelly that stretched a faded olive T-shirt. Blake could just about make out the 'Nuclear Power? No Thanks' logo peeping through the beard. Noonan stared at them with intense blue eyes under eyebrows that complemented his beard. The only part of his head that wasn't hairy was the top. Long red hair hung down over his ears, surrounding a clear pink spot on the top like a monk's tonsure. A pair of three-quarter-length shorts and scuffed brown boots finished the look.

"You better come in," Noonan said after reading Vikki's warrant card. He led them into a house almost as full of plants as the front garden. Fronds of green trailed down from shelves on every wall, draping themselves on specimens the size of small bushes that sat in large pots. The whole house had a smell of warm compost which wasn't altogether unpleasant. It reminded Blake of his dad's potting shed. "What is all this about, then?" Noonan said and settled himself at a kitchen table covered in trays and plant pots. It looked as though Noonan was in the middle of transplanting as green shoots lay scattered all over the tabletop.

The kitchen itself was cluttered with more vegetation mingled with boxes and packets. The only surface that stood clear was a bread board with a knife and half a loaf on it. It didn't feel unclean, though, Blake thought. Clearly, Noonan spent more time on nurturing his precious flora than tidying up.

Blake settled himself on a chair opposite Noonan and Vikki did likewise. "It's about your landlord, Harry Thorpe, Mr Noonan," Vikki said. "He was found dead yesterday morning."

Noonan blinked and licked his lips. "Really? That's...awful... are you treating it as suspicious?"

"We are," Vikki said. "You weren't his biggest fan, were you Mr Noonan?"

"He wasn't the best landlord, to be honest. This place might seem quite homely now but, in the winter, it's bloody freezing and when it rains… well, let's just say I don't need to water anything," Noonan said. He paused and glanced at Vikki and Blake. "Hang on. Do you think I had something to do with his death?"

Vikki shrugged. "We're just building up a picture of Mr Thorpe's business dealings and anyone he interacted with…"

"The man was a criminal, you must know that," Noonan said. "He bought stolen goods, sold drugs, laundered money. People were terrified of him…"

"You weren't," Vikki said. "We understand you threatened to kill him."

Noonan paled. "It… it was just bravado. People like Thorpe are bullies. You have to show you're not afraid of him. I wouldn't ever…"

"You've a bit of a record for showing people you're not afraid, Mr Noonan, haven't you?" Vikki said, opening her satchel and pulling out a file. "Assaulting a police officer, criminal damage, resisting arrest…"

Noonan scowled. "Those were at demonstrations, and I never assaulted anyone. That copper made it all up."

"The judge didn't seem to think so. My point is, that you aren't averse to taking on people you perceive to be more powerful than yourself if you feel justified."

"I'd never take a life. Yeah, I did threaten Thorpe but only so he knew I wasn't messing. This place is a slum. I mean, I do my best but it's unhealthy."

"So, where were you last night?" Vikki said.

Noonan looked shocked. His eyes flew all around the room as he tried to collect his thoughts. "Nowhere. I mean, I was here. Tending to my plants. I listened to the radio and went to bed early. That was it."

"Can anyone corroborate this?"

"No. I live alone."

"What is it you do for a living, Mr Noonan?" Blake said, looking hard at the man.

Noonan reddened. "I'm a caretaker at Allister House in West Kirby. It's an office block, rented out by different businesses. I keep it clean and sort out any problems."

"What about hobbies? Do you like the water?"

"I used to go sea fishing but I've stopped that now I'm vegan. Look, what's this got to do with anything? It's insane to think I'd go out of my way to hurt Thorpe. And anyway, why would I, when he isn't my landlord anymore?"

"He sold the property?" Blake said, leaning forward. Who to?"

Noonan thought for a second. "An agency

of some sort. They seem okay. Someone came round here only the other day and took a long list of things that need attention. Vexley Housing Trust, that was it."

CHAPTER 8

It appeared that Thor Magnussen was lying low and had been since he moved to the cottage last year. The local police had no knowledge of him and at first they thought DC Alex Manikas' enquiry was some kind of wind-up. They'd hung up on him once and it was only after his third call that they took him seriously. "You sure your pals aren't pulling your leg, Alex?" the detective sergeant at the other end of the line had said, his voice laced with laughter.

"Trust me, I've met this bloke and he's no laughing matter," Alex had replied, sullenly. Kinnear had watched Manikas with concerned curiosity as his colleague spelt out the name through gritted teeth for what seemed like the fortieth time.

"Tasha Cook managed to finally get his address from Mrs Thorpe." Kinnear said after Manikas threw the phone down in disgust. "Let's go for a drive."

Now, hurtling along the A55 through North Wales, Kinnear wondered if the suggestion had been wise. Manikas drove like a man possessed, muttering at any other car that made the slightest infringement of traffic regulations. "I've a good mind to pull that joker over," Alex snapped, flashing his blue lights as a BMW overtook him, blocking his chance to pull out from behind a lorry. "Magnussen probably won't be in anyway and we'll get it in the neck from Blakey for wasting time and money."

"We won't live to get a roasting from Blakey if you carry on driving like this," Kinnear snapped. "What the bloody hell is wrong with you?"

Manikas didn't reply but slowed down to a sedate forty miles an hour on the inside lane and stared sulkily up the road.

Kinnear shook his head. "Ever since Thorpe was found, you've been proper antsy, you have. I've never seen you like this before. No, I tell a lie; the last time you were like this was the last time we investigated Thorpe. Remember? You came back to work after the weekend off all covered in bruises. You told me you'd had a fight in a pub or something. What really happened, Alex."

"Nothing," Manikas said. "I just had too much to drink and got into a scuffle, that's all. Anyway, that was ages ago. I'm sorry. Look, it's just something private, that's all. If I could tell you, I would..."

"As long as it doesn't screw up this investigation, mate," Kinnear said. "You know you can talk to me about anything if you need to."

"Cheers," Alex said. "Anyway, how's little Niamh getting on?"

Kinnear smiled. He and his husband Chris had adopted a little girl earlier that month. "She's doing really well," Kinnear said. "I thought we were going to have all kinds of problems, but she sleeps like a log and is great fun. She's settled in so quickly."

"That's great," Alex said, but his cheeriness sounded forced and artificial.

"She had a bad start in life. Her biological mother has issues with drugs and had neglected her. Poor Niamh's been passed from pillar to post in her short life, so she's quite adaptable. She's behind on her development, so we've got to work on that…"

Kinnear felt a sense of relief that Manikas seemed to have relaxed a little. Whatever was troubling him was serious and Kinnear was still convinced that it had something to do with the case.

It took them a while to locate Thor's cottage. It lay on the side of the hills sweeping up from the coast, looking out over the Dee Estuary and the Irish Sea. But it was tucked down a narrow country lane that they drove past three times before realising that it was the way.

The cottage itself was a small, stone bungalow with tiny square windows. A busy garden huddled around it and a climbing rose scaled the painted walls. "It's beautiful," Kinnear muttered as they crunched up the gravel path to the green front door. "Like a hobbit house."

"Yeah, well, just remember, a giant lives in it," Alex said, rapping on the door. "And he's dangerous."

Kinnear was about to reply when the door swung open. Thor filled the doorway, almost bending down to look out at them. His muscular physique stretched his t-shirt, distorting the image of the comic-book character of the same name. He still had the same hairstyle, shaved at the sides but long and slicked back on top. Stubble covered his square jaw and he stared angrily at Alex. Dark circles shadowed Thor's red-rimmed eyes and Kinnear wasn't convinced they came just from grief.

"You," he said, ignoring Kinnear. "You've got some nerve intruding on my grief like this. What the fuck do you want?"

"We're sorry for your loss, Mr Magnussen but you must realise that we have to investigate your father's death and that includes talking to you," Kinnear said.

"I realise that, yeah," Thor said. "You could have left *him* back at the station, though, that's all I'm saying."

Kinnear looked puzzled. "I don't understand..."

"If you have a specific objection to being questioned by me, Mr Magnussen, then you can tell us now. Otherwise, can we come in? We'll take up as little of your time as possible."

Thor's face darkened and Kinnear wondered just how much they were going to get out of him in his current foul mood. He also wondered why he objected to Alex's presence so much. The big man paused for a few seconds and then stood back. Kinnear and Manikas stepped inside.

The interior décor of the house screamed 'holiday let.' The decorators had adopted neutral tones for the walls and skirtings but Mrs Thorpe seemed to have cluttered the place up with every ornament and bit of furniture she didn't want on display at home. A bright red leather three-piece suite vied with a mirror framed in some kind of wood painted with bright African figures. Pierrot dolls lined up on every surface. Kinnear shuddered. A standard lamp with a bright orange shade stood in the corner. It was like an explosion in a charity shop had thrown these disparate items into the cottage. Adding to the sense of clutter were numerous crushed beer cans and a musty, mushroom smell hung in the air. Having read the file on Thor Magnussen, Kinnear remembered that his gang of bikers modelled themselves on Viking berserkers, drinking an intoxicating mushroom tea. Looking at the big man, he decided that starting to question him about any recent drug use might be counter-productive and unhealthy.

Thor must have noticed Kinnear's bewildered look. He waved his arms around. "It's my mother," he said in a deep voice. "She has no clue about interior design." His foot clinked against a can. "I've had a few beers, too. What do you want to know?"

"Where were you the night before last?" Kinnear said.

"I was down on the Wirral," Thor said, colouring a little. "It's been so nice. A gang of us had a fire on the beach…"

"Which beach?" Kinnear said, scribbling down notes. Manikas sat staring at Magnussen, his jaw cracking as he ground his teeth.

"Caldy beach. Don't worry, we tidied up after ourselves and the tide washed the rest of it away. We didn't do any harm."

"You were larking around with a bonfire while your dad was being murdered just up the coast?" Alex muttered. "Nice."

"If I'd known, I'd have done something about it," Thor said in a low voice. "If I find out who did it, I'll make them pay."

"That wouldn't be a sensible move, Mr Magnussen," Kinnear said, trying to break the tension between the two men. What the hell was going on? "So there will be others who will corroborate your account of your whereabouts?"

"Yes. I'll give you their names. I have nothing to hide..."

"Really?" Alex said. "You had an argument with your father. There was no love lost between you two. Or else you'd still be in your little flat at the family home instead of this place."

"What was the nature of the argument with your father?" Kinnear said, giving Manikas an irritated glance.

Thor cleared his throat. "It was after you lot tried to frame me for the murder of that stupid paranormal investigator, Trevor Long."

"We didn't try to frame you, Mr Magnussen," Kinnear said, "but go on."

"Dad wasn't happy that I'd caught the attention of the police. We never really got on. That was one of the reasons I changed my name. Anyway, I had a party and ended up injuring myself." He massaged his huge shoulder and glanced up at Manikas. "That was the final straw for Dad. He lost it with me, so I left."

"I remember that," Kinnear said. "You crashed a JCB into a pit. We came to interview you in hospital."

"Yeah," Thor said, glaring at Alex. "My shoulder's never been right since. It's really messed up my axe throwing."

Kinnear remembered that Thor had run a business that offered axe throwing parties for companies and individuals. “That’s a shame,” Kinnear said.

“Isn’t it just?” Thor said, still glaring at Manikas.

“Perhaps if you’d been more careful at that party, you wouldn’t have ended up in hospital,” Manikas said.

“Can you think of anyone who might have benefitted from your father’s death?” Kinnear said, getting increasingly impatient with Manikas. “Or anyone who might wish to harm him?”

Thor shrugged. “There must be a huge list of people who would want to hurt him, I imagine. Who benefits from his death? I dunno. He’s probably written me out of his will, so not me. He had rivals. Kyle Quinlan popped up from nowhere. Dad sold most of his business interests to him, so I heard.”

“Do you know why?”

Thor shrugged. “I think Dad was going to retire anyway. And Quinlan seems to have rich backers. He’s like the fucking pied piper. We’ve lost quite a few warriors from the Sons of Sol to Quinlan. He pays good money.”

“For what?”

“Security, muscle. People to run errands for

him. Quinlan is clever. He offers good money to those he recruits. Dad was always a skinflint when it came to anyone but himself. And he didn't treat his people very kindly. Anyone who used to work for him could have decided to top him."

"Except it takes a certain type of person to be a killer, Mr Magnussen," Manikas said. "Especially to kill someone the way your father died."

Thor went pale. "What d'you mean?"

"Alex," Kinnear snapped.

"He was buried up to his neck in the sand," Manikas said. "Buried. Does that ring any bells for you?"

"You..." Thor launched himself across the room, sending occasional tables and footstools tumbling in all directions. He landed on top of Manikas, tipping the sofa over and crashing into the wall. He wrapped his hands round Manikas' throat, but Alex broke his grip and headbutted the big man.

Both of them rolled aside from each other, seeing stars and trying to get to their feet but Kinnear leapt in between them. "Stop! Stop this now. What the hell is going on?"

"Get him out of my house," Thor snarled, nursing a bleeding nose. "Or I'll kill him. Is this all part of the plan, eh? To frame me for my own father's death? Is Clements all part of this?"

"Clements?" Kinnear said. "Why would he have anything to do with all this?"

"You don't fool me. I've seen him around, following Mum and Dad. Taking photos. He's been wanting to get back at Dad for years and you lot look after your own, don't you?"

Kinnear held up a hand. "Mr Magnussen, I assure you..."

"Just get out. And if you want to talk to me again, you're going to have to arrest me or charge me with something. Just go."

Kinnear grabbed hold of Manikas' elbow and frogmarched him back to their car. One way or another, he was going to find out what the hell was going on.

CHAPTER 9

Tasha Cook was beginning to think that Shirley Thorpe was taking her for an idiot. She'd managed to get back into the house after their interview with Blake but since then, Mrs Thorpe had her running around, making tea and washing up.

"Have you managed to think of anyone else who might have had dealings with your husband recently?" Tasha said, as she brought in yet another cup of coffee.

Shirley Thorpe sat in her armchair, leafing through an interior design magazine. "Yes, there was one person. Sam Fletcher but I don't imagine he'd be of any interest to you."

"And what was his connection to Mr Thorpe?"

"Harry was always going on about selling-up and retiring to Wales," Shirley Thorpe said, lowering the magazine and looking over the top of her reading glasses at Tasha. "Sam runs a couple of businesses renting out boats. Harry wanted to get involved in that."

"Was Mr Fletcher as enthusiastic about Mr Thorpe getting involved?"

"I don't think so," Shirley Thorpe said. "Harry was always grumbling that Sam kept giving him the cold shoulder."

"So this Sam Fletcher rejected your husband's business proposals."

"I suppose so. I didn't pay that much attention. As long as my allowance went into my account, Harry could do what he wanted. I had no interest in his dealings."

"Mrs Thorpe," Tasha said, gently. "Have you any idea about your husband's money? I mean what he had, where he invested it?"

"Of course not," Shirley Thorpe looked as though Tasha had just asked her if she'd ever thought of trying to fly. "I told you, I steered clear of all that. The less I knew the better."

"It may be wise to let us have a look into his accounts and just make sure there's been no recent movement of cash..."

"I'm not having you lot snooping round Harry's money. D'you think I'm totally brainless?"

"But if someone killed your husband for money, there might be transactions there that point us in the right direction for..."

"No," Shirley Thorpe said. "Absolutely not."

"DCI Blake might decide to get a warrant..."

"Then that's what he'll have to do because I'm not allowing anyone to look at my husband's money otherwise."

*****

Thor Magnussen swept up the fragments of Pierrot clowns that littered the floor and cursed. He'd had two glasses of mushroom tea since the two coppers had left but he still felt jittery and on edge. The room swam a little, making him feel as though he was on the deck of a ship. "Manikas knows what's going on," he muttered to the cracked face of the clown on the floor. It stared up at him, sadly, a painted tear on its cheek. "There was a time when me and dad did everything together. He took me to horse racing and the greyhounds, too." The Pierrot doll's face gazed up in sympathy at Thor. He thought it might have nodded, too. "We even had a few dogs once. We trained them and everything. We were so close then. And dad brought back all kinds of toys and weird sweets for me from his trips abroad. Video games and phones, iPads and stuff, too." Thor picked up the Pierrot face and held it in front of him. It seemed to float and dance in front of him. "Dad wasn't perfect, though, when I was older, he was always picking on me. We stopped going to the dogs and it seemed like I couldn't do anything right. Maybe that's why I always wanted to show the old man that I could stand on my own two feet."

"But that wasn't your fault, was it?" the Pierrot doll said, its voice echoing and reedy. The room revolved around them. "You grew up. Your dad was always a bit impatient, wasn't he? But the rot set in because of one person, didn't it?"

Thor grunted and nodded. "Yes, you're right. He became colder then. Harsher on everyone. Clements had made Dad's life hell and he's still walking around, thumbing his nose at everyone."

"What would Harry Thorpe do about that?" the Pierrot giggled.

Thor threw the brush down. "You're right. What would Harry Thorpe do about that?"

*****

The blue sky stretched off across the sea to the horizon. Kinnear and Manikas stared at the forest of wind turbines that covered the expanse of water between the Welsh coast and the Wirral. They could see Hilbre Island and the sands where Thorpe's body had been found. The Wirral itself was a fuzzy mass of browns, greens, and greys. In the distance beyond that, Kinnear thought he could make out the Anglican Cathedral and St John's beacon in Liverpool but the heat haze made them indistinct. It was a beautiful day, the kind that drew people from their houses and offices. Up here on the hillside, birds sang and sheep bleated to each other across the fields.

After they had come out of Thor's cottage, Kinnear had snatched the car keys from Manikas and virtually pushed him into the passenger seat. He'd driven a few miles up the road and pulled into a gateway, facing the coast. Now they sat looking out at the view in silence.

"You're going to tell me what that was all about, Alex," Kinnear said. "I need to know. And if you refuse, then I'll take my concerns to Blakey. I'm not having you jeopardise my career with your foul moods and this... this... behaviour, whatever it is. Understand?"

Manikas nodded but said nothing.

"Well?" Kinnear snapped. "I'm waiting."

"I-I can't, Andy... it's difficult..."

"You gave away a crucial bit of information about the murder. It was like you were goading him with it. I don't care how difficult it is, mate, you're going to tell me. Or I swear..."

"He tried to kill me," Manikas said, looking down into the footwell. "Thor tried to kill me last year."

Kinnear stared at Manikas, trying to process the information. "What are you talking about? When last year?"

"When we were investigating the Trevor Long case. I went to Thor's party undercover..."

"But you aren't trained to..."

"I know, I know," Manikas said, holding up his hands. "Blakey told me not to do it but I was so convinced that Thor and his Sons of Sol gang had killed Trevor Long that I made contact with Thor and pretended I wanted to join in."

"That weekend, when you came in all bruised and told us you'd got drunk and fought in a pub. Was that when he tried to kill you?"

"I went of my own volition. No back-up. Nobody even knew where I was. It was stupid. Total madness."

"Too right," Kinnear muttered. "So what happened?"

"They rumbled me pretty quickly and drugged me. I woke up in a deep pit. Harry Thorpe turned up the next morning and tried to bribe me, but I refused, so he told them to bury me alive."

"Fuck."

"I managed to escape but in the process, Thor drove the JCB into the pit and ended up in hospital." Manikas heaved a huge sigh and put his head in his hands.

"But why didn't you say anything? You had Thorpe bang to rights..."

"Did I? I wasn't on authorised police business. Blakey had warned me off. I was also off my head on drugs..."

"But they were forced on you..."

Alex Manikas shook his head. "I doubt anyone there would have corroborated my story and

Thorpe had already taken the force to court once, remember? I had nothing. But at the same time, he couldn't do anything about me without revealing that he'd tried to kill me. I just chalked it down to experience and moved on until Thorpe turned up dead."

"So do you think Thorpe being buried up to his neck like that was significant?"

"I don't know," Alex said, with a shrug. "I remember Thorpe saying something about if he couldn't get round an opponent, he buried them. It could have been a figure of speech but who knows? Maybe he meant what he said and there are bodies buried elsewhere."

"Burying someone alive," Kinnear said, shuddering. "That's awful. Mate, you must have been terrified."

Alex Manikas nodded. "Just seeing Thor sat there with his stupid haircut and ridiculous physique, it brought it all back, Andy. He was off his head on mushrooms that night, proper berserk. He might seem like a bumbling, big teddy bear but I'm telling you, Thor Magnussen is a killer."

"We've got to tell the boss," Kinnear said.

"No!" Manikas snapped. "I'll lose my job, mate. I was terrified that it would all come out when everyone started talking about interviewing Thor but at least he's got the good sense to keep it quiet."

Kinnear rubbed his forehead. "But there were no charges brought against Thorpe or his son, Alex. In fact it turned out to be a completely different kind of case, as I recall. Blakey's a fair-minded kind of bloke…"

"He also sticks to the letter of the law. I went there undercover after he expressly told me not to. I had no training, and no permission. He'd have me suspended the moment we told him. I can't afford that, Andy. Please don't say anything. I'm begging you."

CHAPTER 10

DCI Matty Cavanagh visibly winced when Blake entered his office. For once, the young man wasn't sitting with his feet up on his desk. He actually looked busy. Cavanagh had something of a reputation for flippancy and corner cutting. Many of his colleagues suspected that much of his success was down to DS Bobby Dirkin, a granite lump of a man who was ruthlessly efficient and totally loyal to Cavanagh. Whatever the truth, Cavanagh and Dirkin had an enviable record in terms of arrests and cases brought successfully to justice.

Blake often suspected that Cavanagh cultivated his image of fecklessness to lull people into a false sense of security. The man couldn't be more interested in fashion and football and be so successful at the same time. Right now, though Cavanagh looked anything but laid-back.

"I know what you're going to say, Will and the answer is no. I'm running around like a blue-arsed fly as it is..."

"I just need someone to have a word with Quinlan about the Thorpe case, that's all, Matty," Blake said, leaning on his desk. The red-haired Cavanagh sat back in his chair and stretched. He didn't look his usual well-groomed self and Blake wondered if he'd been here all night. "You know what'll happen if I go anywhere near the bugger..."

"Look, Will, I wouldn't be surprised if Quinlan was connected in some way to Harry Thorpe's death but we're flat out looking at this body in the docks right now. Another of Quinlan's old associates..."

"Any connection with Thorpe?"

"No," Cavanagh said, firmly. "They swam in different pools, but it looks like Quinlan is paddling in both. If you see what I mean. Our victim, Dane Wilson, was trying to build his own little drug empire north of the city. He had no connection or beef with Thorpe at all."

"Well, I'll just have to go and interview Quinlan myself, won't I? I hope that doesn't mess up your investigation, mate. I mean, I wouldn't want Quinlan to accuse me of harassing him because of Laura Vexley and somehow drag us both into the mire."

Cavanagh groaned and put his hands to his face. "Fuck's sake, Will. Okay. I'll send Bobby D over to have a word with Quinlan. But you can bet your bottom dollar that Quinlan will be squeaky clean on all of this. He's careful."

"Cheers, Matty, I owe you," Blake said, heading out of the office. He paused at the door and looked back at the young DCI. "Where was the body you're investigating found?"

"Floating in the dock. Stab wound to the chest. Why?"

Blake shook his head. "I'm not sure. Just a theory I'm working on. Let me know when Bobby's had a word." He looked out across the office and saw DI Kath Cryer striding purposefully towards him, holding up a piece of paper.

"It's Thorpe's car, sir," she said. "It's been spotted not far from Doug Noonan's house."

*****

When Kath Cryer had said that Thorpe's car had been spotted, he assumed it had been found abandoned. So he didn't expect to see it hurtling towards him as they turned into a hawthorn-lined lane not far from Noonan's place. With a few choice words, Kath dragged down on the steering wheel and swerved around the dark Jaguar XE as it skimmed past them. Blake glimpsed some jeering, young faces in the rear window, then it was gone.

"Jeez, Bloody joyriders, that's all we need. Kath, are you okay?"

"I will be when we've got those little scrotes cuffed and bent over the bonnet of that bloody car, sir," she muttered, wrestling the car into reverse and swinging round.

"Let's get after them, then."

Kath put her foot on the accelerator but held off putting the blue lights on. Blake called for any other cars that might be in the area to assist. The Jag bounced over the speedbumps as they powered through a busy housing estate.

"Someone's going to get killed," Kath said. "They haven't even clocked onto us, yet. Do you think we should fall back a bit, sir?"

Blake winced as they lurched over the speedbumps themselves. It was a beautiful day in the summer holidays and kids were cycling along the pavements, adults pushing prams. "Try and keep some distance, Kath. You're right; if they see us, they might panic. Jeez, this could go west so quickly."

As though to prove Blake right, the Jag suddenly powered forward, taking three wingmirrors off parked cars and sending a wheelie bin flying across the pavement. A puff of blue exhaust smoke lingered in the air behind them. Kath put her foot down and gained on them.

"There's the main road up to Arrowe Park ahead, sir," she said. "I reckon they're heading for that."

The Jag hurtled onto the busy road without even pausing at the junction. A red van blared its horn before bouncing onto the grass verge to avoid a collision. Kath had to slam on the brakes and almost skid around the oncoming car. She flicked on the blue lights and headed after the Jag. Blake squinted above them where a helicopter had joined the chase.

Blake could hardly breathe as Kath weaved in and out of traffic after the Jag. In the back, he could see the silhouettes of two passengers. Car theft was more common at night and a daylight chase like this was unusual, not to say hazardous. The Jag cut straight across a mini roundabout and overtook a bus, causing it to brake suddenly. They lost sight of the car for a moment and Blake gripped the hand grab as Kath hurtled past the bus too. Startled faces flashed by Blake as they caught the tail of the Jag again. Traffic lights at the Arrowe Park Hotel junction lay ahead of them but both lanes were blocked. Without any pause, the Jag mounted the kerb and drove onto the grass verge, its rear wheels kicking up mud and grass. It slithered alongside the row of waiting cars, the back swaying dangerously, then bounced back onto the road. Kath hissed with frustration as the cars in front responded to the blue light and tried to get out of her way.

"He's heading up Arrowe Park Road towards the hospital entrance," Blake said. "I hate to think what'll happen if an ambulance comes out of there in a hurry."

The lights turned red at the hospital entrance

and cars skidded to avoid the Jag as it shot through the junction. “There’s an industrial estate up ahead,” Blake murmured. “If we can force them down there… oh thank God.”

Blue lights flashed ahead, indicating that the Jag’s path was blocked. It slithered round the corner into the service road to the industrial estate and Kath followed. Blake could see the cars up ahead and the officers at the side of the road, ready to deploy the Stinger device to puncture the car’s tyres. The Jag’s brake lights flashed on and its tyres squealed on the tarmac but it bumped pathetically over the metallic spikes and came to an abrupt halt.

Kath Cryer slammed on her own brakes and stopped behind the Jag with centimetres to spare. But they didn’t have time to recover as the Jag’s doors swung open and three teenagers sprinted from the car. Blake was out, rugby-tackling one lad to the ground while Kath grabbed another, slamming him against the side of the Jag. The final joyrider ran straight into the arms of a uniformed officer.

The lad underneath Blake squirmed. He stank of body odour and some kind of cheap body spray. “Get off me you fuckin…”

Blake leaned down and hissed in his ear. “The question isn’t, do I arrest you for taking a car without the owner’s consent? I’m going to do that anyway. I'm just wondering whether or not to arrest you on suspicion of murder too."

"Murder?" the boy said, falling still. "I haven't murdered nobody."

"You're driving a dead man's car, sonny."

"We just found it down that lane, mister. I swear down. It had the keys in it and everything. We couldn't believe our luck..."

"We'll see, shall we?" Blake said, dragging the lad to his feet and marching him towards the waiting police officers.

*****

As she entered the room, Laura Vexley could smell the alcohol haze that surrounded Kyle Quinlan. She closed her eyes and shook her head. He sat at his desk in a huge leather chair, with that sheepish, naughty boy grin on his face. He was a good-looking man, tall and muscular but dark and smooth, too. The trouble was he knew it.

"Tell me you didn't kill Harry Thorpe," Laura said, standing in front of the huge desk, with her arms folding.

Quinlan held up his hands and widened his eyes. Even unshaven and ragged after a night on the lash he looked stunning. "Okay, I didn't kill Harry Thorpe."

"Don't joke with me, Kyle. If you planted him in

the sand after he sold out to you, your reputation is going to be worthless."

"How d'you work that out? Won't people be more scared of me?"

"No. They'll just think you're a psycho and not do business with you. They'll run a mile."

"But if I threaten them, it'll have more force, won't it? If I say, 'don't fuck with me unless you wanna end up buried, waiting for the tide to come in,' it'll put the wind up 'em, won't it?"

"You can't go round threatening people all the time, Kyle. You have to earn respect..."

"They'll respect me if they think they're gonna die..."

"No. They'll fear you and when people fear something they either run away or they gang up and fight it. Is that what you want? A war?"

"I'd win," Quinlan muttered, pouting like a toddler.

"No, you wouldn't. Nobody wins those kinds of battles. Everyone just ends up in prison because they're too busy killing each other to remember to be careful. If you don't carry people with you, then someone will stab you in the back."

"And who might that 'someone' be?" Quinlan said, glaring at Laura. "You? It wouldn't be the first time, would it?"

Laura felt her cheeks redden. It was true that in another time, she had been Quinlan's wife, he beat her until she stood up to him, kicked his backside and took the money he was guarding for Harry Thorpe. It had forced Quinlan to flee abroad for his life. Laura had rebuilt her life after that and thought she could be happy without Quinlan. Time had proved her wrong. "That's exactly what I'm talking about. If you kick people for long enough, they turn on you. I came back because I thought you'd changed; you said you were older and wiser. I thought your near-death experience in America had taught you a lesson. But you're still the same old Kyle, it seems."

Quinlan scowled at her, rubbing his head. "Have I laid a finger on you? No. You've got a good life, haven't you? Plenty of money, your little businesses. Don't worry about Thorpe."

"Don't worry about Thorpe? What's that meant to mean?"

"Look, the less you know the better. Just forget about Harry Thorpe, okay?"

Laura stared hard at Kyle Quinlan. He wasn't always the sharpest tool in the pack but he could be hard to read sometimes. "You better know what you're doing, Kyle?"

He returned her gaze. "I do, I promise you."

"And what about Dane Wilson?"

Kyle looked her in the eye and Laura almost flinched at the darkness in there. “That was a random stabbing. Could have been anyone. Not many people liked Dane, did they?”

Shaking her head, Laura turned on her heel. “Just make sure you don’t get tangled up in the Harry Thorpe investigation. It’ll make you look terrible.” She slammed the door behind her. He was starting to keep secrets from her and that meant she was losing control. She didn’t like it.

CHAPTER 11

Oliver Young wasn't your run-of -the-mill every-day joyrider. For a start, he lived not far from where Harold Thorpe's car was first found in what was quite a desirable residential area. On the face of it, he wasn't some deprived, feral teen-ager from a sink estate, off the rails on drink and drugs. He was quiet and well-spoken. His clothes were clean and, according to a young PC, were all expensive designer sportswear. Blake wouldn't know. It just looked like a white tracksuit to him, but he was willing to take the constable's word for it.

Young's parents sent a brief almost imme-diately and then, surprisingly, an appropriate adult called Maggie who clearly didn't approve of either Oliver or the brief or the fact that both of his parents were 'too busy' to come and sit with him.

"What do they do that's so important, Oliver?" she had said loudly at the desk in the custody suite. Oliver had muttered something that Blake didn't hear. "What the hell is 'lifestyle coaching' when it's at home?" Maggie must have been in her fifties, with a shock of greying, mousy brown hair. "Tell 'em from me that they should have got their arses down here, if they had a shred of decency." She struck Blake as the kind of woman you didn't mess with.

"Mrs Tempest," the brief, Gareth Cornell had started to say. Blake knew Gareth from previous cases. He was a skinny, pale man with messy blond hair that never seemed to settle into a decent cut. "I don't think..."

"Did you borrow that suit off your dad for the occasion, Gareth?" Maggie said, not changing her tone from when she was talking to Oliver.

Gareth Cornell flushed red. "No... I..." he had muttered and turned to Blake. "Is there somewhere the three of us could talk, privately?"

The desk sergeant had allocated them a room to discuss what Oliver's best options were. Blake had watched them disappear into the room and had almost felt sorry for Oliver. "And don't let old Corny Cornell here persuade you to do that 'no comment' bollocks," Maggie had said starting the 'discussion' before they had even closed the door. "You're not the 'Godfather,' lad, they saw you in the Jag giving the police the finger. Keeping schtum will only go against you..."

Now, sitting in front of a contrite Oliver Young, Blake was left wondering if they couldn't somehow employ Maggie Tempest and then clone her. Gareth Cornell coughed awkwardly and muttered something about Oliver wanting to cooperate fully.

"But don't you go putting words in his mouth, Blakey," Maggie Tempest said. "And give him time to think about things, he's got dyspraxia apparently..." she shrugged and looked at the ceiling.

"Okay," Blake said, giving Kath Cryer a quick glance. "So, tell me about the events leading up to you taking the stolen car, a black Jaguar XE, registration number HTHT1."

Oliver Young thought for a moment and then looked at Maggie. "He means how did you end up nicking the car?"

"Oh!" Oliver said. "Right! Well, me and Smudge and Rinker we were just walking around, bored, and we saw it in the field gate. I went up to it and saw that the keys were in it. So we took it."

"That was just prior to when we came around the corner and intercepted you..." Blake said.

Maggie Tempest tutted and folded her arms. "Just prior? Intercepted? Come one, DCI Blake, this isn't a vocab test. Give the lad a chance!"

"Mrs Tempest, we appreciate your help but we can't have you interrupting us all the time," Blake said.

"Speak plain English then," Maggie Tempest said. "Then I don't have to bloomin' translate."

Out of the corner of his eye, Blake caught a glimpse of Kath Cryer smirking. "Oliver was that just before we met you in the lane?"

Oliver glanced over at Maggie who nodded. "No," Oliver said. "We found it on the Monday evening and drove it around a bit. When we weren't caught, I said we should put it back where we found it and leave it with the keys in and all that. But it was there again today and it was too tempting. It's a lovely car."

"Ooh, yeah, I know," Maggie agreed. "I mean, I've never been in that one, like, but I've been in others..." She saw Blake's expression and clamped her mouth shut.

"Right," Oliver said. "I noticed the car early Monday morning. I'd been doing my paper round..."

"You've got a paper round?" Maggie said, staring at Oliver. "How the hell did you end up nicking cars?"

Oliver shrugged. "I just saw it. I mean, nobody was claiming it were they? And the keys were still in it and I thought I'd mention it to the lads. It was more like borrowing it, really."

"Where did you learn to drive like that?" Kath said, making Blake wince and wonder if, between Maggie and Kath, the interview might just go off the rails altogether.

"My dad paid for some private lessons a while back. It was on this racetrack with a real sports-car. The man said I was too young but Dad managed to persuade him…"

"Did you know who the owner of the car was?"

"I don't know who it belonged to apart from someone who's been murdered."

"What makes you say that?" Blake said.

"You said something about charging me with murder. So I guess the car belonged to someone who'd been murdered, yeah?"

"The lad's got a paper round, Blake," Maggie Tempest said. "He's not a murderer."

Blake ignored her and looked hard at Oliver. "When you first saw the car, was anyone in it or near it?"

"Not really…"

"What do you mean, 'not really?' Either someone was in it or they were near it. I don't understand."

"Well there's a bloke who walks his dog round there most days. He stopped and stared at the car."

"Okay," Blake said. "So did you."

"Yeah, but he took off after he saw the car. Almost ran, pulling the little dog along. I felt a bit sorry for it."

"This man, what did he look like?"

"Long ginger beard, long hair, always wears one of those caps..."

"Like a baseball cap?"

"A bit like that but square. Smudge calls them Jeremy Corbyn hats. Do you know the kind I mean? Anyway," Oliver said, with a giggle. "I always think the bloke looks like that dwarf in Lord of the Rings. I saw him without the hat once and he's bald on top..."

*****

Doug Noonan's house was just around the corner from where Oliver found the car and the man himself was watering the plants in his front garden when Blake arrived. It was late and still warm and clammy but Blake had decided to make the call on the way home. Noonan froze, a stream of water splattering onto the flooded plant pot beneath. "Inspector Blake," he said in a faint voice. "What are you doing here, again?"

"Do you have a dog, Mr Noonan?"

"What?"

"I asked you if you had a dog."

As if to save Doug the trouble of answering, a Yorkshire terrier leapt up at the front room window, its yapping muffled by the glass.

"Why didn't you tell us that Harry Thorpe's car was just around the corner?" Blake said.

"I don't know what you're talking about," Doug Noonan said.

"That's funny because a witness saw someone, who looks just like you, walking smartly away from the vehicle dragging a Yorkshire Terrier behind him."

"I-I didn't know it was Thorpe's car..."

"You clocked the personalised number plate, right? Thorpe has been around to your, sorry, his, house. You'd have seen the car before."

Noonan licked his lips. "Yeah, but he might have other houses round here. Just cos his car was parked round the corner doesn't mean it's anything to do with me..."

Blake put his hands in his pockets. "I never said it did have anything to do with you. I just wondered why you were walking away from it so quickly and why you didn't mention it when we spoke to you yesterday. Is there something you want to tell me?"

"I saw his car, yes but I never knew he was dead, did I? He was a scary man and I knew I'd gone a bit too far threatening him. I thought he might be lurking around with one or two of his gorillas to rough me up. That's why I hurried away from the car."

"Funny that it's been parked so close to your house, Mr Noonan, isn't it?"

Noonan glared at Blake. "I don't know what you mean. I only saw it yesterday, after Thorpe was found dead, I presume."

"We have samples of your DNA, Mr Noonan, if we find any traces in that car…"

"You won't, Inspector. You absolutely won't," Noonan said, through gritted teeth.

"Fair enough," Blake said, turning on his heel. "I'll want to speak to you further, I'm sure, Mr Noonan." The man stood in the front garden still holding the watering can. All the way down the road, Blake could feel Noonan's eyes boring a hole in his back.

*****

Doug Noonan waited until DCI Blake had vanished up the road then rummaged in his pocket for his phone. He scrolled through the contacts until he came to the name 'Client 1.' It rang for a long time, leaving Noonan to listen to his own breath rattling against the phone and his heart thudding against his chest. Finally, a voice answered.

"He was just here again," Noonan said, glancing up and down the street.

"Who?"

"Blake! Bloody Blake was just here again. Look, I know you said not to worry but I'm getting edgy. You said nobody would give a toss about Thorpe."

"Calm yourself," Client 1 said. "Just keep your head down. You did a professional job, so you won't have left any evidence, will you?"

Noonan felt himself reddening. "Of course not," he said, coughing gruffly. "But listen, I need the cash immediately with an extra two grand."

"Two grand? Are you having a laugh? What the hell for?"

"Because I might have to do a quick dash to somewhere far away and it'll cost."

"You don't need to go anywhere, Noonan. You'll keep your head down and meet me at the agreed time and place tomorrow, okay? You'll get your money."

"Fine. Don't forget, I know who you are. If I go down, I'll be taking you with me." Noonan ended the call and stared at the phone. He wished he'd never got involved in all of this.

CHAPTER 12

Serafina smelt strange. There was no doubt about it. Blake had come home late and slumped onto the sofa with a bottle of Brimstage Brewery Pale Ale, but it wasn't long before the cat was up on his knee. When her bushy tail swept across his face he'd frowned. What was that smell? Normally, Serafina's smell was neutral unless she was wet. Charlie might be partial to rolling in a bit of fox poo and revelled in smelling like a midden, but Serafina was constantly grooming.

He stroked her head and snuffled the back of her neck. It wasn't an unpleasant smell. It was somewhere between potpourri and air freshener. There was a chemical taint under the flowery scent. It was the smell of someone else's house.

When he was a kid, Blake had realised early on that different people's houses smelled of different things. Once, one of his mates had remarked that Blake's house always smelt of baking. This came as a relief to the young Blake; some of his mates' houses smelt of cigarettes and others' smelt of frying and fat and it would linger on his clothes for days. One friend's house was damp and musty, a smell he could never forget. At least the cat smelt fragrant, but it was definitely the smell of another home.

"Where have you been, puss?" Blake muttered, stroking the cat. "Is someone trying to seduce you away from me with food again?" His stomach fluttered anxiously. Blake didn't like the idea of her visiting someone else. Last year, Serafina had gone missing and Blake's search for her had almost cost him his life. Previous to that, someone in the area had been supplying her with extra food, resulting in her gaining an unhealthy amount of weight and giving her an eye-watering flatulence.

Charlie whimpered and looked up at him. When Laura had been around, she'd talked a lot about a 'dogs on the floor' policy, not allowing him onto the furniture. Blake could see the sense in it. All he had to do was roll in some of his favourite blend of fox and badger crap and then leap up onto the sofa and the cleaning bill would be phenomenal. That was if Blake didn't miss the errant stains and sit in them himself. But Laura wasn't here, and Blake felt sorry for the little fella. Besides, he'd grown since Laura had left, he was only a puppy then. "Come on, fella," Blake said, patting the sofa. Charlie didn't need telling twice; he bounced up next to Blake and began burrowing his snout under Blake's arm, his tail thumping on the cushion like a bass drum.

Blake's grin faded as he thought about the case. There was something about Noonan that Blake didn't trust. He was holding something back, that was certain. Noonan didn't strike Blake as a killer but from what PC Mark Robertson's witness and others had said, Thorpe's death had been a team effort. Or at least the disposal of the body had been. That pointed to something more organised which would require a degree of leadership. It came back to Quinlan.

The fact that he'd been buying up properties and businesses in Laura's name worried Blake. She was becoming more and more entangled in his world. She said to Blake that she was just looking after number one, that she knew what she was doing but the more her name was plastered across his business interests, the harder it would ever be for her to step away from Quinlan.

He looked down at Charlie. "And why should I care, eh, boy? She's made her bed, so she should lie in it, right?" Charlie looked up at him, with sad, brown eyes. Blake sighed. "I know, mate but it's getting harder and harder to think anything good of her. Don't look like that." Was Charlie right to reproach him? Was there a spark of frustration and annoyance inside Blake? A desire to rid himself of Laura once and for all? Then why did he find it so hard to move on?

*****

DC Andrew Kinnear lay in bed, staring at the darkness above him. His husband, Chris, snored softly beside him, and a suffocating heat filled the room, but it was Kinnear's racing mind that stopped him from sleeping. He wished he hadn't pushed Alex Manikas to reveal his secret. Didn't he have some kind of duty to report it to Blake? What if it all came out and then people realised that Kinnear had kept Alex's secret? He could be disciplined, possibly even lose his job. How would he explain that to Chris? They had Niamh now, their daughter, the little girl depended on them. He couldn't let them down.

He could hardly believe that Manikas would go off on some kind of undercover mission. What was he thinking of? And then to conceal it all. It was a wonder Thorpe hadn't tried to blackmail Manikas. Then again Thorpe could hardly have said anything once he'd tried to murder Alex.

Kinnear shuddered. Imagine being buried alive. It hadn't happened but Alex had come that close to a horrible death. How had he coped with that? Surely such an experience must have affected Manikas. He should have had counselling and support from the force. Instead, he'd kept quiet and bottled it all up. That wasn't healthy; whatever happened in the past shouldn't have a negative impact on the current investigation. But the way Manikas goaded Magnussen suggested that Alex shouldn't be anywhere near this case. He had to get Manikas to tell Blake everything that had happened. Otherwise, the only other option would be to break Manikas' trust. He just hoped he didn't have to do that.

*****

It would have been absolutely no consolation to Kinnear to know that DC Alex Manikas found sleep impossible, too. Similar thoughts whirled around his head. He'd dozed of at some point, only to find himself deep in that pit with Thor's gang looking down on him. His dream was vivid and he smelt the damp earth and the diesel from the digger, felt the cold of the soil as it rained down on him. Then he was scrambling on top of the earth as it piled up, fighting tooth and nail to get away. He sat up with a gasp, sweat drenching him, his heart pounding.

He went to the bathroom and splashed cold water on his face, shivering at its sting but grateful for it too in the stifling night. Alex thought he'd coped well crushing those memories but seeing Thor Magnussen sitting in his cottage had brought it all back. A cold rage had spread through him and suddenly, he had wanted to leap across the room and smash the big man's brains out.

Other people might think Thor Magnussen was a bit of a buffoon, indulged by his mother and feckless but Alex had seen the man's mad glare as he drove the digger at him that fateful night. Alex had also heard the way Harry Thorpe had spoken to his son and he could well believe that

Thor Magnussen could kill his father. The man had even changed his name. He may say he was grieving but there was no love lost between Thor Magnussen and his estranged father. The problem was getting the rest of the team to realise that without revealing what had happened in the past.

He stared out of the window into the dark street outside. If only he hadn't told Andrew Kinnear. He knew Andrew was a worrier, the man was probably fretting about it now. It was essential that Kinnear didn't tell Blake. Manikas picked up his phone. It buzzed for all of a second before Kinnear answered it.

"Bloody hell, Alex, it's four in the morning," Kinnear whispered.

"Yeah and you're wide awake," Alex said, his voice low.

"I've you to thank for that, mate," Kinnear said, bitterly.

"I know, look, I'm sorry. But we are where we are, right?"

"You've got to tell Blake. This is bound to come out and it'll look a lot worse if he thinks you've... we've tried to cover it up..."

"I can't, Andy," Manikas said. "This is my life we're talking about. What will I do if I'm kicked out of the force?"

“You? I’m not thinking about you, mate. I’ve got a daughter and a husband to support. I can’t afford to lose my job either and *you’ve* dragged me into it!”

“You forced me to tell you. I didn’t want to. Remember that before you go accusing me of dragging you into anything. Look, if we can track down some of Thor’s gang, you know, the Sons of Sol, then maybe we could get some other dirt on Thor that might tie him to the murder. If we nail Thor, maybe he won’t be so keen to talk about the time he tried to kill me.”

“Or he might just think if he’s going down, he might as well take you with him,” Kinnear hissed. “Bloody hell, Alex. I can’t stand this. Why the hell did you try and go undercover in the first place? You need training and authorisation and… and…” Manikas could imagine Kinnear desperately trying not to throw the phone across the room.

“I’m sorry, mate. I really am. If I could go back, I wouldn’t do it but, like I say, here we are. I need to do something. I can’t just let things unravel and I reckon if we can nail Thor, then we’re good.”

“What makes you think he even did it?”

“Oh, come on, mate,” Alex said. “You saw him back at his cottage. The mask slipped, didn’t it? He might come across as a bit of a muscle-headed lump but he’s a shrewd operator, believe me and how often are murders within families? It's common…"

"The occasional family row getting out of hand and ending in a stabbing or an angry punch is one thing. To bury your dad up to his neck in sand and leave him to drown is something else."

"But Thor has the manpower and it's the kind of freaky thing he'd do, right? He's into all that Viking shit. I bet they buried their victims in the sand."

"Why are we even talking about this? You need to go to Blake, tomorrow and tell him everything you know."

"I can't Andy, I just can't. God. My parents would be so ashamed of me. I've let everyone down. Please. I'm begging you, give me some time and I'll show you that Thor is guilty. If I can't then I'll go to Blake on my own. He doesn't even have to know that I told you first."

Manikas heard Kinnear's heavy sigh down the phone. "Bloody hell, mate. Okay but I'm doing this because you're my friend," Kinnear said. "I hope you realise I'm going against my own good judgement. Okay?"

"Okay. And thanks. Try and get some sleep. I'm really sorry, Andy." Manikas hung up. He felt bad for pulling Kinnear into the mire but at the same time, he felt like he had an ally and together, they'd prove that Thor Magnussen was the killer that Alex knew he was. Now they had to find a dissident member of the Sons of Sol and Alex knew just where to look.

CHAPTER 13

There was a weariness about the team in the Major Incident Room that couldn't just be down to the lack of sleep after a sticky, humid night. Blake felt pretty sure it emanated from Manikas and Kinnear. He peered at them as they slumped in their plastic chairs, arms folded, not talking to each other or anyone else in the group. Even Kath Cryer picked up on it and halted her conversation with Vikki Chinn to make a comment.

"You two weren't out on a school night were you lads? You look like you've been on the lash. And if you were, why wasn't I invited?"

Kinnear smiled weakly. "Sorry, Ma'am, the littlun was up in the night. It just wiped me out. You know when you're woken up at four in the morning and you can't get back to sleep?"

"I'm fine," Manikas said, straightening up in his chair and blinking. "It was just so hot last night."

"Just make sure you concentrate, lads," Blake said. "I don't want anyone dropping the ball on this one. So far we've drawn a load of blanks and I really want a breakthrough. Vikki, any developments?"

"Tasha Cook has identified another associate of Harry Thorpe's who might be worth talking to, sir," Vikki said and consulted her notes. "Sam Fletcher. Apparently, he has a thriving boat rental business here and in North Wales. Tasha also reported that Mrs Thorpe became very defensive when her husband's financial accounts were mentioned."

"Right. Ian Ollerthwaite is still on sick leave, isn't he?" Ollerthwaite had been the victim of a savage beating a couple of months back and for a while it was touch and go whether he would survive.

"Technically, sir, yes," Kath said, "but his wife told me privately that he's driving her up the wall..."

"You've been in touch with Theresa Ollerthwaite?" Blake said to Kath, trying to conceal the wonder in his voice. Kath wasn't the most touchy-feely person in the team and the staid, some might say boring, Ollerthwaite was the last person that Kath would have an interest in. Blake had once described him as Ketamine in human form or something like that. Just the sound of his voice made your eyelids droop. The idea of DI Kath Cryer befriending Mrs Ollerthwaite amazed Blake.

"Don't look so surprised, sir. She's a laugh. I suppose she'd have to have a sense of humour to be married to Ian for so long. Anyway, she reckons he would be up for a couple of days working from home."

"I'll pop round and visit him," Blake said. "See if he's up for looking at Thorpe's accounts."

"He'll like that," Kath said, grinning mischievously. "Apparently, he's used the time off to completely reconstruct his loft layout. New train engines, too. The finer detail of the locomotives was lost on me but I'm sure you'll be in your element, sir."

Blake winced. "Great."

"I like his train layouts, sir," Kinnear said. "I don't mind going."

"Very noble of you, Andrew, but I think it better be me. I want to make sure he's okay with taking on the case. It can be quite stressful getting back into work after a major trauma like that."

Kinnear nodded and gave Manikas a sidelong glance. "I'm sure it can, sir."

"How did you two get on with Thor Magnussen?" Blake said, slightly puzzled by Kinnear's response and the way Alex Manikas flinched slightly when Blake addressed them.

"He was quite hostile, sir," Kinnear said. "We think he may warrant closer investigation. He claims he was just down the coast with the Sons of Sol when his father died. You know yourself how many murders are committed within families..."

"And Magnussen was estranged from his father, sir. There was plenty of bad blood between them," Alex added. "He said that some of his Sons of Sol had defected to Kyle Quinlan. We thought if we spoke to them, we might get a clearer picture of the relationship between Magnussen and his father."

"Okay," Blake said. "Tread carefully, though. I don't want Quinlan wading in on this until Cavanagh is ready to talk to him."

"It has to be Quinlan, sir," Kath Cryer said, looking pained on Blake's behalf. "He was in direct competition with Thorpe…"

"Until Thorpe sold his entire business portfolio to Quinlan," Blake said. "Something most of Thorpe's employees and tenants seem unanimously happy about. Why would Quinlan do something so public when he's got what he wanted? Cavanagh is looking into another rival of Quinlan's who has just turned up floating in the docks. Now I know, that points to Quinlan maybe having a purge, or making a pre-emptive strike but why not just bump Thorpe off quietly? Make it look like a mugging or something?"

Kath shrugged. "Like I said before, to make a statement…"

"But he didn't make that statement with this other rival, did he? To me it seems too high risk, Kath. Quinlan isn't a fool and he's got good advice in the form of Laura Vexley. I had it from the horse's mouth a few months back, that she intends to make sure Quinlan doesn't screw up. And she seems to be up to her neck in his business interests…" aware he was beginning to rant, Blake clammed up.

"I'm pretty sure Magnussen is our man, sir," Alex said, breaking the brief, awkward silence. "It makes sense. He's fallen out with his father, wants to get him out of the way so he can go back to his Mum on that farm they live on. Plus, his gang could easily have pulled off the stunt of burying him. I mean they have access to diggers and stuff, don't they?"

"Do they?" Blake said, in surprise.

"Well, yeah," Manikas said, reddening. "Thorpe was a property developer. They have gear like that, I think…"

"Wasn't Magnussen hospitalised after messing about on a digger on the Thorpe place?" Kinnear said, nudging Manikas.

"God, yeah," Manikas said. "I'd forgotten that."

"Okay, you two," Blake said. "I'll admit, Magnussen might well be a prime suspect but let's not jump to conclusions. Vikki, any forensics back from Thorpe's car?"

"Nothing of much use, sir. The joyriders' prints were all over the inside. Thorpe's prints and his wife's on the steering wheel and door handles, too. Otherwise, it's clean. Fragments of gravel in the tyres are from the drive at Thorpe's home. Nothing in the glove compartment or the boot. The kids didn't take anything from the car, we're pretty sure of that."

Blake shook his head. "The car was so close to Doug Noonan's house. It doesn't make sense that he would dump the car there if he killed Thorpe. I mean, why would you incriminate yourself?"

"Plus a witness said he looked panicky when he saw the car, sir," Kath said. "Which would suggest he was surprised to see it there."

"Can we rule him out then, sir?" Vikki said.

"I don't know," Blake said. "He did threaten Thorpe and there's something about him that doesn't seem right. Who else have we got?"

"Jack Kenning sent through some more details from the post-mortem and toxicology. Apparently, there were high levels of flunitrazepam in Thorpe's blood stream along with alcohol."

"That's Rohypnol, right?" Blake said. "Jeez, so Thorpe was drugged and then drowned."

"That would explain why there were no signs of a struggle, sir," Kath said.

"Kenning says that from the amount found in his blood, he might well have been semi-conscious when the tide came in," Vikki said, grimacing. "And, judging from the amount of sea water in Thorpe's lung lining, he drowned."

"Jeez," Blake muttered. "So someone drugged him. Where the hell were his bodyguards? I don't remember seeing Thorpe without them apart from at the police station."

"It is weird, sir," Vikki agreed.

"At seven o'clock, Thorpe goes out. Maybe to meet someone and ends up unconscious. Then he's taken to the beach where he's buried up to his neck just as the tide is coming in."

"We need to know where he was going that night and who he was meeting, sir," Vikki Chinn said.

"It must have been someone he knew and trusted, given he didn't take any muscle to protect him," Kinnear said.

"Or someone he wasn't scared of," Blake said. "Any sign of his mobile phone?"

"No, sir. We've got the number and are pulling the call records but we're still waiting for them," Vikki said.

"Good. Chivvy them up, Vikki. Make a nuisance of yourself. I want to know who he spoke to on his last day on earth," Blake muttered. "So, we've got Noonan, possibly. Thor Magnussen, a strong contender. Who else?"

"There's Clements, sir, the disgraced Inspector

who tried to frame Thorpe," Kath said. "His alibi is a bit shaky. He said he watched TV and went to the supermarket for some beers. There's no trace of him on the supermarket CCTV and nobody remembers seeing him there. It doesn't make him guilty, though. I mean, I stayed in and watched telly last night..."

"Wasn't Theo there with you, Ma'am?" Vikki said. "He'd give you an alibi."

"That useless lump? Slept all the way through Holby city. I could have sneaked out and shot all the neighbours and he'd still be snoring and farting on the sofa."

Blake shook his head. "Again, it's the theatrics involved that puzzle me, Kath. Clements might have got a kick out of harassing Thorpe but I can't see him as the killer. And if he was, he'd be more likely to kill Thorpe in a low-key manner. He's forensically aware, and he'd also know how many cases turn on a vigilant member of the public. Why would he go to all the trouble of burying Thorpe on a public beach? Jeez, when I say it like that why would *anyone* do that? It's insane."

"A statement, sir, it's the only explanation," Kath said again. "It's saying 'this is what happens if you mess with us.'"

Blake pulled a face. "But who does that, Kath? It's like it's out of a film or TV. Who benefits from

Thorpe's death?"

"Quinlan," Kath said.

Alex raised a hand. "Thor Magnussen."

"What about Mrs Thorpe?" Blake said. "She'd inherit everything, wouldn't she? What's her alibi, again?"

"She was at a Pilates class at a private health club between 8pm and 9.30. Then she came home and went to bed," Vikki said, glancing at her notes once more.

"Plenty of people will have seen her there, I guess," Blake said, rubbing his temples. "We've verified that, have we?"

Vikki nodded. "Yep, Tasha spoke to her Pilates instructor who confirmed that Mrs Thorpe was there in his class."

"So she's out the frame but could still have hired someone to do the dirty work."

"I dunno, sir," Vikki said. "Tasha seemed pretty certain that Mrs Thorpe was genuinely upset about her husband's death."

"Also, she'd have a job rustling up a crew to manhandle her husband over to the beach and dig a hole to plant him in, sir" Manikas said. "Anyone she knew would be connected with her husband."

"Vikki, have another word with Mrs Thorpe. At

the very least, we need to know what happened to Thorpe's bodyguard. We need to have a look at Thorpe's will, although I suspect that won't cover all of his ill-gotten gains. Alex and Andrew, get stuck into Thor's alibi and any ex-members of his team who might give us a lead on his relationship with his father. Kath, can you go and have another word with Clements, maybe you can use your no-nonsense charm on him, he's a slippery bugger. I'll go and see Ian Ollerthwaite, see if we can drag him away from his toy trains and back onto some proper police work. Let's stop fannying around and nail down whoever did this."

CHAPTER 14

Another hot day had brought the people of Heswall out in force. DI Kath Cryer sat in her car at the lights and wondered if anyone else actually worked or went to school these days. A small gang of young girls in their flimsy summer wear drift past a trio of lads in shorts and vest tops. In her day, they'd have been eyeing each other up, flirting and giggling. Sighing, she watched them staring into their phones as they shuffled along the pavement, oblivious. She wound her window down but resisted the urge to shout something about youth being wasted on the young. The air-con in her car was broken but the open window did little to cool the car. Kath hissed with frustration at the temporary traffic lights, cursing the lazy bastards who were meant to keep these cars serviced and in tiptop condition. The last service this car had must have been a Friday afternoon job.

But Kath knew why she was in such a bad mood. It was Blake. As far as she could see, he had his head in the sand over the fact that it was Kyle Quinlan they should be chasing down for this murder. She smirked at herself in the rear-view mirror; head in the sand probably wasn't the best expression given the circumstances of Thorpe's death. A frustrated frown replaced the smile. Why were they making Clements' life a misery? An ex-copper who, fair enough, had been a little overeager to get a result but it wasn't like Thorpe was a poor innocent. The idea of Clements actually taking such a massive risk as killing Harry Thorpe in public struck Kath as ridiculous.

Finally, the lights changed and soon, Kath arrived at Clements' bungalow. Kath took in the neat front lawn, freshly dug flower bed. Surely, these were signs of a man who had moved on, not someone just waiting for the chance to bury an old adversary up to his neck in sand. She got out and knocked on the door.

Clements himself, struck Kath as an angry-looking man with small eyes, and a tight mouth. Maybe he did still hold a grudge, she thought. He certainly looked like the experience had aged him. His pot belly hinted at days spent sitting down, maybe at a computer or watching TV. Kath could imagine him spitting bile on Twitter or poring over internet conspiracy theories. It didn't make him a killer, though. He glared at her through thick glasses. "Oh for fuck's sake. Again?"

"Sorry, Mr Clements," Kath said, pocketing her warrant card. "Not my shout. The boss sent me over to have another word."

Slightly mollified by Kath's honesty, he looked

Kath up and down. "Well, I'm just going out for a coffee. You all right if we walk and talk?"

Kath stood on the doorstep as Clements went back into the house to get a jacket and his wallet. She could see papers on the floor, a pile of magazines next to them. A greasy smell drifted out of the house, making her glad he hadn't invited her in.

"Yeah, it's a tip, I know," he said as he came out and shut the door. "I care more about my garden than the inside of the house, this time of year. Besides, when I stopped being a copper, I lost everything apart from this place. My wife left me, took my son up north. I scrape by now but money's tight and no pension to look forward to. So I don't splash out on fripperies."

"I'm sorry to hear that," Kath said.

"Are you?" Clements muttered, setting off down the road. He obviously wasn't in peak condition and looked older than his years but he was still taller than Kath and had quite a stride.

Kath hurried after him. "Harry Thorpe was no angel and," she glanced back at the house, "it seems to me that you've paid a heavy price for what you did. Look Mr Clements, you were a copper and you know the score, so I'll be honest with you. I'm not sure why we're bothering you. There are far more likely candidates for this business than you. So if I can just tie up the loose ends, I can leave you alone and get on with my job."

Clements raised an eyebrow. "Call me, Nigel," he said. "Come on, I'll buy you a coffee."

*****

If there was one thing Blake hated, it was boats. He'd never trusted them. His encounters with them had been unpleasant, wet, and cold. Early school experiences in canoes on an outward-bound course when he'd been told to deliberately capsize had left him suspicious of them and the people who got so excited about them. Once on holiday, his dad had decided to hire a rowing boat on the River in Stratford only to spend the whole time barking at him and Jeff, his brother, to keep still and not trail their hands in the water. They spent more time drifting under the trees and bushes along the bank. Ultimately, they'd crashed into another family boat and Will had watched his dad engage in a mortifying argument with the other group.

So when he discovered that Sam Fletcher, one of Thorpe's old business associates, was down at West Kirby Sailing Club, his heart sank. The club lay at the southern end of West Kirby Marina, a white, flat-roofed building surrounded by a yard full of sailing boats. A forest of masts poked up from behind a tall picket fence, lines jangling against them in the breeze. Blake tried to hide his relief at the news that Fletcher was in the yard checking his boat out and not actually setting sail.

Sam Fletcher looked just as Blake expected; a mop of thick white hair framed his weather-beaten face. He had a ruggedness about him that told of years of living outside. Standing on the back of his boat, which in turn, sat on a trailer, meant that Blake had to shade his eyes from the sun to look up at him. Fletcher wore a faded mauve polo-shirt and ragged shorts that revealed his sinewy brown legs.

"I wondered how long it would take you lot to track me down," Fletcher said when Blake introduced himself.

"You didn't consider coming to find us, then, Mr Fletcher?" Blake said, still squinting into the sun.

Fletcher shrugged and jumped down from the boat, landing close to Blake. "Didn't see the need. I don't think I can help you."

Now he could see him more clearly, Blake noticed scarring on the man's face and his steely blue eyes. "What was your relationship with Harry Thorpe?" Blake said.

"You don't hang about, do you? Why don't you just come right out and ask me if I killed him?"

"Did you?"

Fletcher laughed. "Of course not. Harry and I go... went... back a long way. You'll know I've got a past, Mr Blake."

"You've done a couple of stretches for smuggling cocaine into the country, I know that much. Was that for Thorpe?"

Fletcher shrugged. "Don't suppose it can harm him and I'd deny it all if you tried to go after his widow because of it but, yeah, I did time for Thorpe. That's all behind me, now. I do a bit of repair work, rent out a few boats over in North Wales..."

"Did you stay in touch with Thorpe?"

"Now and then he'd pop up round here. After my last stint inside, I told him I wanted nothing more to do with him..."

"How did he take that?"

Fletcher thought for a second. "He was a fair man, was Harry Thorpe. I reckon he realised I'd done enough for him. It was an amicable parting of the ways."

"But he came back into your life recently, didn't he?"

"Yeah," Fletcher said, rolling his eyes. "He got back in touch about a year ago, wanting to start up a boat rental business." He paused for a moment. "He seemed different, though."

"In what way?"

"I don't know. Tired of it all, maybe? Yeah,

weary. He said he was getting too old. Mentioned something about a 'close shave' with you lot. He talked about selling up his betting shops and houses and opening a legit business in North Wales. He wanted me to go in with him."

"And how did you feel about that?"

"I wasn't mad keen, to be honest. Harry wasn't going to change his spots for long. Anyone who knew him could work that out. The moment he saw an angle or a way to cut corners or screw someone over, he'd be doing it like a shot. I've spent a lot of time building up trust in my customers and business associates, Mr Blake. They'd run a mile from a wide boy like Harry Thorpe."

"So you slapped him off again..."

"I know where you're going with this. You're going to suggest he was putting pressure on me to let him use my contacts or to introduce him. Maybe you think he was threatening me..."

"Well was he?"

"He wasn't very happy, but I told him the truth. If I'd introduced him to some of my clients, they'd be mortified and I wouldn't work again. He was quite insistent, though."

"How insistent?"

"Put it this way, he didn't see the irony of telling me he wanted to go straight and then threatening to kneecap me if I didn't get him an invite to the Sailing Club Spring Ball. I managed to introduce him to a couple of prewarned pals who schmoozed him for a while and then dropped him. The last thing I'd do was try and kill him, though. I'm not mad."

"Someone killed him, though, quite publicly."

"Well it wasn't me. If I was going to kill anyone, I'd take them far out to sea and sink them nice and deep."

"Nice," Blake said. "So where were you on Sunday night when the tide was out?"

Fletcher looked over his shoulder. "I spent a few hours in the club bar there with a couple of mates. They'll vouch for me. Then I went home to Mrs Fletcher."

Blake nodded. "Okay. We can check that. If you can give us the names and addresses of your friends at the club."

"I wish I could help you, Inspector, I'm sorry about what happened to Harry but, to be honest, it's a weight off my mind. He was unravelling. Sick of life but scrabbling around, trying to give it some meaning. Some of us have a midlife crisis in the actual middle of our lives. Harry's life was one continuous crisis, from what I could see. He was like a swan, gliding along the surface but kicking like hell to keep going. You've spoken to his bit on the side, right?"

"I'm sorry?"

"Harry Thorpe had a girlfriend. Classic, really. Younger than him, way younger. If that isn't a sign that the wheels were coming off, then I don't know what is."

CHAPTER 15

A regular stint at power walking might have been something that Kath Cryer had promised herself last New Year's Eve but never really followed-up on. Now, keeping up with Clements, it reminded her of that drunken vow to herself. Sweat trickled down her back and her breath embarrassingly loud as Clements strode up the road.

"The thing is, Nigel," Kath panted as she struggled to keep level with him, "we have no way of verifying your… alibi…"

"I didn't show up on the supermarket CCTV then?" Clements said, not slowing down. "What can I say? Nobody phoned me either, so you couldn't locate me through the call. That's not very helpful, is it?"

"No," Kath managed to say. They'd hit Telegraph Road, the main drag through Heswall and Kath saw a Costa across the road. "Oh, thank God," she muttered under her breath.

Clements led her over the road but turned left abruptly before they reached the shop. "There's a neat little indie coffee house just up here," he said, suddenly. Kath felt her face glowing. It was warm anyway, but she really didn't need this kind of workout. She wished she'd just insisted on talking at the house, but she had made the mistake of feeling sorry for the man.

They turned into Pensby Road, a mix of cafes and boutiques with a thin smattering of charity shops. Clements stopped outside a small coffee shop called Green Tricycle and pushed on the front door. Kath tried not to wrinkle her nose. The place looked pretentious and overpriced, and she suspected that she'd be left with the bill.

It was quiet inside, probably because of the nice weather. Clements took a table by the window. "I'll just have an Americano," he said.

"Right," Kath said, her suspicions confirmed. She went to the counter where a young girl was fiddling with her phone. She looked up and smiled.

"An Americano and a latte, please," Kath said.

"Would you like cookies?" the girl said, expectantly.

"No thanks."

"Carrot cake, then?"

"No," Kath said, with a fixed smile. "Being careful. You know..."

"Ooh, when's it due?"

"What? No. No!" Kath said, blinking at the girl and then looking down in horror at her stomach and back up at the girl. “I’m not expecting. I’m watching my weight if you must know…”

The colour drained from the girl’s face. “I’m so sorry, I didn’t mean…”

“Don’t worry, love, it’ll happen to you one day,” she snapped. “And you’ll remember this and relive the toe-curling embarrassment all over again. You’re welcome.” She turned to see if Clements had noticed the altercation but he seemed to be waving his arms around as if he was being tormented by a particularly vindictive wasp. “Are you okay, Nigel?”

Clements quickly sat on his hands and sat bolt upright. “Yes. Fine.”

She glanced out of the window to see a red-haired figure dressed in khaki disappearing to the side of the shop window and out of view. “What were you doing?”

“Just some kids playing the fool. Flicking the v’s at me through the window. I was telling them to get lost,” Clements said. “They’ve gone now.”

Kath sat down, peering out of the window, briefly. “Right,” she said. “So how are you going to prove that you weren’t burying Harry Thorpe up to his neck in sand on Sunday night?”

“You do know how ridiculous that sounds, right?” Clements said. “If I was going to get rid of Thorpe, I’d be far more low-key. You don’t spend almost twenty years as a detective without picking up a few tips on committing the perfect murder. And what you just described would not count as the perfect murder. I'm not sure you should have shared that little detail with me either."

"I know you didn't kill him, Nigel. Why would you?"

"The bastard ruined my life. I can see why people might look at me as a suspect. Part of me would love to throttle Thorpe but I don't think I'm made that way, to be honest." He sat back in his chair as the waitress hurried over with the drinks and put them on the table without making eye contact with Kath. "Tell me, detective, why did you join the police?"

Kath shrugged. "It's personal. Something happened to my family..."

"I don't want to pry but suffice to say, you joined to put right something that was wrong. A sense of justice and fair play, yeah?"

"I suppose so." Kath sipped at her coffee.

"So did I. All I ever wanted to do was put criminals behind bars. To uphold the law. And I quickly realised that some people seemed to wriggle through our fingers time and again..."

"Harry Thorpe for example."

"Yeah. Time and again we came that close to

nailing him, but somehow, he managed to slip away. I'd had an exemplary record before that incident…"

"I'd heard you routinely sailed close to the wind."

"Who told you that, Blake? That stuffed shirt can't talk. Does he ever mention the Hilbre Island affair? No? I'm not surprised. Suffice to say, a young man drowned, and your precious Blakey walked away without so much as a caution."

Kath kept a poker face and sipped at her coffee again. Kinnear had mentioned something at one of the briefings and Blake had seemed rattled by it. It was hard to believe that Blake would sweep something like that under the carpet. "So what has all this got to do with you?"

"Just that your boss has a vested interest in making me sound like an unreliable character. I was there when the young man in question died. Blakey can dismiss me as a flake but I'm not a murderer. I was a good detective. I still am. If I was investigating Thorpe's death, I'd look at his rivals, for a start."

Kath rolled her eyes. "Wow, thanks Nigel, hadn't thought of that."

"Kyle Quinlan is the man you want to target. He's new in the area but used to work for Thorpe. He's been buying up Thorpe's businesses…"

"So you *have* been spying on Thorpe."

"Did you think I was just winding him up? I've been watching Thorpe for months," Clements said, tapping the side of his nose, "just waiting for a chance to bring him down..."

"And what does 'bringing him down' entail exactly?"

"I was looking for evidence to bring to you lot, so you could finally lock him up. I'd be vindicated, even if they wouldn't reinstate me. Look, I don't deny I followed him around a lot and made a nuisance of myself by reporting him for minor offences, but I wouldn't kill him. What I want to know is, why is your boss going after me instead of Quinlan?"

Kath shifted in her seat. "I was wondering the same thing," she muttered.

"What about the girl?" Clements said, lowering his voice. "Has she said anything?"

"Girl?" Kath said. "What girl?"

Clements grinned, obviously pleased that he was one step ahead of his old colleagues. "You mean you don't know about Thorpe's bit on the side? He needed his head reading. I followed him to a number of... assignations, shall we call them?"

"You're telling me that Thorpe had a mistress?"

"I dunno, Kath, 'mistress' sounds a bit mature

for this one. What's the opposite of a sugar daddy? A honey trap? But yeah, Old Thorpey had a spring in his step, all right. The girl was dark, Mediterranean. A stunner. She had a funny name 'Eenaybra' or something like that. Sounded foreign. I never managed to track down where she lived but I have a list of restaurants and local hotels they used. You want to start looking for her, she might give you a few answers."

*****

New Brighton promenade still clung onto a vestige of its seaside resort heritage in the form of New Palace, an Art-Deco building that housed an indoor play area, a rock shop, and a penny arcade. The New Palace had survived thanks to the forward-thinking owners who adapted with the times as quickly as they could but even then, the Liverpool Echo routinely ran articles declaring that it was doomed or up for sale. As DC Kinnear climbed out of the car, he looked across the River Mersey to Liverpool.

"It's weird to think this was a holiday destination once," he said to DC Alex Manikas. "Have you seen those old photos of the hordes of holiday-makers swarming off the ferries?"

"You sound like Blakey," Manikas said, flashing a rare smile.

"Did you know there used to be tower here, Manikas? Bigger than the Blackpool Tower, it was," Kinnear said, in his awful 'Blakey' voice.

Manikas grinned again. "Looks quite busy now," he said.

He wasn't wrong; the sunshine had brought out visitors in their thousands. Streams of people wandered along the promenade. Parents pushed prams and buggies, steering around what seemed like a squadron of mobility scooters that monopolised the pedestrian path and the cycle lane. Cars cruised up and down the road, searching for a parking spot. Kinnear could smell the mingling aroma of chip shops, the candy floss kiosk and diesel fumes from the cars, all baked by the sun. It wasn't unpleasant and brought back memories of family holidays.

"Come on, let's go and find this nutter," Manikas said.

After their disastrous interview with Thor Magnussen, they had been unable to contact the big man to get the names of the people who might corroborate his alibi. The Niche computer system had thrown up a number of Magnussen's associates, one of them being Eric Smith aka Ulric. They'd called at his home in New Brighton but his mother had directed them to the amusement arcades on the prom.

Further along the prom from the New Palace and just up a side street was a lesser-known gambling arcade, originally owned by Harry Thorpe.

"Apparently, he haunts this place when he isn't chasing around after Thor Magnussen," Kinnear said, as they pushed open the heavy oak door of the arcade. It wasn't a family arcade like the ones on the front, with penny falls machines and cheerful, bleeping video games. It was a money trap with darkened windows and faded, plastic hanging baskets trying to give it a veneer of respectability.

"I hate these places," Manikas muttered.

The twilight inside the shop revealed two walls lined with slot machines. A bored teenager leaned on the counter at the back, scrolling through his phone. The machines winked and whistled at Kinnear and Manikas as they passed them. Even if he hadn't been the only punter in the room, Eric Smith or Ulric would have been pretty obvious, with his long hair, shaved at the side, long beard and black, studded leather jacket. He may as well have been wearing a horned helmet.

Eric Smith?" Kinnear said, producing a warrant card. "Ulric?"

Ulric's eyes widened and he threw a handful of change at Kinnear's face. Kinnear stumbled backwards in the hail of coins and collided with Manikas. Ulric dashed to the back of the shop, vaulting over the counter and pushing the teenager out of the way.

Kinnear scrambled to his feet and ran behind the counter and through the back door behind it. He stopped, almost ploughing into Smith who struggled in the grip of a big, good-looking man. The man seemed to be relishing Eric Smith's discomfort as he pushed Smith's arm up behind his back. "Something going on, officer?" the man said.

"Let me go, you dickhead!" Smith growled.

"DC Kinnear, Merseyside Police, this is my colleague, DC Manikas. We just wanted a word with Mr Smith here. Your name is...?"

"Quinlan," the man said. "Kyle Quinlan. I'm the new owner of these premises."

Smith gave a squeak and twisted his head to look at Quinlan. Then the blood drained from his face and he fainted. Laughing, Quinlan dropped him to the ground.

CHAPTER 16

Kinnear lunged forward to support Smith. The man groaned and his eyes fluttered open. "Are you okay, Mr Smith?" Kinnear asked.

"I wanna go home," Smith said, faintly.

"Sit him up here," Quinlan said, rolling an office chair from behind a desk, over to them. Kinnear took in his surroundings for the first time. They stood in a small room, lined with filing cabinets. The narrow window at the top of the wall was covered by grilles. The whole room felt like a bunker. Smith slumped into the chair and looked up at Quinlan.

"I'm sorry, Mr Quinlan, I didn't mean to disturb you. I just wanted to get away from the bizzies..."

Quinlan rolled his eyes. "What on earth for?" he leaned forward. "Just tell them what they want to know, and you and I will be fine, okay?"

Eric Smith nodded and Quinlan stood back, smiling.

Manikas looked from Smith to Quinlan. "Can we talk to him in here? Alone?"

"Oh," Quinlan said, laughing. "What am I like? Yeah, no problem, I'll just be outside." He shot Smith a warning glance and left, shutting the door softly behind him.

"Please, don't hurt me," he said, staring up at Manikas. "You were at Thor's party that night, weren't you? He tried to kill you."

"We're not here about that, Eric... what do we call you? Eric or Ulric?" Kinnear said.

"Eric's fine. I only use the other name when I'm hanging out with Thor. He makes us use them names. All part of his Viking thing. Wh-what do you want?"

"We're looking into the death of Harry Thorpe. Do you know anything about that?"

"No. Only that he was found on the beach. Honest, I don't know anything else," he said. He grabbed Manikas' sleeve. "Look, I'm really sorry about what happened at the party. I didn't have anything to do with that. It was Thor. He's a fuckin' nutter when he's done some mushrooms, you've got to believe me. I ran away when they dumped you in that pit. I haven't been near Thor since."

"Just forget that," Manikas snapped. "That's not what we're here about. Who told you that Thorpe was dead?"

"Everyone knows. It's just gossip, innit?"

"And what other gossip do you know?" Kinnear said, glancing over at the door.

"Nothin' about this place, if that's what you're

asking. I come here to win a bit of money. I never worked for Thorpe or nothing."

"What about Thor, Eric?" Manikas said, leaning in on Eric. "Have you heard anything about Thor?"

"Only that he's not happy about his dad's death. He wants to know who's responsible, like. I dunno, maybe he wants payback or something…"

"Who from? Quinlan?"

"No," Eric said, looking horrified. "Why would he do that? Mr Quinlan didn't kill Thorpe, I can tell you that. It's a bit weird though isn't it?"

"What?" Kinnear said.

"Well, Thorpe trying to bury him," he said, nodding at Manikas, "and then Thorpe getting buried…"

Manikas grabbed Smith by the jacket. "You just forget that, okay? It doesn't go anywhere else. Anyway, how do you know he was buried?"

Smith looked pained, as though he'd given away vital information. "I-I just heard it, that's all."

"Who from? Thor?" Manikas snapped.

"No. In the pub. I told you. It was just gossip. I wanna go now. You got to arrest me if you want to hold me, right? So, I wanna go home."

The door opened and Quinlan stood there.

"Everything okay?"

"Yes," Kinnear said. "Thank you for your assistance, Mr Quinlan. I think we're finished here, for now. How long have you owned this establishment?"

Quinlan wrinkled his nose. "Not long. It's a bit of a dump but it's a toe-hold."

"A toe-hold?"

"I've got big plans for New Brighton. Casinos, hotel chains, luxury yachts in the marina? It could become the Monte Carlo of Europe…"

"Monte Carlo is the Monte Carlo of Europe, surely," Manikas said, his brow furrowing.

Quinlan tapped the side of his head. "Gotta think big, Alex," he said. "Gotta think big…"

"How did you know my name?"

"Warrant card of course," Quinlan said, with a shrug. He turned to Smith. "I'll organise a lift home for you Eric. You look like you need some rest."

Kinnear looked hard at Eric Smith. "Or we can get you home, if you want."

"No," Eric mumbled, not meeting Kinnear's gaze. "I'll take Mr Quinlan's offer. I think I've caused you enough trouble."

"Fair enough," Kinnear said. "Mr Quinlan, we'll need a statement about you stopping Eric. It shouldn't be a problem..."

"Fine by me. Just call me, tell me when you want me to come in. I thought he was an intruder after my takings. I used minimal force to defend myself."

"Quite... we shouldn't need you to..." Kinnear began but Manikas jumped in.

"That's great, Mr Quinlan. We'll let you know when we want you to come in for interview. Thanks for your cooperation."

"Always glad to help our fine constabulary, Alex, you know that," Quinlan murmured, a smile quirking the corners of his mouth. "See you soon."

Outside Kinnear blinked at Manikas. "What the f..."

"Think about it. We've got Quinlan in an interview room. Blakey's going to love that. We might be able to skew the questions a little..."

Kinnear shook his head. "Honestly, Alex, will you never learn? How can we drag Quinlan in for a statement about Smith and then grill him about... about what exactly?"

"Well about how he knows my name for a kick-off."

"He told you, warrant card."

"I never showed him my warrant card, mate.

Not once."

*****

They'd tried to make the viewing room a warm, comforting place by placing some flowers by the window and arranging some comfortable chairs for people to sink down onto if they were overcome but it didn't disguise its real purpose. People came here to identify their dead relatives and the clinical smell that hung in the air defied anyone to feel comforted.

It had taken Thor Magnussen all his self-control not to strangle the Family Liaison Officer who seemed to have installed herself at his mother's house. Thor wasn't fooled by her look of concern and her offers of help; at the end of the day, she was still a copper and anything that was said within her earshot would go straight back to the station. But it was DC Cook who had arranged for him to see his father's body, so he had to give credit for that.

Harry Thorpe lay on a trolley, a sheet pulled up to his neck, but Thor could tell he had been messed about. The Cook woman had said something about a post-mortem, but Thor didn't really know what that involved. It was hard to say what it was, but his dad looked kind of disjointed, as though he'd been taken apart and reassembled hastily. His skin had a strange pallor to it, as well. Again, something had been said about his time in the sea, but Thor didn't really listen. He pressed his forehead against the glass and stared at his father's corpse.

"I'll leave you for a moment," DC Tasha Cook muttered, sliding away.

Thor wondered why his father's eyes were screwed up tightly. He looked like he was screaming in pain, even though his mouth was closed. Maybe he had been screaming in his final moments. From what he'd gleaned, his father had been drugged before being buried up to his neck in sand and left for the tide. Was he scared, in those final moments? Or was he just so out of it that he didn't notice? Maybe the cold seawater would have woken him up or at least brought him to some kind of consciousness. Thor had Googled drowning, but it wasn't clear whether drowning was painful or not. And that wasn't the point.

It was humiliating.

Someone had gone to a great effort to make sure that his dad died in a horrible and undignified manner. And Thor couldn't let that go unpunished.

Tasha Cook had reappeared at the back of the room, a silent presence but demanding his attention. He turned and looked at her. She was part of it, all coppers were. They'd taken his body and chopped it up. It was Clements that Thor really blamed. Clements had followed his mum and dad around for months before the murder. He was still a copper, Thor knew that. Manikas and Blake probably helped him. They all had blood on their hands.

"I hope you don't mind me asking," Tasha said, breaking into his thoughts. "Your father didn't have his usual bodyguards with him, the day he died, which was unusual. Can you think of any reason why that would be the case?"

Thor thought for a moment. This hadn't occurred to him. His dad always made sure he had a bit of muscle alongside him. He could handle himself but didn't really like to get his hands dirty, or his knuckles bruised. Still, Thor didn't want to give anything away, so he shrugged. "Maybe someone paid them off. Or maybe dad dismissed them. He seems to have been selling off all his businesses from what I can see. He was retiring."

"But he must have known that he'd still have enemies. Surely, he'd keep a couple of men for security."

"My old man was a skinflint when it came to other people. He'd cut corners if it saved him a few bob." Thor looked at DC Cook. She wasn't bad-looking for a copper, she obviously kept in shape and he liked her mane of honey-coloured hair. She was the enemy, though and not there to help him. Still, he wondered why she was asking these questions. Maybe she was a dupe, put onto the case by Blake and Manikas to give it a veneer of respectability.

"If we had contact details for these men, maybe we could ask them ourselves," DC Cook said.

"That's true," Thor said, not offering any more.

"Do you have their names? Surely you must have known anyone working so closely with your father."

Thor looked back at the body on the trailer. "I lived my own life, DC Cook, and we weren't that close. I hadn't been near my father for the best part of a year. He could have employed anyone to keep him safe. I wouldn't know."

"If you think of anyone, will you let us know?" DC Cook said. Thor could tell she didn't believe him from the look in her eyes. She was disappointed.

"If I find out, DC Cook, then you'll be the first to know," he said, not even trying to hide the sarcasm in his voice. He knew exactly where he was going and who he was going to see. DC Cook could deal with what he left behind.

CHAPTER 17

There was no answer at the Thorpe house. DS Vikki Chinn had tried ringing and got the same result. When Blake had phoned her with the latest delicate news about Harry Thorpe's love life, Vikki thought it best to come out and talk to Mrs Thorpe in person. Now she stood on the doorstep of the Thorpes' converted farm wishing she'd stayed in the office. She had other places to go but she hated to waste time like this. Two cars sat in the yard in front of the house, a white Range Rover and a sporty, red Audi. She knew the Range Rover belonged to Mrs Thorpe but didn't recognise the Audi at all.

She gave a hiss of frustration. This case seemed to be slithering out of their grasp. Will Blake didn't seem to be taking the Kyle Quinlan angle seriously at all and, even though Harry Thorpe had been buried in front of the great British public, nobody noticed anything useful. They had exactly zero leads and were thrashing about in the dark.

The creak of a door broke Vikki's spiralling train of thought. Looking across the yard, she saw a door to one of the converted barns open and Mrs Thorpe stepped out. She looked startled to see Vikki for a split second but regained her composure as only the wife of a seasoned criminal could. She muttered something and shut the door behind her, striding towards Vikki.

"Can I help you?" she said, sounding slightly breathless. Vikki noticed she wore a track suit and trainers.

"My name is DS Vikki Chinn, Mrs Thorpe, I'm sorry to disturb you but I wondered if you had time to answer a few questions."

"More questions? Bloody hell. I'm grieving, here. It's really bad for my mental health, you know."

"I'm sorry, Mrs Thorpe, we wouldn't bother you unless we thought it absolutely necessary. I can ask Tasha Cook to call round, if..."

"No," Mrs Thorpe said. "Just ask your questions and then go." She folded her arms.

"If we could go inside..."

Mrs Thorpe pursed her lips. "Do we have to?"

"It's a little delicate," Vikki said. "I'd rather we..."

Mrs Thorpe scowled and looked over her shoulder at the barn. "Oh, all right then, come inside."

Vikki settled in the living room and wondered how to phrase her line of questioning. She bought herself a little extra time by asking about the bodyguards.

"We wondered why Harry didn't have his usual bodyguards with him on the night he died. Can you think of any reason for that?"

Mrs Thorpe looked at Vikki long and hard as she thought. "I dunno," she said at last. "Like I told your colleagues, he was winding down, and selling up. He might have given them their cards or maybe he gave them the night off."

"Was that a common occurrence?"

"Not really but some nights, when we didn't fancy having two big hairy men breathing down our necks, he'd send them packing. Sometimes, tell them to go and sit in the car but usually, he'd send them to one of the studios..."

"Studios?"

Mrs Thorpe rolled her eyes. "The barn conversions. I have my own gym and dance studio over there but there's an office, too. It's quite comfy."

"But you don't recall where they went on Sunday night?"

"I just assumed they were waiting for him in the car. I hadn't really seen them all day, come to think of it."

"Do you have the names of the bodyguards? They could have been the last people to see Harry alive..."

Mrs Thorpe's eyes widened. "Do you think it could have been them who killed him?"

"I really don't know, Mrs Thorpe but it's essential that we talk to them and find out if they were involved in any way."

"Well, there's Terry Ford," Mrs Thorpe said. "He's worked for us for years and then, recently, Bjorn has been a bit of a fixture."

"Bjorn?"

"Yeah," Mrs Thorpe said, rolling her eyes again. "He was one of our Fabian's mates from that silly Viking group, he formed. Bjorn had a sensible head on his shoulders, though and Harry took him on. Iveson, his second name was, I think."

"Do you have addresses?" Vikki said, hopefully.

"Not off the top of my head. I could check the address book if you like. Harry was old-fashioned like that. He wrote everyone's names and addresses down."

"That would be really helpful, Mrs Thorpe."

The woman scurried off, leaving Vikki listening to the ticking of a distant clock. The place felt like a country B&B, there was a certain peace about it that made Vikki stifle a yawn. A car door slammed, and an engine growled into life. Vikki stood up and went to the window in time to see the red Audi disappear out of the yard, but she couldn't see the driver.

Mrs Thorpe came back, catching Vikki by the window. "Just the cleaner," Mrs Thorpe said, handing Vikki a piece of paper. "The addresses are on there, now, if that's all..."

Vikki winced. "There was one other thing. Were you aware of there being anyone else in your husband's life? Another woman, perhaps?"

"What? You mean was Harry having an affair?"

"I'm sorry to ask but..."

Mrs Thorpe looked pale. "My husband was many things, DS Chinn, and many of them weren't nice but he was loyal to me," she said, through gritted teeth. "He might have had a few dalliances along the way but what man's head isn't turned by a pretty young thing? But they meant nothing, do you understand? Nothing."

*****

Normally, Blake would have saved the visit to Ian Ollerthwaite's house until he was heading home but he wanted to get to work on Thorpe's accounts as quickly as possible. DC Ian Ollerthwaite had something of a reputation as an energy vampire, which was a little unfair. It was true that he didn't have a great ability when it came to sparkling conversation but then neither did Blake. Most people didn't really mind Blake's taciturn silence, but Ollethwaite would try to fill the void with commentary. Usually, his talk would be centred around the particular intricacies of his latest model railway layout or a very specific account of the latest ledger he was analysing. The fact that Al Capone was convicted of tax evasion is of passing interest to most people, but nobody wants every line of the man's financial transactions recited to them.

The fact that Ollerthwaite was obsessed with figures was at once, a weakness and a strength. Blake had come to view it as something of a super power but, much as he valued Ollerthwaite, he still found him somewhat tedious.

Ollerthwaite lived in a detached house in Spital which was dormitory settlement between Bebington and Bromborough. Spital was an estate agent's dream in terms of connectivity and it was a much-sought-after area. The house, set back from the main Spital Road that passed the railway station and eventually ran up to junction four of the M53. It was a large, brick-built, mock-Tudor house set in a spacious, well-kept garden. Blake pulled into the wide drive and marvelled at how little he actually knew about his team's private life. I mean, they talked about their partners and families and he occasionally met them at functions, but he never would have thought that Ian Ollerthwaite lived in a house like this.

Theresa Ollerthwaite answered the door and gave Blake the kind of smile he imagined was reserved for grandparents coming to take an over-excited child to the zoo for the day. "Will, thank the Lord," she laughed. She was a small woman with ringlets of mousey brown hair and delicate features. Blake could tell she was used to laughing and enjoyed life. He felt guilty wondering how she managed that being married to Ian.

"Is Ian playing up, Theresa?"

She beamed at him. "Let's just say he needs something other than how to replicate the intricacies of the West Coast Line signal failure of 1938. Even Dylan was glad to go to Summer School this morning."

"Sounds serious," Blake said. "I hope I can help."

"Abandon hope all ye... etc, etc," Theresa said, laughing again.

What didn't surprise Blake was the orderliness of the house. The place was spotless, and everything seemed to have a place. Ruefully, he thought to his own home, a jumble sale mess of piles of clothes, dirty dishes and stacks of papers. Theresa settled Blake in a cosy living room dominated by a painting of a train steaming through a pastoral landscape.

Ollerthwaite appeared, his fawn cardigan and drooping moustache making him look older than his years. Blake felt a pang of sympathy for the man, he was innocuous and wouldn't harm a fly but had been set upon earlier in the year and ended up in hospital for some time. "Ian, good to see you up and about."

"Thank you, sir, I've been doing these exercises

given to me by the physiotherapist. They involve a series of stretches and lunges three times a day. They are a bit boring but seem to be doing the job. I find the lunges the hardest, they stretch the back of my thigh which can lead to some discomfort…"

"Well, as long as they're doing the trick, that's the main thing, Ian," Blake said. "I'll cut to the chase, how do you feel about doing a bit of work?"

Ian thought for a while, rubbing his chin as though Blake had given him a real conundrum to solve. "On the one hand, sir, I'm quite eager to get back to some kind of service. However, I took quite a battering and I'm not sure I feel fit enough to travel into the office every day…"

"You wouldn't have to…"

"Plus, there's the layout I'm working on right now, it's… delicate… I keep going over the difficulties with Theresa, but she doesn't appreciate what a ticklish business it is. It involves some serious soldering…"

"I'm not suggesting you come into the office, Ian, you could work from home and only a couple of days a week. It's a murder and I just need your sharp eye to go over the books for me."

"Who is it, sir?"

"Harry Thorpe. We found him buried up to his

neck in the sand just off Hilbre island."

"Drowned then?"

"That's what it looks like, Ian. So what do you say? You ready to dip your toe back in?"

"I'm not sure that's the best metaphor to use, sir, given the circumstances of Mr Thorpe's demise," Ollerthwaite replied, looking quite pleased with his comment. "But yes, I'd be very interested in having a look at his accounts."

"Excellent. I'll have the stuff sent over tomorrow. The sooner you can find anything suspicious or unusual, the better. I'll be honest, Ian, we're stumped at the moment, running round in circles. I'm hoping you'll be able to shed some light on why Thorpe ended up dead."

CHAPTER 18

The wardrobe was empty and so was the smalls drawer but Terry Ford wasn't sure he could fit everything in his small suitcase. He didn't care where he went as long as it was warm and if it was warm, then he wouldn't need half the clothes he'd pulled out of his cupboards. The trouble was, he didn't really know how long he should go for, either. All he knew was that Harry Thorpe, his ex-boss, was dead and sooner or later, the bizzies would come snooping around. It might just be better all-round if he wasn't here when they arrived.

He sat on the bed next to the laptop and looked at the last-minute booking website, he'd landed on. Spain might be nice but how long could he stay there? It was a bit obvious, too. Harry had plenty of friends who had retired to the Costa del Sol, he'd be spotted the moment he got off the plane. What about Cyprus? He'd had a great time there once. Sod it. Cyprus would be a start. He could always move on. That might not be a bad idea, come to think of it.

A motorbike roared past in the road below. It was loud and for some reason, it jarred his nerves. "Get a grip, Terry," he muttered, clicking on the ticket selection for Cyprus. "Just a few minutes away from sun, sea and souvlaki."

A crash downstairs brought Terry to his feet. Without even thinking, he slid his hand under the mattress and pulled out a handgun. If someone had come for him, then he wouldn't make it easy for them. Pulling the bedroom door open, he crept along the landing, gun held before him. He stopped at the top of the stairs and listened. Silence. It sounded as though someone had kicked in the back door.

The fifth step creaked ominously as Terry inched his way down each on into the hall, still keeping the gun up, straight-armed and bracing it with his other hand, like he'd seen in the movies. His hand shook. He'd never actually had to use the gun and had never really had any proper training, but he'd blow anyone away who got in his way.

He paused at the foot of the stairs, by the front room and took a breath. The door was open, so he slipped inside, sweeping the gun barrel across the empty room. Still holding his breath, he slipped out into the hall again and took another step, gun arm held up in front of him. A flash of silver came from the next door filling his gun arm with a sudden, startling agony. Terry stared in horror at the explosion of blood where his hand used to be. He tried to pull the trigger, but nothing happened. Instead, the gun clattered to the floor. Terry was pretty sure his hand was still gripping it. Thor Magnussen stepped out of the next doorway holding a huge axe. Terry staggered back, screaming and clutching the stump where his hand used to be. He crashed against the wall and slid down onto the floor, whimpering.

Thor squatted beside him. "So what happened, Terry?"

"Wh-what was that for? I... need an ambulance," Terry gasped, trying not to look at the raw stump.

"All in good time. You tell me what I need to know and I'll get you to hospital. How come you weren't looking after my dad when he was killed?"

Terry's breathing was erratic. It was clear he couldn't think straight. "It's not what you think, mate. He gave us the night off. Told us to go home..."

"Bollocks. Who paid you off?"

"Nobody!"

"It was Clements, wasn't it? I couldn't believe it at first. I thought it was just a few bent coppers who had it in for my dad. The more I thought about it, though, the more sense it made. It would need an insider to lull my dad into a false sense of security. Someone he trusted with his life..."

"Honest, I swear down. Harry sent us home. He said...he didn't need us. He'd been doing a lot of that in the last few months. Bjorn reckoned... he'd got a bit on the side..." Terry's eyes were glazing and the pool of blood spread across the laminate floor.

Thor growled and leaned in on Terry. "Watch your mouth. My dad would never do that to my mum. You were paid to leave him, weren't you?"

"No! He'd sold up anyway... He didn't think he was in any danger. He'd... sold everything to Kyle Quinlan. If you want to have a go at anyone, maybe you should pick on him. Please, I... think I'm going to... pass out..."

"Where's Bjorn hanging out these days?"

Terry looked up at Thor, his jaw slack, drool slithered down his chin. "Screwballs," he said, slurring his voice. "Pool hall... in Wallasey... please, Thor... ambulance..."

"Fuck you, Terry, you should have looked after my dad," Thor said, standing up. "And so should Bjorn."

*****

Doug Noonan sat in his kitchen, surrounded by wilting plant cuttings, and fidgeted with his phone. He'd meant to get them potted-on but had been too preoccupied.

What the fuck was Clements thinking of? The

ex-copper had arranged to meet Noonan with the cash that morning. As agreed, Noonan had stationed himself in the Costa coffee shop in Heswall and awaited Clements' arrival. Then the idiot had rocked up with one of his ex-colleagues. Noonan could spot a copper a mile off and this woman had that look about her; confident, a bit of a combative look about her. Anyway, even if she wasn't, they had agreed to meet alone. At first, Noonan had thought it was some kind of elaborate sting and had prepared to run but then Clements had changed direction and led the woman off up towards the cross. He'd shot a warning glance into the Costa and Noonan had realised that he couldn't come in. he'd also realised that sitting directly in the window was probably a mistake.

Curious, Noonan had slipped out and followed them from a distance. He watched as they disappeared into the Green Tricycle coffee shop and muttered a prayer of thanks that Clements thought so quickly on his feet. Mind you, that could prove to be a problem later. He sidled close to the shop window. If Clements hadn't shooed him off, the policewoman would have clocked him. Pulling his collar up, he'd hurried off into the crowd, praying he hadn't been seen.

Now, back at home, Noonan wasn't sure what to do. He made the call and it was picked up almost immediately. "What the hell were you thinking off sitting in the window of Costa like that, you idiot? I thought you were a professional."

"I- I needed to keep an eye on the street," Noonan said, thinking fast. "Anyway, I wasn't the one who brought a bloody copper along with me. What the fuck was that all about?"

This time it was Clements who was on the back foot. "That wasn't my fault, was it? She just turned up out of the blue. I think she was trying to catch me out. Anyway, I managed to distract her so she didn't spot you."

"She doesn't know me..."

"For fuck's sake, they've interviewed you. You're a suspect in this bloody murder business! They'll have a photo of you on a little whiteboard somewhere alongside a list of everything you've been nicked for in the past, your shoesize and what you bloody well had for breakfast on the day of the murder. Are you sure you know what you're doing because I'm beginning to wonder?"

"You're beginning to wonder? I tell you what, get me my money or I'll give you a practical fucking demonstration of how professional I am," Noonan snarled, "and it'll be the last fucking thing you do." He killed the call and slammed the phone onto the table. This was all getting too much.

CHAPTER 19

After a day of chasing his own tail, the last thing Blake wanted to do once he got home was talk to anyone. They'd made some small progress in finding out that Thorpe had a new love interest but Blake wondered how useful that information would be. It seemed to Blake that Thorpe had kept his private life very secret and it was likely to be a dead end. Thor Magnussen seemed to have gone off the radar and Kath Cryer seemed convinced that all resources should be turned to trying to convict Kyle Quinlan.

Blake could see her logic. Clearly Thorpe and Quinlan were rivals, but Thorpe had stepped out of the ring. He'd even sold everything to Quinlan. To kill Thorpe now seemed counter-productive to Blake. Who would do business with Quinlan if he proved so unpredictable? It was one thing to rule by fear, but people had to be able to trust you. Kath was sold on the idea of Quinlan putting Thorpe's death on display as some kind of warning to others, but Blake didn't buy that. Word would get around no matter how Thorpe died. It was almost too theatrical.

Alex and Andrew had complicated matters by encountering Quinlan at the gambling arcade and asking him to come in for interview. This wasn't a bad idea but if it was handled badly, it would leave Blake open to accusations of hounding Quinlan because of his relationship with Laura. He hadn't seen Laura for months, but he wondered what she was doing and when her name cropped up in Quinlan's criminal dealings, it was like a knife in his heart. In his darkest moments, he wondered if the whole affair between them had been part of some elaborate plan to discredit him. That was just paranoia, but some days, he felt as though his hands were tied when it came to Quinlan.

Loosening his tie, he slumped onto his sofa and let Charlie jump up next to him. He scanned the room. There was no sign of Serafina but she could come in later than him, sometimes.

The doorbell rang and Blake groaned. It was late, gone nine on a sweaty, hot night, and he really didn't want to get up again. On the other hand, it must be important for someone to call at this time of night. Resolving to physically kick the arse of whoever it was if they were a time-waster, Blake heaved himself out of his seat and trudged to the front door.

A man and a woman stood on Blake's step. He was thickset, dressed in a pair of baggy chinos and a brown cardigan. His curly hair framed his round, red face. He looked nervous and his eyes darted all around the door frame but never at Blake. Blake recognised the woman straight away as the one who had been hiding behind his hedge and stroking Serafina. She was skinny with lank hair and a grudging, disappointed look about her.

"Can I help you?" Blake said, not trying to hide his irritation at being disturbed.

The two looked at each other, each pleading with the other to say something. "It about the cat…" the woman said at last.

"Which cat?" Blake said.

"Smoky," the man said. "Smoky is ours."

"I'm pleased to hear it," Blake said, slightly confused. "I hope you and Smoky are very happy together. What's that got to do with me?"

"We want her back," the man said, staring at Blake's shoes.

"Look, I've had a long day and I'm very tired, so it might be my fault, but I haven't got a clue what you're talking about. I haven't got a cat called Smoky…"

"You don't call her Smoky," the woman said, "but you do have our cat…"

"You're talking about Serafina?"

The man looked relieved. "Yes. She's ours."

"No, you're wrong," Blake said. "Serafina was my mother's cat. As much as that cat actually 'belongs' to anyone. She's lived here ever since.

Where is she? I hope you haven't taken her..."

"No," the woman said. "We came round to ask for her. You being a policeman and all that Mr Blake."

"If you know my name, perhaps I should know yours," Blake said, eyeing the pair, suspiciously.

"I'm Heather and this is Peter," the woman said. Peter gave a little wave.

"And your surname?" Blake said, gruffly.

"Leeky," Peter said. "Heather and Peter Leeky."

"Peter Leeky? Seriously?" Blake muttered. "Well, thanks for calling round but Serafina lives here and I'm sure she wouldn't be very happy being moved. I think that's all I have to say on the matter." He began to close the door.

"Just hear what we've got to say, Mr Blake," Heather said, stepping forward. "We wouldn't bother you normally but Smoky appeared at our back door the other day. We know it's her."

Blake paused. "I really don't have the energy for this..."

"We had Smoky as a kitten and she was a Persian just like yours. Then about six years ago, she just disappeared. Your mum used to walk past our house every day, I recognised her in the papers when she went missing. She was always fussing over Smoky when she went past. I think she took her one day..."

"My mum got *Serafina* from a cats rescue centre," Blake said. "That's all there is to it."

"Then you'll have the papers to prove that, won't you?" Peter said, in a sudden rush of bravery.

"I don't have to prove anything about that cat to you or anyone else, Mr Leeky," Blake said. "Now get off my property."

"But..."

"Just go," Blake said.

Heather and Peter shuffled down the short gravel drive. Peter looked back. "You'll be hearing from our solicitor!"

"Feel free," Blake said and went back in the house. "Jeez, that's all I need." He thought back to when Serafina first made an appearance. Six years would be about right. Blake's mother wandered out of the house around three years ago and her dementia became obvious a couple of years before that. Mum would veer between dark moods, sadness or fury. Sometimes he would find her in the garden calling for dad who had passed away before Mum's condition worsened.

It had crossed Blake's mind that Serafina might not have come from a rescue centre before. She had just appeared with no mention from his mother about getting a cat. Blake had come in from a late shift and there she'd been, curled up on a pillow. When he'd queried the presence of the cat, his mum had told him she'd rescued it. At the time, Blake had just assumed she'd brought it from some cats home and had thought no more of it. He'd been mad busy at work and the idea that his mother might actually have stolen the cat never entered his mind. With hindsight, things looked very different. It wasn't beyond the realms of possibility that Mum had picked up the cat and brought her home. Once it was here, in Mum's confused mind, it could have been there since forever. Mum had always had cats. Dad hadn't been as enthusiastic about them. A spark of memory lit in Blake's mind and sent him hurrying upstairs to the attic.

Blake's parents had called the roof space 'the attic' but, in truth, it was a grandiose name for a loft. Because he'd inherited the house, Blake had never had to clear out the junk that accumulates over the years. His parents hadn't been in the house all their lives but they'd brought almost all their junk from the previous home and stashed it in the attic. Blake assumed they'd intended to sort it out one day, once the house had been renovated but neither had happened.

Ducking low to avoid banging his head on the beams, he scanned the piles of packing cases, boxes and bin bags full of his parents' past. He had a memory of sitting with his mother as a small child and looking at old photographs. They had been in a wooden box. At the time, he was so young that he had little to no interest in the pictures of old relatives, long dead. He had relished the closeness of his mother more than anything else and remembered the softness of her voice.

Cursing under his breath, he pulled a few crates aside and rummaged through them. Lifting an old pram frame up, he wondered why on earth they'd brought that with them. Perhaps they had thought it might be useful for future grandchildren. Blake's stomach swirled and he swallowed the grief down as he remembered his daughter, Ellie, who passed away so young. He paused, realising the danger of plunging into the rapids of the past so carelessly. There was so much up here that could drag him down to the depths. After she had died and his marriage had collapsed, Blake had sought refuge at his mother's house and had found himself trapped.

He took a breath and shifted some bin bags that he knew contained old baby clothes. What would they smell like now? Would there be any traces of Ellie on them? This was a big mistake. He turned to climb back down the ladder and saw the box, like a small treasure chest, with the key still poking out of it. Picking it up, he backed out of the dank void, vowing to stay away from there for a long time.

Sitting on his bed, he emptied the contents of the box over the duvet cover. Postcards, letters in his mother and father's handwriting, photographs spilled out across each other, along with a few beads and dull coins; old pennies and farthings. There was a medal, too but he wasn't sure who that had belonged to. Blake sat, leafing through photographs of his mum and dad, sometimes in a pair, sometimes on their own. There was a wedding day photo, his parents beaming at him. Then he found himself going further back to a time before mum and dad met. There were pictures of dad hiking in the Lake District and grinning outside a tent with a gang of scouts. Mum in her Girl Guide uniform, then younger, riding a tricycle. It was then that Blake found the photograph that had lurked on the edge of his consciousness for these last few months.

Mum sat on a doorstep of her parents' house in Tranmere, she had a huge Persian cat in an ungainly hold, its legs poking up and its head pressed against Mum's chubby, toddler cheek. It was clear that Mum loved the cat dearly, the way only a toddler could. Blake flicked over the photo and took a breath.

Written in faded pencil was one word: Serafina.

CHAPTER 20

Screwballs Pool Hall was a hangar of a building on the outskirts of Wallasey at the north end of the Wirral. It had been a cinema back in the sixties and then a storage facility for several years. Since the eighties, it had been a snooker and pool hall. DC Andrew Kinnear looked surreptitiously at his watch as he followed DC Alex Manikas into the cool gloom of the hall. It was late, and he knew he'd missed Niamh, his daughter's bedtime once again. The long, hot day hadn't helped Kinnear's temper. His shirt was plastered to his back and he watched people saunter past in light summer wear with envy.

"Couldn't we have done this tomorrow, Alex?" Kinnear said. "I promised Chris I wouldn't be late tonight."

"It wasn't my fault Bjorn wasn't at home, Andy. If he gets wind that we want to talk to him, then he might scarper," Alex said. Kinnear didn't like the feverish light in his eye. "This guy was one of the bastards that tried to bury me, Andy, I'm not letting him get off the hook..."

Kinnear grabbed Manikas' arm. "You better not make a show of us, Alex. You got away with it at Thor's cottage but this is a public setting. If you lose it here, you'll be in big trouble."

"Relax, I can handle it."

"I'm warning you, Alex, if you kick off in here, I'm arresting you and taking it straight to Blakey. I won't have you screwing this investigation up. Okay?"

"Fine," Manikas growled. "Let's just go and find Bjorn."

The inside of the hall was dingy and airless, lit mainly by the strip lights over each snooker table. At this end of the hall, there were five pool tables. Young men watched each other play, ignoring Kinnear and Manikas as they entered. Further up the hall, Kinnear could count ten full size snooker tables, all occupied. A soundtrack of eighties hits mingled with the murmured conversation and the click of balls punctuated by the occasional laughter or curse. They approached the bar at the side of the hall where a gaunt, bald man polished beer glasses and watched them approach.

"We're looking for Bjorn Iveson," Kinnear said, showing his warrant card. "Can you tell me which table he's playing on?"

"Number eight," the man behind the bar said. "There isn't going to be any trouble, is there? We've got kids playing here. It's a family place."

"No trouble," Kinnear assured him. "We just

want a quick word, that's all."

The man nodded down the hall to where a tall, burly man with a long beard and long hair shaved at the sides pondered the angles on a tight red on the side pocket. He reminded Kinnear of Thor, and he wondered if he'd met the man on the previous investigation but couldn't really remember. Alex, on the other hand, obviously remembered. Kinnear could feel the tension emanating from his colleague. As they drew nearer, their movement caught Bjorn's noticed and he glanced their way. Then his eyes widened and he froze, gripping the snooker cue.

Bjorn's tablemate was a scrawny lad with an almost shaven head and a T-shirt that was two sizes too big for him. "You okay, Bjorn?" he said.

"Yeah," he muttered. "Just give us a moment will you, mate?"

"Okay," the lad pulled a tobacco pouch and light from his jacket and stalked off to a side door that led outside.

"Mr Iveson? I'm DC Kinnear, this is..."

"I know who he is. How're you doing, Alex?"

"Never better," Manikas said, through gritted teeth.

"We just wanted to ask you a few questions about Harry Thorpe. You're probably aware that he died on Sunday."

"Yeah," Bjorn said, losing some of his bravado. "I heard."

"What d'you know about it?" Alex said.

"Just the same as everyone else. He was found on the beach. That's all. Why?"

"You were working as his bodyguard, we believe, when he died. How come you weren't there on Sunday night?"

"He gave us the night off."

"What did you do with the night off, then?" Alex said.

"I was here until 11pm. Playing Skinny."

"Who?"

"Skinny, that's the name of the lad who just went for a smoke. He and I were here having a few beers and a few games. The owner will verify that. So will Skinny."

"Is he the owner at the bar?" Kinnear asked.

"Nah, he's just staff. I think you know the new owner."

Kinnear rolled his eyes. "Let me guess, Kyle Quinlan."

"That's the one. He's offered me a job here, as it happens. Good pay. So now you know that you can piss off and let me finish my game."

"We'll decide when we've finished," Manikas

said.

"No you won't. I don't have to talk to you. Unless you're going to arrest me for something, Alex. If I were you, I'd stop… digging…"

Kinnear gripped Alex's arm. "All right, you've had your fun, Bjorn. Just before we go, can you think of anyone who might have wanted to harm Thorpe?"

"Behave," Bjorn snorted. "Who wouldn't? Christ, even I didn't really like him. He was a rude skinflint who wouldn't give you the steam off his piss if he could help it. There's an endless list of people he's done over in the past. I don't imagine it'll be a big funeral."

"But why did he give you the night off?"

"I'm not sure. He'd been doing it a lot. I wasn't happy about it. We'd get there and he'd send us packing with no pay. It was getting a bit too regular for my liking."

"What about Thor?" Alex said. "Do you think he might have had something to do with Harry's murder?"

"That head the ball? Nah. He was scared of his old man. Don't get me wrong, Thor can be totally mental when he's stoned or pissed but he'd never kill Harry. He's more into his Viking shit…"

"Says the man who calls himself Bjorn," Alex sneered.

Bjorn coloured a little. "If you must know, that's the name I was baptised with. My mum was a big ABBA fan, okay? Thor thought it was cool. I suppose I would, too, if my real name was Fabian."

"And you've no idea what he was up to the night he died?" Kinnear said.

Bjorn shrugged. "Who knows? I'll tell you this for nothing, something had changed in Harry in those last few weeks. He seemed distracted, like he wasn't really interested in keeping the businesses going. I reckoned he had a bit on the side, another woman, like. Then he sold up, didn't he? Now that's all I know. I'm going for a smoke, myself. Don't bother me again."

Outside Kinnear shook his head at Alex. "Are you sure we shouldn't talk to Blake about what happened at Thor's party, Alex? I mean, it seems to me that half of Thor's friends know about it and a lot of them work for Quinlan, now. It's only a matter of time before he finds out, if he hasn't done so already."

"So?" Manikas said.

"So, he doesn't have anything to worry about, does he? He isn't Harry Thorpe. He never gave the order to kill you. If I was Kyle Quinlan, I'd be looking for one of Thor's Viking pals who was happy to do a little time for drug use but also happy to place you at the party. You're ripe for blackmailing, mate, and I'm not sure I want to be dragged into it, too."

*****

Thor hid behind a parked car on the opposite side of the road and watched as the two coppers left Screwballs. He narrowed his eyes. This confirmed his suspicions. Bjorn was working with them. That didn't surprise him. Bjorn had abandoned him and taken a job as a bodyguard with Harry instead of sticking by Thor. This just demonstrated what a turncoat he was. Not only did he stab Thor in the back, then he turned on his dad. But what was the best way to deal with him? Killing him in the street might be a little too public but then again, if he confronted him at home, there'd be his whole family to contend with and that wasn't practical. If he went inside, Bjorn would be surrounded by friends.

A shiver of anxiety coursed down Thor's spine. There was no other way. He had to confront Bjorn in the street as soon as he came out of the club no matter who was with him. To his amazement, almost as soon as he'd had that thought, the man himself appeared at the front door and sauntered over to his motorbike. Taking a breath, Thor strode over to Bjorn.

The big man's smile faded as he noticed the axe in Thor's hand. "Hey, mate, you okay?"

"Who killed my father?" Thor growled, raising the axe. "Why weren't you there to protect him?"

Bjorn raised his hands and spoke gently. "Shit, Thor, put the axe down, we can talk. No need to threaten me, mate."

"Just tell me who paid you off. Was it the police? I saw Manikas walk out of here just now. You doing their dirty work for them, now?"

"No. He came round asking the same questions you are. I wouldn't help him, you know that Thor."

"Do I? What did you tell them then?"

"The truth, as it happens, that your dad gave us the night off. Told us to piss off home. He'd been doing it a lot recently, mate. Ask Terry Ford..."

"I already have," Thor said, tightening his grip on the axe.

A dawning realisation spread across Bjorn's face. "Bloody hell, mate, you haven't hurt him, have you?"

"Why didn't you protect my dad?" Thor yelled, stepping forward.

Bjorn retreated a step. "I told you! We were sent home. Look, you might not want to hear this but I think your dad was seeing someone..."

"No," Thor snapped. "You killed him. With Clements."

"Who the fuck's Clements? What are you talking about?"

"Where's Clements?" Thor lunged forward, swinging the axe down. Instinctively, Bjorn raised his arm to defend himself and yelled as the axe struck, cracking into the crash helmet that he was carrying. Thor grunted with disappointment. He raised the axe again, but Bjorn wasn't giving him the chance. He closed in, headbutting Thor full in the face. Stars exploded before Thor's eyes and he staggered back, crashing into Bjorn's motorbike. Then the big man was on top of him, smacking him with the helmet and following it up with punch after punch. Thor dropped the axe and put his fists up to protect his head.

"I always knew you were fucking mental, Thor," Bjorn gasped, "but I never thought you'd try and kill me. I'm your fucking friend!" Bjorn's fists rained down on Thor until every inch of his shoulders, face and arms throbbed with the same pulse of pain. He rolled on his side as Bjorn's knuckles made his ears ring. Squinting out of one swollen eye, he saw the handle of the axe and made a grab for it. Swinging it backhand, he caught Bjorn in the temple with the flat of the blade. Suddenly, Bjorn's weight on Thor's body vanished and the big man fell to one side, his skull cracking on the pavement.

Panting for breath, Thor scrambled to his feet and stared down at the fallen Bjorn. He blinked and looked around, suddenly aware of the crowd that had gathered. Men from the snooker hall and people from the garage across the road, a couple of passers-by all stared at him in disbelief, too afraid to tackle him. A police car wailed in the distance.

Ignoring the pain, Thor jogged across the road back to his own motorbike, jumped on and started the engine. In a few seconds, he was roaring through the town towards home and away from the chaos behind him.

CHAPTER 21

It was with a heavy heart that Blake forked Serafina's food into her bowl. It smelt pungent and fishy in the hot morning air. There would be a storm soon, surely, Blake thought. Maybe that would cool things down. Oblivious to his mood, Serafina tangled herself around his ankles and growled at Charlie who wagged his tail eagerly at the prospect of breakfast. Ian Youde, Blake's neighbour and friend leaned against the doorframe, his arms folded. He was an older man, thin with cropped hair and a letterbox mouth. At first glance, he wouldn't strike you as the kind of person who would regularly walk Blake's dog for him or watch out for the cat, but Ian was often saving Blake's bacon. Quite literally once.

"I've heard a little bit about the Leekies," he said. "They live over the other side of the by-pass. The house is a bloody mess. I don't think either of them work for a living."

Blake looked down at the cat. "That's neither here nor there, really, if the cat belonged to them in the first place. Do you think it's possible that my mum saw the cat and somehow mistook it for one she'd owned when she was a small child?"

"I don't know, mate," Ian said. "Didn't you say

Serafina turned up before your mum started having her problems?"

"Yeah but it's hard to pinpoint when the dementia really took hold. Maybe in some moment of confusion she thought she was a little girl again and picked up Serafina or Smoky and brought her home. If that's the case, then the Leekies have every right to demand their cat back, even after all this time."

"But it was years ago, Will," Ian said.

"You don't keep stolen goods just because you've had them for a few years," Blake said. "Of all people, I should know that. I don't know what I'd do without her, though, Ian. Serafina is my link to the past, to my mum..."

"From what I know, they're pretty strapped for cash," Ian muttered. "Why not see if they'd consider some kind of settlement."

"I'd feel awful. It'd be like trying to bribe them. And what would that say about my view of the Leekies."

Ian Youde shrugged. "I dunno but money talks, sometimes. I wouldn't rule it out, that's all."

"Money might talk," Blake said, morosely, "but the number of times people who are paid off and yet come back for more is staggering."

"You've considered the other option, right?"

"A hit man might be too extreme for this situation, Ian, much as I'm tempted..."

"What if your mum genuinely had gone to a rescue centre and picked Serafina because she reminded her of the childhood pet?" Ian said. "It's just as feasible."

Blake nodded. "That's a fair point. I wonder how long these places keep records."

"Five or six years mightn't be an unreasonable time to expect them to," Youde said. "You just have to work out which cats home she might have gone to."

"It probably wouldn't have been far away," Blake said. "On the Wirral at least and that'll narrow it down. I'll have a look and see what the possibilities are, assuming I get a chance at work."

"I'll do some snooping for you too, mate," Ian said. "Go on, you get off now. I'll take Charlie out after he's had his scran and I'll keep an eye out in case the Leekies decide to try a bit of catnapping."

Blake pulled a face. "You think they're capable of that, Ian?"

"As I said, I've heard of the Leekies before. They're a funny couple and I wouldn't put it past them."

*****

It was just a normal suburban semi-detached house on the outskirts of Birkenhead and on any other day, nobody would have given it a second glance. Today, however, it sported a new porch in the form of a white scene-of-crime tent and more visitors had traipsed across its threshold than in the last five years. The new visitors had all been dressed in white coveralls, their mouths and noses masked to avoid any DNA contamination. The front garden wall had been adorned with blue and white police tape to indicate that only authorised personnel were allowed within the cordon.

Blake sat in the front of the car with DS Vikki Chinn. She sipped coffee from a polystyrene cup that trembled in her fingers slightly. "Are you okay, then, Vikki?"

Vikki nodded. "I'll be fine, sir. Just a bit of a shock. I mean, I'm used to seeing dead bodies, but the CSI people have usually been in first. Discovering one is an altogether different experience." She paused. "And in this heat..."

Blake nodded. It was another scorcher, and the heat was building. The smell alone would have been sickening but there would have been a lot of flies, too.

"You did fine, Vikki. Looks like your training kicked in. You kept a level head and did everything right. Who is it?"

"A man called Terry Ford..."

"Harry Thorpe's bodyguard," Blake said, raising

his eyebrows.

"You know him, sir?"

"I've met him before, once," Blake said. "Does it look suspicious?"

"His hand had been hacked off, sir. It was lying at the other end of the hall, still gripping a handgun. It looks like Ford had crawled to the front door but had bled to death before he could get help."

"Hand hacked off. Any idea of the weapon?"

Vikki shook her head. "Malachy O'Hare reckons it must have been sharp..."

"No shit, that guy's a genius, Vikki," Blake said, teasing a smile out of his detective sergeant.

"He didn't want to commit himself but he reckoned it must have been quite a heavy weapon, too. An axe or something..."

"An axe?"

"Are you thinking it might be Thor Magnussen, sir? That's what occurred to me when Malachy mentioned the axe."

"Thor does have a bit of a thing for them. He used to run that axe throwing experience, too, didn't he?"

"Maybe Alex Manikas was right, sir, maybe Thor is our man."

"Maybe. Why would he target one of his father's

bodyguards, though?"

"To silence him? Mrs Thorpe had given me his name. That's why I'd come here first thing. I wanted to catch him early and ask him some questions. It looks like he was about to do a flit, too. There were packed cases on the bed and his laptop was on a travel website."

"Maybe but if Thor had killed his father without detection, why would he suddenly blow all that with such a clumsy attack on Ford? It doesn't make sense. It feels more like revenge to me. Either way, it's worth picking up Mr Magnussen if we can find him."

PC Mark Robertson appeared at the car window. Blake liked him, he was a sensible copper who had been in uniform for so long, it seemed like he'd been born on the beat. "Thought you might want to know, sir, there was an almighty punch up between, as one witness put it, 'two hairy giants' last night, outside Screwballs snooker club in Wallasey. One of them had an axe. Bjorn Iveson was left unconscious. He's in hospital now."

"Iveson was the other of the bodyguards Mrs Thorpe mentioned, sir," Vikki said. "Is he conscious, Mark?"

"Sorry, Sarge," Robertson said. "He's being sedated at the moment. He took quite a battering, apparently."

"So Thor comes here and attacks Ford, then heads over to Wallasey and has a go at Bjorn," Blake said. "It sounds like revenge to me. I wonder if Bjorn and Ford were somehow involved in Thorpe's death."

"At the very least, they were meant to protect Thorpe and didn't for whatever reason."

"And Thor is making them pay," Blake said. "Looks like we need to find Thor before he hurts anyone else."

*****

Thor Magnussen wasn't sure which was worse, the pain of the cuts and bruises he'd received from Bjorn or his mother's cold anger as she dragged a cloth across them, clearing any smears of blood. "You bloody idiot. Didn't you learn anything from your father? You wait before you get your own back. I wouldn't be surprised if half the force aren't out looking for you."

They sat in Thor's flat at the side of the Thorpes' house, surrounded by Thor's games and toys, table football, a dart board, even a makeshift axe-throwing alley. It was an overgrown teenager's dream, one large room with a huge TV at the end of a king-sized bed, and a leather three-piece suite.

"I know, Mum but I wasn't thinking straight. I went to see Dad… at the hospital. It made me so mad. And those bloody coppers coming to interview me. That Manikas trying to lord it over me after what he did. He was the one who put me in hospital, you know."

"Well, you can't stay here, son," Mrs Thorpe said. "The police are in and out of here like nobody's business. They're sure to look for you here."

"Aren't you sad, Mum?" Thor said, grabbing her arm.

Tears glittered in her eyes. "Of course I'm sad. I'm sad and angry and bloody sorry, too."

"Sorry?" Thor said. "What about?"

"You wouldn't understand, love," she said. "Your dad and I weren't really getting on very well just before he... was taken. I keep thinking that if I'd said or done something different, then he'd be with us today..."

"He didn't kill himself, Mum," Thor muttered, rubbing her arm. "He was murdered..."

"And you think Bjorn had something to do with it? Really? You need your head reading. Why would he do such a horrible thing to your dad?"

"Not on his own, Mum. I reckon it was Clements."

"That waste of space? You think he killed your dad? Behave."

"Clements is clever. He's got his police mates in

on it. Manikas and Blake. They've never forgiven him for standing up to them. Together, they could easily put pressure on Bjorn and Terry to kill dad. Think about it."

"I am and it's bloody nonsense. Look, I'll get you some money and book a flight. You go and sun yourself somewhere far away until this blows over..."

Thor stood up. "No. I'm not resting until Dad has been avenged."

"But you hated your father. He was no angel. Why are you doing this?"

"I let him down, Mum. If I'd been by his side, then this would never have happened. If I leave it, then Clements will get away with it and it'll all be brushed under the carpet." He paused and looked at his mother. "What do you mean, he was no angel?"

Mrs Thorpe looked down at the bloody rag she was tying in knots. "What I said. He- wasn't a good man by any stretch."

"He broke the law, yeah, but he had his own code..."

"He wasn't bloody Robin Hood, Fabian! And he wasn't always true to me either..."

"Why are you telling me this?"

"I just want you to see that you might think you let him down, but he let us down a lot more, that's all."

"So it's okay that he was murdered?"

"No."

"Tied up and stuffed in the ground..."

"Stop it."

"Left for the tide to sweep over him and drown him..."

Mrs Thorpe slapped Thor sharply across the cheek. "I said shut up! He's gone and there's nothing you can do about that. Killing someone else won't bring him back and it won't change what he thought of you. It's too late."

"Not in my book," Thor said. "You might have given up on Dad but I haven't."

CHAPTER 22

Bitter coffee and stale biscuits weren't exactly the best brain food going but it was all that was on offer at Birkenhead Station. Blake sat in a tiny, stifling room, his tie loose and his shirt open at the neck. There was no air conditioning or windows in this space that adjoined an interview room. He'd almost banged Kinnear and Manikas' heads together when they'd told him that Kyle Quinlan was coming in to make a statement about their encounter with Ulric the day before.

"He offered to come in and then phoned up to say he could only come in today, sir," Kinnear had said, apologetically.

"But we thought it was too good a chance to waste," Manikas had added, excitedly.

"Chance for what?"

"Maybe we can sneak a few questions about Thorpe into our conversation. It might be useful, sir," Manikas had said.

Blake shook his head. Manikas used to be so steady and cautious. Since last year, he seemed to have become a loose cannon. "He'll smell a rat being interviewed by two DCs anyway, he's not stupid, Alex."

"I know but..."

"Okay, do it," Blake had said. "But you don't mention my name and you don't go accusing him of anything. The Superintendent is going to give me such a bollocking for this, I hope you realise."

Kinnear winced but Manikas' eyes blazed with excitement.

Now Blake sat in the small room, listening through the audio link to Quinlan's smug reassurances that he really didn't mind coming in.

"It wasn't necessary," Kinnear said. "We could have phoned you..."

"Honestly, I was coming here anyway," Quinlan said.

"To the station?" Manikas said.

"To Birkenhead. I'm meeting a building contractor later, discussing some development opportunities in the area."

"Right," Kinnear said. "So, do you know Eric Smith otherwise known as Ulric?"

"Didn't until yesterday when he came flying into my office. I thought he was trying to rob the takings but turns out he was running from you two. What was he up to?"

"Nothing. We just wanted to talk to him..."

"About the murder?"

"We can't really discuss that, Mr Quinlan," Kinnear said.

"That's funny because I thought that's what you really wanted to talk to me about," Quinlan said. Blake heard him shift in his seat and imagined him sitting back, enjoying Kinnear's discomfort.

"Not at all..."

"Oh come on, lads, I've been around the block a bit. I know the score. You don't roll out the red carpet for a poxy statement about a possible assault. And unless resources are a bit more flush than they used to be, the idea of two DCs taking down my details is ludicrous. Is Blakey behind this? Where is he? Is he listening in?"

"Jeez," Blake hissed and clicked off the audio link. Jumping out of his chair, he hurried round into the main interview room. Quinlan sat just as he'd pictured him, grinning smugly. "Okay, Mr Quinlan. I must apologise for my over-eager colleagues. If I'd known sooner, I'd have cancelled the whole thing..."

"But you didn't, did you, Will? So go on, ask me anything you want. Off the record of course. I'll try to answer as best I can."

Blake shot Manikas and Kinnear a filthy look and then pulled up a chair. "The first thing I'd want to know is why you're here at all?"

"That hurts, Will," Quinlan said, grinning and putting a hand to his heart. "I'm a concerned citizen. I want to help, obviously."

"Really?"

"Okay, apart from that, I want to make it clear that I had nothing to do with Harry Thorpe's death and neither did any of my associates."

"Harry had sold a lot of property and businesses to you…"

"Exactly! All of them neglected, and all in need of investment. Harry was sitting on a number of little goldmines if he'd just put a bit of heart and cash into them but he seemed eager to get shut of them."

"You must have been suspicious if he was so keen to sell."

"He kept going on about retirement and starting a new life. I really think he wanted to leave it all behind and move on to something fresh."

"So you can account for your whereabouts on Sunday night," Blake said, bracing himself for the inevitable reply.

"The delectable Ms Laura Vexley and I were having dinner along with Councillor Lewis and his wife. I have big plans for this place, Will. The Wirral could become a boom town with the right planning decisions. Quite apart from me being a respectable businessman who wouldn't harm a fly, I would have absolutely no reason to kill Harry Thorpe. He was out of the picture. Paid off."

"And what is your business, exactly?" Blake said, staring hard at Quinlan.

"A bit of this, a bit of that," Quinlan said, grinning. "Property development, I like a bit of a flutter, so the betting shops appealed to me and the gambling arcades, too. The council has always called this place the Leisure Peninsula, but it's never really meant it. Did you know that the Wirral once had a tower just like Blackpool, with a ballroom and everything?"

"It was bigger than Blackpool Tower, apparently," Blake said.

"Imagine if we could bring that back," Quinlan said. "Speed boats in the marina at West Kirby, acres of casinos in New Brighton, The Floral Pavilion hosting big name acts. It could be massive. That's my business, Will."

"Right," Blake muttered. Full marks for ambition but he couldn't help thinking that the acres of casinos would involve cash only slot machines through which Quinlan would be laundering millions of blood-drenched pounds.

"Anyway," Quinlan said, rubbing his hands together. "I'd love to chew the fat all morning with you guys but I'm sure you've got real criminals to catch and you're obviously not really interested in poor old Ulric, so I'll say my goodbyes." He stood up and looked thoughtfully over Will's head. "I'm no grass, gents, and far be it from me to tell you how to do your job, but if I was you, I'd be looking closer to home."

"Harry's son?"

Quinlan's eyes widened. "I'd never point the finger at anyone. I'd just say that maybe you're thinking too hard about this."

"If you know something that might help us, Mr Quinlan," Blake said through gritted teeth, "then you should tell us."

Quinlan held up his hands, a pantomime of innocence. "I don't know anything, Will, I'm just theorising, that's all. I just read somewhere that most victims knew their killers, that's all…."

"DC Manikas will show you out. Sorry to have wasted your time."

"It was fun. We should do it again sometime," Quinlan said, flashing Blake a pearly smile. Blake watched Manikas usher the big man out of the interview room and then turned to Kinnear.

"I'm sorry, sir," Kinnear said. "We just…"

"We?" Blake snorted. "Don't give me that, Andrew, this has Manikas written all over it. You don't have to defend him. I don't know what's going on with him but I can't imagine you were all in favour of dragging Quinlan in…"

Kinnear blushed and bit his lip. “It could have been useful sir,” he said, trying to keep from dropping his colleague in the mire.

“It could have blown up in our faces. As it stands, it was just mildly embarrassing. Quinlan was never going to incriminate himself. If he did organise Thorpe’s death, then he’d make damn sure he was miles away in full sight of a number of reliable witnesses. And of course, if we do check his alibi with the councillor, we could be accused of damaging his reputation for no good reason.”

“I’m sorry, sir…”

“Don’t you apologise, Andrew, just tell me what the hell is wrong with Alex.”

*****

Alex Manikas walked in awkward silence beside Kyle Quinlan, their feet clicking on the tiled floor. A few officers hurried past, glancing up at them, suspiciously, as though they recognised Quinlan. At the door, Quinlan turned to Manikas and made a show of shaking his hand.

“It’s been a pleasure to meet you, Alex,” he said, smirking.

Manikas couldn’t help himself. “How the hell do you know my name? I never showed you my warrant card the other day and it was never mentioned.”

"Your reputation goes before you, Alex," Quinlan said, his smirk broadening into a full grin that Alex immediately wanted to punch. Hard. "Quite the party animal, so I've heard. You see, a lot of Harry's former employees came looking for work with me once they knew he was scaling down. Some of the hairier ones had a tale to tell. You're quite the action hero, aren't you? Does Blakey know?"

"I think we're finished here," Manikas said.

"I'll take that as a no then. Listen, I'm not a monster like Harry Thorpe, Alex. I'm sure we could help each other. Let's face it, you're nowhere near solving this case and old Thor is on the rampage, so I hear. He put one of my employees in hospital. That needs to stop." Quinlan pulled a card from the rear pocket of his trousers. "Give me a shout. Maybe we can make that story about you, the drugs and the big pit go away once and for all."

Alex watched Quinlan saunter out of the station and knew he had a decision to make.

*****

It struck Laura Vexley as odd that in all the time she'd been back with Kyle Quinlan, she had never discovered the surname of his right-hand man, Nick. She wasn't even sure where he lived. Most of his time seemed to be spent in their house in Caldy, when he wasn't popping out to 'run errands' whatever that might entail. Laura didn't want to know.

Nick was a huge man, who filled his sharp suits. He was as bald as a billiard ball and despite his imposing appearance, his face had a gentleness about it and Laura had come to learn that he was a stabilising influence in Kyle Quinlan's life.

She stumbled across him staring out of the lounge window, a mug of tea in his hand. "You all right Nick?"

Nick turned and gestured outside with his mug. "DS Bobby Dirkin," he said.

Laura peered over his shoulder at the receding figure walking back across their lawns towards the main gates. "He works with Matty Cavanagh," she said. "What was he after?"

"Wanted a word with Kyle," Nick said, taking a sip of his tea. "Probably about the Dane Wilson murder. Or Harry Thorpe. Maybe both."

"What did you say?"

"Told him the truth, that Mr Quinlan wasn't available." Nick gave her a sidelong glance. "To be honest, Laura, I'm worried."

"About the police?"

"Not really, no more about Kyle. He's spent a lot of money that belongs to other people. Dangerous people..."

"Who?"

"It's best not to know, Laura, trust me. He promised them he could work wonders over here if he had a bit of seed capital but he's burning through it and I don't see a lot of return coming in."

"Do you think these people will come for their money if they're concerned about him?"

"I know they will. And it won't be healthy for any of us if they do, believe me. These people don't mess around. If Kyle doesn't get his shit together soon, you need to start making plans..."

"Plans?"

"Come on Laura," Nick said, turning his big brown eyes on her. "I've worked with Kyle for a long time. He's my friend and I'll keep him safe as long as I can. If this all goes tits-up, you've got to be ready to either take control or get out of here fast."

CHAPTER 23

Leasowe Castle Hotel was one of those places that DI Kath Cryer had visited for weddings and the odd staff training day. It was a sandstone building a couple of hundred yards from the sea on the north coast of the Wirral. Four wings ran from a central tower and newer additions sprang from them. Battlements adorned the older part of the castle but it had never been properly fortified. It was said to have been built by Fernando the fifth Earl of Derby who was second in line to the throne after Elizabeth the first. Will Blake had once told her that Fernando had been poisoned in 1594. He'd told her a load of other stuff but that was all that had stuck in her mind. The hotel had been through ups and downs over the years but seemed to have been renovated since she last visited and now thrived as a venue for conferences and weddings.

The Reception Hall was tiled and a staircase curved up from it to the rooms above. Kath could see a long corridor which she knew led to the function rooms, bars and restaurant. To say that the receptionist behind the dark, wooden desk was unhelpful to begin with would have been an understatement. Her smooth brow wrinkled and she gave Kath a condescending smile when

Harry Thorpe's name was mentioned.

"I'm afraid we're very particular about client confidentiality, Mrs Cryer and Mr Thorpe was very particular about our discretion with regard to any visits here."

Kath took a breath and squinted at the receptionist's name badge. "It's *Detective Inspector* Cryer, to you, *Beverley*," she said, through gritted teeth. "And Mr Thorpe won't be very particular about anything anymore given he was murdered last Sunday. Now, I can go and get a warrant to force you to give me the information I need. Trouble is, I'm a very busy woman and I wouldn't be back until Saturday afternoon with a load of uniformed officers. That wouldn't interfere with any plans you might have, would it? I mean, I'd hate to spoil someone's wedding..."

Beverley pursed her lips and Kath could see the mental battle written on her face. "I-I don't know... Mr Thorpe could be quite..."

"Mr Thorpe's quite dead, love," Kath said, flatly. "Now, when was he last here and who was he with?"

Beverley scowled for a moment then tapped at the computer on the reception desk. "He was in Wednesday of last week, he booked a room," Beverley said, looking up at Kath. "Didn't stop over though..."

Kath raised her eyebrows. "Really? He went

home? Did they, you know... stay long?"

"Ooh no, booked in at two, went upstairs, came down for dinner at six after... whatever," Beverley said, smirking, "and then he went."

"What about her?" Kath said, putting a hand to her mouth as though scandalised. "Did she stay?"

Beverley leaned over the counter and lowered her voice. "Yeah. She always does." She glanced up and down the foyer, checking that what she said next didn't go beyond Kath and the two suits of armour standing by the door. "Empties the mini-bar every time *and* does room service."

"Cheeky cow," Kath said, widening her eyes. The relationship between them had changed from interrogative Inspector to trusted confidante. "And does Harry pay for everything?"

"He's got a business account with us. It all went on the tab."

"And was it the same woman every time?"

Beverley thought for a second. "It never used to be but I'd say in the last six months it has been. She's a real stunner. Makes you wonder what she saw in that old man. His bank balance, probably."

"Have you got a name?"

"She must have signed in," Beverley said. "Hang on." She disappeared into a back room and Kath could hear the rustling of paper. A moment or two later, she emerged with a booking card. "We always get them to write their names and addresses on this. For security and the like, you know. Here she is. Gyneebra Garcia? What kind of name is that?"

"I think it's pronounced Heneebrah," Kath said looking at the name which was spelt 'Ginebra' in scrawly handwriting. "Garcia is a Spanish name, right?"

"I think so," Beverley said. "Her accent sounded foreign to me."

"She's put Thorpe's home address as her own but I don't think she'd be very welcome there," Kath muttered. "I wish we had a picture of her..."

Beverley bit her lip, totally part of the investigation now. "We might have CCTV of them coming in here and registering," she said in a small voice.

"Beverley," Kath said, beaming. "I could kiss you."

*****

Alex Manikas looked pale and pinched as he slumped in his chair in the interview room. Instinctively, Blake had settled on the other side of the table making Manikas look like a criminal being questioned. Blake half hoped he felt that way.

"So, just run that by me one more time, Alex," Blake said, in a low voice. "Last year, you went to Thor Magnussen's party when I expressly told you not to…"

"It was a Sons of Sol gathering, sir. I was convinced I could get the dirt on him over the disappearance of Trevor Long."

"But you didn't, did you? It all went tits-up as I said it would. Which was the very reason I said you weren't to go. Jeez. You're a good copper, Alex, what the hell were you thinking of?"

"I know, sir, it was a mistake. I see that now. I saw it then, once Thorpe tried to kill me but there was nothing I could do."

"You could have told me. You could have been honest about what you did. In all likelihood, you'd have got a warning but we'd have had Thorpe bang to rights."

"I know, sir, I wasn't thinking straight…"

"And I don't think you have since that day, Alex."

"We all make mistakes, sir. Didn't you at Hilbre Island? DI Clements mentioned something about that…"

"That has nothing to do with this," Blake muttered, feeling himself reddening. "It's in the past. Totally different."

"I just thought I was following a strong lead, sir. In the end it turned out it wasn't Thor Magnussen but someone entirely different. So there was no real harm done." The words sounded weak, and Blake could tell Manikas knew it.

"No harm done? Apart from you leaving yourself open to blackmail all this time, apart from you thinking you can be some kind of 'maverick.' This isn't a Dirty Harry film, Alex." Blake rubbed his forehead. "If it had turned out that Thor had killed Trevor Long, our case against him would have been compromised."

"I know, sir," Alex said, putting his head in his hands.

"And what prompted you to tell me about this now?"

"This case, sir, it brought it all back. I was worried that Thor might use it to discredit any investigation against him in respect of his father..."

"Well you're damn right about that. When we find Thor Magnussen, your presence alone could jeopardise any investigation we might have around his involvement in the death of Terry Ford, too."

"Yes, sir. And..."

"And?"

"Kyle Quinlan made it plain that he knew about it, too. I was worried that he might try to blackmail me..."

Blake took a long breath. "You've made a right cat's arse of this, Alex but, you did the right thing in the end. I'll need to talk to the Superintendent about this, Alex. Take yourself off home; I can't have you putting any further investigations at risk."

"Yes, sir," Alex said, standing up and heading for the door.

"And Alex," Blake called after him. "Stay at home. I don't want any more heroics or sudden bursts of inspiration leading you to hunt Thor down. If you think of anything phone me or Andrew, okay?"

Manikas nodded and shut the door behind him. "Jeez," Blake muttered, shaking his head.

*****

The Seraph Pub stood in a dark corner of the North End of Birkenhead. A little corner pub, it was shunned by locals and by rights should have been closed down years ago. But vested criminal interests kept it open and the clientele, usually from out of the area had certain unwritten rules when entering its cramped, twilight interior. The pub hadn't changed in appearance, it seemed, for a hundred and fifty years. The same engineering brick exterior, the same tiles around the doorway and the same wooden window frames, baked hard by a century of sun, rain and frost. Inside had the same feel to it. The wallpaper looked like it should be in a museum along with the dark wooden furniture. Nobody had ever wandered into The Seraph and suggested a makeover or if they had, they disappeared and were never seen or heard of again.

Thor Magnussen sat hunched on one of the small, wooden stools like a giant squashed into a doll's house. He filled the small bar so much that two other men had looked over to the landlord, Boredom McClague for some kind of adjudication. McClague, whose drooping, indifferent expression had earned him the nickname had shrugged. He couldn't see what Thor could do to make himself any smaller and, besides, the big man looked on edge to say the least.

Normally, Boredom was strict about enforcing 'the rules' around the pub and he didn't like anyone bringing illicit merchandise onto his premises. Drugs, stolen goods and weapons stayed outside. The only thing people brought inside was conversation and compromise. Boredom had his misgivings about Thor. The hulking man looked as though he was about to explode. He twitched and jigged his knee up and down as he talked to the small man in the corner. But Boredom didn't have the muscle to deal with Thor and, besides, he'd heard the news about Harry Thorpe and felt sorry for the young man.

That's not to say Boredom wasn't curious about why he was talking to Dolly. That was the small man's name, or the only one he ever answered to. It seemed obvious why he'd been christened Dolly by those who used his services. He was small and spindly, with a head that seemed too large for his child-like body. Dolly always wore a brown tweed suit and a small porkpie hat which made him look even more like some kind of ventriloquist's dummy. But nobody controlled the little man.

Dolly's currency was information. He could find things out quickly about people who wanted absolute secrecy. He seemed to know everything about everyone. His knowledge came from an arcane mixture of technology, being in the right place at the right time and just knowing everybody. Some said that Dolly was kept on a retainer by several members of the criminal (and respectable) community who feared he had the dirt on them hidden somewhere. It was said that nobody moved against Dolly because on his death, secrets would automatically land in the post and email inboxes of the authorities, bringing down many local villains and quite a few local dignitaries. If you were talking to Dolly, you wanted to know something but listening to Dolly was dangerous. He might be impervious to the enmity of the dark and powerful but his clients weren't. Often Dolly was the last person a man talked to before walking to his doom.

Talking to Dolly cost you, as well and often, he didn't want money. Sometimes, he'd want your deepest, most deadly secret. Dealing with Dolly was sometimes a double-edged sword and left you more than just in his debt. Boredom polished glasses slowly and tried to listen in but whatever was being said escaped even his sharp ears.

Thor looked at the little man squashed into the corner next to him. "I'm sorry to hear about your father, Thor," Dolly said, in a soft, high pitched voice. "He was a good customer."

"Was he?" Thor said, surprised.

"Of course, he was. Knowledge is power and your father liked power, once."

"Once?"

Dolly sighed. "I'll give you this much for free, your father was old and more concerned about other things."

"What other things?"

"Affairs of the heart," Dolly said. "Now. You wanted three addresses. I have them. I'll need you to BACS the money to this account." Dolly handed Thor a card.

"Was my father having an affair, Dolly?"

"I've said enough. I don't think you can afford that information."

"I could squeeze it out of you."

Dolly nodded but didn't appear even slightly perturbed. "You could but then you'd be dead the moment you left this pub and unable to fulfil your revenge mission."

"How did you know?" Thor began to say.

"Just send the money to that account, please, Thor. Then I'll give you the addresses."

Thor pulled his phone out and opened his banking app. "They better be right."

Dolly looked at him with lazy, hooded eyes. Thor could see the veins squirming across his eyelids. There was something creepy about Dolly. Thor wasn't sure what it was but if someone told him that Dolly was a vampire, Thor would've believed them.

"Thank you," Dolly said.

"So?" Thor muttered leaning towards Dolly. "Where are the addresses?

Dolly said nothing but stood up as if to go. Thor began to rise but his phone pinged, using a ringtone he'd never heard before. He looked down at the text that had just arrived. It contained three addresses.

"Goodbye, Thor," Dolly said, without even looking at the big man. "Use that information wisely."

"I will," Thor muttered, staring at the text. "I certainly will."

CHAPTER 24

Superintendent Martin was a lean man with a beak of a nose and a granite stare. His cold, blue eyes and grey hair gave him a steeliness that made even Blake a little nervous. Martin was a generally a fair man but seemed to have a dim view of Blake's past in TV. He was forever suspicious that Blake was somehow courting limelight or grandstanding in front of the media. Nothing could be further from the truth but Blake did seem to inherit more complex and public cases. Often Blake found himself in front of cameras and journalists but this was purely as a result of the cases he was investigating.

"I've sent him home for now, just to get him away from the case, sir. He's compromised as far as Thor Magnussen goes..."

"He disobeyed a direct order, put his life and those of others in danger and then failed to report a crime, Will."

"But the person accused of instigating the crime is dead and the one who tried to commit it is a suspect in another murder. You have to admit, it's complicated, sir."

"I'm not denying it, Will but he's overstepped the mark, of that there's no doubt. I don't think we have any choice but to pursue disciplinary procedures. I'll consult personnel. In the meantime, can he be kept in the background? Get him to work from home on something. How is the rest of the investigation going?"

"Slowly, sir. It's frustrating. Kath Cryer has made a bit of a breakthrough and found the name of Thorpe's love interest. There's CCTV footage, so we're going to circulate that. Kath is checking with the Spanish authorities to see if she's known to them, but it feels like we're going nowhere otherwise."

"Kath said she suspected organised crime might be involved."

"Kyle Quinlan seems to have bought up Thorpe's empire. I've got Ian Ollerthwaite looking into Thorpe's transactions to see if anything comes up there. Quinlan himself denies any involvement..."

"You've spoken to him?"

Blake took a breath. "He was on the scene of another incident yesterday and volunteered to make a statement. He was happy to talk about his relationship with Thorpe and has a cast-iron alibi. So I'm not sold on the idea that Quinlan is somehow involved."

"How about Thorpe's son, Thor?"

"It's possible, I suppose, sir. Most victims know

their murderers. Statistically speaking, Thor is a contender, and he seems a likely fit for the Terry Ford killing. We need to find him fast, but he's vanished."

*****

Geoff Noonan had had enough. He'd rung Clements a number of times, only to get his voicemail. He'd realised that leaving a message might not be a wise idea and hung up on each occasion, but his temper was getting the better of him. The man had promised to pay him for the job and was wriggling off the hook. It was only a matter of time before Clements disappeared altogether, leaving Noonan holding the baby. No. Not a baby, a smoking gun.

He called again and this time, couldn't contain himself. "Clements, it's me. You better get your act together, mate or I swear I'll come round there and rip your fucking head off your shoulders. I did what you wanted and now it's time for you to pay up. Call me back in the next ten minutes or I'm coming round to you. You've seen what I'm capable of. You know what I did to Thorpe. Don't push me too far."

He glared at the phone with a sinking feeling. That was a bad idea. But what else was he to do? Clements needed telling.

*****

Nigel Clements listened to the voicemail message and swallowed hard. Although he was an ex-copper and used to dealing with violent situations, this felt different. He'd underestimated Noonan and hadn't thought him capable of killing anyone, let alone Harry Thorpe. In truth, Clements wasn't really sure if he wanted Thorpe dead anyway. It didn't get him his job back and it didn't really make him feel better knowing that Thorpe's wife and son were grieving the loss of a husband and father. Clements had unleashed a monster.

He couldn't tell anyone though. Imagine being convicted of conspiracy to murder and put in prison alongside people he'd arrested in the past. He might have been caught out by Harry Thorpe but Clements had put away some pretty heavy-duty villains during his career and not all of them on totally sound evidence. Some of them would still be doing long stretches and only too glad to get reacquainted with their arresting officer. That was before you factored in the characters that Thorpe's family would set on him once he was banged up. It would be a death sentence.

Clements sat down and buried his face in his hands. There was no choice, he'd have to pay Noonan off. But he didn't have the kind of money Noonan was talking about. Perhaps if he took all his savings out, he could give Noonan some kind of deposit. But he'd have to remortgage the house to get hold of that kind of money. What if he used the money he had to go away? Perhaps he could disappear, he had the skills after all. He could go abroad or even just up north for now and sell the house later. There was nothing to keep him here any more and a very good reason to run away.

He jumped up. That was what he'd do. He'd pack his bags, and get away from here once and for all. Now was as good a time as any, especially if Noonan was on his way round. Bounding up the stairs into his bedroom, he dragged his suitcase down from on top of the wardrobe.

That was when he heard the door downstairs creak open.

*****

Once again the lights twinkled on the River Mersey as Blake pulled into his drive. It was about as dark as a summer night gets but still warm and Blake marvelled at the heat as he climbed out of his air-conditioned car. He could tell something was wrong before he even got to the front door. The house looked quiet and empty. When he opened the door, Charlie's paws clicked across the tiles towards him in the dark, but they sounded muted. Serafina wasn't here. Somehow, he could tell. He clicked the hall light on and Charlie looked up at him, forlorn as though he had some bad news to impart.

"Hey, fella," Blake said, squatting to scratch Charlie's ear. He called the cat but knew she wasn't there to come running. It was hard to pinpoint how he knew, maybe it was the slight echo as his voice bounced off the tiles and the high ceiling. It always did that but somehow the house felt emptier and quieter.

Scraping some food into a bowl for Charlie, Blake sat on a kitchen chair and watched the little dog eat. What could he do? Go round and demand they give back a cat that wasn't his in the first place? That sounded ridiculous and Blake wasn't sure where he stood legally as far as the cat went. He cursed himself for not having the time to check the cats homes to see if his mother had actually taken Serafina in legally.

He rang Ian Youde. He sounded a bit croaky. "Will, what's the time?"

"Sorry, Ian, did I wake you up? It's almost eleven."

"No, I must have fallen asleep in the armchair while I was watching telly, mate," he said. "What is it?"

"Serafina's gone. I'm sure of it."

"She was there this morning, but I didn't see her when I took Charlie for his afternoon walk. I've been around all day and haven't seen a soul. You certain?"

"Yeah, I don't know how but I just know."

"They must've taken her when I took Charlie

out, then. Listen, I phoned up two cat rescue places on the Wirral and neither had a record of your mum homing any of their cats. They were both pretty adamant that they'd remember a big, bolshy Persian even if it was so long ago."

Blake slumped back in his chair. "That's it then, Ian. Serafina's gone and if they have taken her, I can't see how I'll get her back."

CHAPTER 25

There was so much blood. It pooled on the kitchen floor, oozing from the huge gash in the head of the corpse. The thin, straggly hair was matted with blood. A few flies buzzed lazily between the overflowing pedal bin and the staring, upturned face of Nigel Clements. Blood drops spattered all over the kitchen units as Clements had dragged his hand down them before coming to rest on the floor, leaving four smudged, red lines on the white doors.

Doug Noonan stared at the carnage and the dead body, frozen in horror. He turned to run but then paused. He'd called Clements before coming round. If the police found his phone, then they'd know. The air, already warm on this summer morning and laden with the metallic smell of blood, suddenly felt stifling and the kitchen began to revolve around Noonan. He reached out and steadied himself on the dark, marble work surface. "Shit!" he hissed, grabbing a tea towel and wiping the spot where his hand had rested. The towel came up red with blood. Noonan threw it down and looked at his hand which was also gory red. "Shit! Shit! Shit!" He stepped over Clements' legs and ran the tap over his hands, rubbing vigorously. Then he looked down.

He had planted his feet in another ruddy puddle. "Oh, no, please..." Noonan stepped back, leaving a perfect footprint on the vinyl flooring. He tried to rub the soles of his boots over it but only managed to get splatters on the bottom of his jeans. "For God's sake..."

Pausing, Noonan took a deep breath. Get the phone. Don't worry about anything else. Just find the phone. He stepped into the hallway, unconsciously wiping his feet on the carpet as he went. As far as Noonan knew, Clements was quite a solitary man and didn't have contact with any immediate family. From the looks of it, he didn't employ a cleaner or, if he did, he was being ripped off. It was unlikely that he'd be disturbed while he searched. All the same, he wanted to be out of this house and away as quickly as possible. Wincing, he pushed the front room door open, then stopped. Going back to the kitchen and tiptoeing round the dead Clements, Noonan found a pair of pink, rubber washing-up gloves under the sink. They were small and hard to get on but with a bit of cursing, and persistence, he managed.

Freed from the fear of leaving any more fingerprints, Noonan strode back into the front room, holding his hands up like a surgeon about to operate. He started by lifting the magazines on the coffee table, then pulled out the drawers of the cabinet at the side of the room. They were full of compacted envelopes, old elastic bands and used-up pens. Noonan hissed with frustration; this would take ages. He tipped the drawer he held upside down, spilling the contents onto the sofa.

As Noonan moved through the house, his search became more frantic. He tore at coat pockets, shook out backpacks and even rummaged through the dirty laundry. He pulled the musty bed clothes off the bed and turned over the mattress. The wardrobes were turned out and their contents scattered as he rifled through everything. It was only as he came down the stairs that it even occurred to him that the best way to find the phone would be to ring it. "Idiot," he muttered to himself. "Idiot!" He stabbed his gloved finger on the screen of his own phone, realising that he had contaminated that with forensic evidence, too. How did anyone get away with murder in this age of science?

A distant buzzing brought him to his senses. He hurried back into the kitchen and let out a petulant whine of despair. Once again he stood over the oozing corpse and stared at the vibrating, oblong outline of the phone in Clements' pocket.

Clements wore a pair of faded jeans, but the blood had soaked into the legs, making them dark. Noonan found himself muttering a prayer of thanks that the man's T-shirt was a navy blue and so didn't really show the stains. The tan, cotton windcheater was another matter, though. It had mopped up what seemed like gallons of red, especially around the pockets.

Maybe it was a delayed shock or the fact that, in his frantic search, Noonan had pulled out pictures of a younger Clements, surrounded by family and friends but he froze. The body at his feet had, until not long ago, been a living, breathing man with feelings and a past. There might not have been many people who could say they loved Clements, but Noonan guessed there were those out there who cared about him in some distant way. And yet here the man was, laid low. Noonan wondered if he could actually lay hands on Clements' body and get the phone from his bloody jeans.

Muttering curses, Noonan, leaned awkwardly over the body to reach into the pocket. The fabric felt heavy and damp even through his gloves and it was all he could do to stop himself from squeezing his eyes shut. Why he didn't stand up and walk around the other side of the body, he never knew; squeamishness, perhaps and an unwillingness to spend a second more at this task than was totally necessary. Whatever the reason, as he balanced precariously over Clements' corpse, three flies buzzed up from his face. One flew directly from the man's head wound onto Noonan's lip and, crying out, the man swatted his gory, gloved hand towards his face.

Several things happened at once. Doug Noonan managed to slap himself in the face, smearing gore across his cheek. Losing his balance, he tried to pull his other hand from Clements' pocket to steady himself. The soaked fabric gripped the rubber gloves on his hand, holding him fast and, effectively, pulling him back towards the body. With a squeak of horror, Noonan fell forward heavily, squashing Clements' torso. The air trapped in Clements' body groaned out through the dead man's throat and vocal cords. Noonan gave a scream of horror and revulsion as the body moaned at him, the head and chest shifting slightly as though it was trying to sit up.

His eyes blinded with blood, Noonan dragged his hand free and staggered to his feet. The rubber gloves just smeared more red liquid into his eyes when he rubbed, so he stumbled through the kitchen towards the door, trying to pull the tight, clinging gloves from his hand. One came free with a pop and Noonan knuckled at his eye, trying to get some sight back. That was when he ran smack into the kitchen door. Pain splintered across his forehead and he felt something warm trickle into his eye again.

Panting for breath and in fear for his life, Noonan ripped the remaining glove off, leaving the wrist part still clinging to his arm. He tore open the garden gate, crashing it against the house wall and ran out into the street, leaving

Clements and the phone behind.

*****

Liverpool's Baltic Triangle was an area of intense development, the home of digital and tech start-ups and trendy eateries, it drew the young and the hip for work and entertainment. Its close proximity to Toxteth and Chinatown gave it a cosmopolitan, edgy feel. Given that Blake thought of himself as neither young nor trendy, he rarely ventured into this part of the city unless some event from work drew him here. It was a gridiron of converted warehouses, some said that the name Baltic came from the Norwegian timber that was stored here. Others cited the ancient whaling associations with the area. Those warehouses that had not been used for offices had been made into flats and townhouses. It was one of these that Blake was seeking out.

True to his word Jack Kenning, the pathologist, had forwarded photographs of the ropes used to bind Thorpe on to a knot expert called Talen Doyle. But Doyle hadn't made it easy for Blake. He insisted that Blake come to his flat rather than emailing a report or just giving feedback over the phone. After a protracted debate, Blake had decided that he'd save time by just agreeing to pop down the road from HQ and call in on the man. If he was being honest, Blake was that close to telling Doyle to forget about it. The fact that Doyle knew Kenning didn't endear the man to Blake and he wondered if he would have any useful information at all. The long discussion about whether Blake would come to the flat really hadn't helped. But Blake was desperate for any kind of lead.

Doyle's flat was in a large warehouse conversion on Greenland Street in the heart of the Baltic Triangle. The brickwork, clean and sandblasted, soared above Blake's head, studded with black, aluminium window frames. It reeked simultaneously of history and modern chic. Blake pressed the button with Doyle's name beside it and was buzzed in. Glad of the cooler air in the echoing stairwell, Blake climbed up to the third floor.

His heart sank when he saw Talen Doyle standing at the top of the stairs, waiting for him. The man looked like an end-of-pier stage magician. He was thickset and clearly had once carried some muscle. Now a small but growing beer belly stretched the T-shirt that poked out through the front of his black leather waistcoat. He was bald on top, but what hair he had left was gathered in a thin, greasy ponytail. His face was bare apart from a small, dark beard that covered his chin. An earring, bangles, pendants and a pair of dark blue round lensed glasses finished the look.

"Mr Blake," Doyle said.

Blake nodded, vowing to himself that if the man said, 'I've been expecting you' he'd turn around and head straight back to the office. "Mr Doyle?" Blake said.

"Indeed."

Blake clenched his teeth, wondering if Kenning had set him up with this man as some kind of joke. "Are we going to have our conversation on the stairs or are you going to invite me in?" Blake said, not meaning to sound waspish but he couldn't abide the man's affectations.

"Y-yes, follow me, please," Doyle said, caught off-guard by Blake's directness. He led Blake to a small flat furnished as Blake would have expected in black leather to match the man's waistcoat and trousers. The walls were covered in black and white prints of faceless, nude women bound and tied with cords of different thickness. The bands made patterns around their torsos and legs. Blake waited for the man to tell him they were 'artistic.' It was only a matter of time. Blake looked away from the pictures and through the window which gave an amazing view across the waterfront to the river and the Wirral beyond, all baking in the summer heat.

"Shibari," Doyle said. "The ancient Japanese art of rope tying. It's about patterns and aesthetics."

"If you say so, Mr Doyle," Blake muttered, glancing at the pictures again. "As a policeman, I worry when I see a woman tied and helpless..."

Doyle gave Blake a condescending smile and

shook his head. “It’s a philosophy, an artform involving trust and the beauty of the physical form.”

“Really?” Blake said. “So tell me, Mr Doyle. What did you learn from the rope that tied Harry Thorpe’s ankles?”

CHAPTER 26

Talen Doyle puffed his chest out and smiled at Blake again. "I sense you don't like me, Mr Blake. Or at least, you don't like my interests..."

Blake shrugged. "I don't know you, Mr Doyle," he said. "Obviously, I'm grateful for any help you might be able to offer. Jack Kenning told me you were a forensic knot expert."

"I'm many things, Mr Blake. I advise circuses, magic acts, film makers and I run Japanese Rope workshops for those interested. But, yes, I also do forensic work."

"And what did you find?"

In response, Doyle threw Blake a length of rope. "Tie me a knot. Don't think about it. Just tie one quickly."

Blake pulled a face. "If this is meant to..."

"Just indulge me, please Inspector."

Blake shrugged and tied a knot.

"A reef knot," Doyle said, taking the rope back. "You're right-handed. I can tell from the turns you used in the knot. It's unlikely you fish or sail or go rock climbing. Am I right?"

"Me doing any of those things would be unlikely these days…"

"People who do, often show off or have fun tying something fancier. You were in the Scouts, but only for a short while."

"Long enough to learn a reef knot but that's it. You could say that about so many people, though…"

"A reef knot is secure but easily undone. You can get out of it quickly. It might say something about your commitment to relationships…"

"Or which knots the Scoutmaster taught me."

"You like an exit strategy, though. You don't like being tangled up in a web or feeling trapped."

"Who does?"

"You'd be surprised, Inspector," Doyle said, rising one eyebrow. He smiled. "To be fair, though, you're right. Most people can tie simple knots from quite an early age without any instruction. Other knots are very specific to one's occupation, pastime or activity. Some people who are experienced and habitual knot-tiers often have a favourite, go-to knot that they use without thinking. This applies to killers who bind their victims too."

"Wait, are you trying to tell me that whoever killed Harry Thorpe has killed before and they have a 'go-to' knot?"

Doyle winced and inclined his head. "It's not a

precise science, Inspector. It has been known for me to be mistaken. Rarely." He picked up a folder and pulled out photographs from the crime scene, flicking through them until he found a close-up of the knot around Thorpe's ankle. "Let's deal with what we do know. The rope is the kind generally used for sailing and water sports. It's not a cheap, nasty nylon rope used in gardening or agriculture. I'd say that whoever tied the knot was left-handed. That knot is called an anchor bend. Normally, it's used to secure a line to a ring or something like that. Technically, it's a hitch but that doesn't matter here. It tells us that the tier has some nautical experience but, crucially, it's an unusual knot to use to tie a rope to someone's ankle. There are several better knots. I can't help but think that this is the killer's 'signature knot.'"

"If you recognise it as such then you must have encountered this person's victims before?"

Doyle looked flustered and sat down heavily in one of his armchairs, the leather of his trousers squeaking on the upholstery. "Two or three years ago, I was asked to look at a series of drownings along the Northern coast of Spain, around Santander and Bilbao. Four men in their mid to late sixties, all wealthy, all tied up with this knot and drowned..."

"Did they ever find the killer?"

"Not that I'm aware of, Inspector. You know what it's like, though, surely; you're asked to give your expert opinion on one aspect of a case and they don't always let you know the outcome. Maybe they did but I doubt it. I was never called to court."

"These men, did you learn anything else about them?"

"I heard some gossip that the men were having affairs with younger women. One theory I did hear was some kind of 'honey trap' scenario but, as I said, I wasn't party to everything that was discovered. The knots were the same, though, and just like this one." He waved the photo of Harry Thorpe's leg. "If I was a gambling man, Inspector, I'd say you have a serial killer on your hands."

*****

There was a muted air in the Major Incident Room when Blake returned from his trip to the Baltic Triangle. It seemed that Kath Cryer had phoned Alex Manikas sometime the previous evening and he'd told her everything. Having promised not to tell a soul, it was now common knowledge amongst the whole team. Blake's mind pinballed between Manikas, Doyle's revelation and the cat. He felt guilty but Manikas had brought this mess on himself. Manikas had asked Blake's permission to approach Thor Magnussen undercover last year and Blake had warned him off. If he'd done as Blake had told him, then none of this would have happened. And yet he felt sorry for the young man. Blake felt guilty, too for worrying about Serafina who, as far as he knew, was in good health but just enjoying food from another bowl. He couldn't shake a feeling of disquiet, though. From what Ian had said, the Leekies weren't that well-off. And if they couldn't even afford to care for Serafina then was it all a scam to get the cat and sell it?

And then there was the suggestion that they had a serial killer in their midst. Blake could hear the incredulity in Kath Cryer's voice when he related Talen Doyle's theory. "A serial killer, sir? With all due respect, that does sound a bit far-fetched..."

"I know Kath, but he was pretty adamant that the knot used was unusual and matched the pattern of the killings in Spain. Plus, the profile of the victims matches Harry Thorpe's don't you think? Successful older business men seduced by Spanish girls. And Thorpe's girlfriend, the mysterious Ginebra Garcia is Spanish..."

"But what about Kyle Quinlan? I'm still certain he has something to do with this. We've wasted so much time chasing Clements and Doug Noonan when we should have been putting pressure on Quinlan."

Blake felt himself blushing. He picked up on the unspoken criticism; they'd wasted time because Blake was letting his past with Laura Vexley stop him from going after Quinlan. It was rubbish, of course. "Make no mistake, Kath. If I thought for a second, that Quinlan was involved in Harry Thorpe's death, then I'd be all over him, you know that. I wouldn't let any personal feelings get in the way of that. Now I'm not denying that Quinlan has benefitted by Thorpe's sudden desire to kick back and escape the rat race but there's no logical reason for him to kill the man. Now, let's put Quinlan to one side for the moment and consider the idea that Thorpe was the victim of some kind of 'honey trap' scam."

"Yes, sir," Kath said, glancing sidelong at Kinnear who stared at the desk.

"So, have we heard back from the Spanish authorities about Ginebra Garcia?"

"Not yet, sir, I'll get onto it, asap, and give them a push," Kath said.

"If you get to speak to anyone, have a word about the Bilbao killings, see if we can get any more detail. Anything from Ian Ollerthwaite yet, Andrew?"

Kinnear smiled and waved a heavy-looking file. "He hasn't been idle, sir. It seems as though Thorpe had been liquidising his assets, as we knew, but most of the money has gone from his accounts into Shirley Thorpe's the day he died."

"Really? Mrs Thorpe always protested that she had nothing to do with her husband's businesses and yet she had access to all his accounts?"

"It seems so, sir. It looks like the remainder, literally just a couple of hundred pounds has been transferred into another account but Ian couldn't identify who that belonged to."

"Perhaps we've been looking at this from the wrong angle, after all," Blake muttered. Quinlan had suggested they look 'closer to home.' Is that what he meant? "Did Shirley Thorpe kill her husband for the money and then try to make it look like some kind of public execution?"

"Perhaps she was worried about losing out to this new woman, sir," Kath said. "It doesn't make her a killer. Anyway, she had an alibi, the Pilates class, remember?"

"True, Kath," Blake said. "Vikki, can you just double check that alibi? It was Tasha Cook who checked it out. Who did she speak to?"

Vikki clicked on the computer keyboard and paused for a second. "It was the Pilates Instructor, a Rio Pecina..."

"The bloke who drove us over to Hilbre when Thorpe's body was found," Blake said. "wasn't he Spanish?"

"Yes, but he said he was Galician, sir," Vikki

said. "It's a province in Northern Spain."

Kath looked uncomfortable. "That's the same region as the four other murders, sir."

"Something else struck me as odd, sir," Vikki said. "When I last went to talk to Mrs Thorpe at the farm, she came out of the studios in exercise gear and had been working out. She told me she had her own studio in one of the barn conversions. Why would you go to the local health club if you had your own facilities?"

"Ring the club and check the times of the classes, Vikki. It may be that Mrs Thorpe went for purely social reasons or maybe something else was going on."

Vikki nodded and picked up her phone.

"Perhaps this Rio seduced Mrs Thorpe, killed her husband and plans to take her money, sir," Kinnear said.

"It doesn't explain Harry Thorpe's love interest unless her nationality is just a coincidence. Could Rio and this Ginebra have been working together? She seduces Harry, while Rio targets Mrs Thorpe?" Blake said. "Or are we getting ahead of ourselves?"

"At the very least, we need to talk to Rio as a matter of urgency, sir," Kinnear said. "Even if there's no link to the Spanish murders, he still has a nautical background, would know his knots and be familiar with the tides."

"True, Andrew. While we're waiting for Vikki to finish on the phone, have we located Thor Magnussen, yet?"

"No, sir," Kath said. "He's gone to ground. No sign of him."

"Jeez, how does a big, ugly bugger like that disappear? He sticks out like a sore thumb in any crowd."

Vikki put the phone down and looked over to Blake. "Sir, I spoke to reception who checked their rota. There was no group Pilates class booked for the Sunday night. She told me that Rio Pecina did a lot of one-to-one lessons and was 'very popular' with Mrs Thorpe. She says he may have 'had a one-to-one' with her at her own studios as that was quite common."

"Looks like we need to have a chat with Mrs Thorpe, then, people," Blake said. The phone rang again and Kath answered it. They watched as the blood drained from her face. "It's Nigel Clements. He's been murdered and someone looking remarkably like Doug Noonan was seen running from the house."

CHAPTER 27

Doug Noonan looked a mess. He hadn't got very far before his appearance had attracted the attention of a local PCSO. After all, he was covered in blood, had half a rubber glove halfway up one arm and was cycling like a lunatic through Heswall. Even now, dressed in grey sweatpants and top to replace his bloody clothes, he looked hollow. The Desk Sergeant at the Custody Suite had taken one look at the charges and agreed that he could be held on suspicion of murder.

Now he sat opposite Blake, pale and sheepish, flanked by a duty solicitor who looked like she needed to get home and have some sleep, too. Blake leafed through the photographs of Clements' body, looking distastefully at the amount of blood.

"So, Doug," he said. You said you came round to talk to Nigel Clements but found him dead. How did you get in?"

"I told you, I rang the bell at the front but got no answer. I thought maybe he was ignoring me, so I went round the back. That was when I saw the back door was open."

"Why would Clements want to ignore you?" Kath Cryer said.

Noonan reddened. "We had a disagreement about something. I thought he might still be cross about it."

"And what was the disagreement about?" Blake said, leaning forward.

"No comment," Noonan said, licking his lips.

Kath slid Clements' phone to the middle of the table. "This was the phone found on Nigel Clements' body. It only had one contact on it, Doug. You. Why was that?"

"No comment."

"Can you explain this, then?" Kath touched the screen and a voice crackled from the phone: "Clements, it's me. You better get your act together, mate or I swear I'll come round there and rip your fucking head off your shoulders. I did what you wanted and now it's time for you to pay up. Call me back in the next ten minutes or I'm coming round to you. You've seen what I'm capable of. You know what I did to Thorpe. Don't push me too far."

"That's your voice, Doug," Blake said. "Did you go round to show Nigel Clements what you were capable of?"

Noonan's face flushed red. "N-no comment."

Kath sat back in her chair. "And what did you do to Thorpe? I take it you mean Harry Thorpe, the man found murdered on West Kirby beach on

Sunday."

"Listen, Doug, you were stopped cycling through Heswall, covered in blood and I'm pretty certain forensics will confirm that it's not your own. There's a threatening message on a very suspicious phone. No doubt your DNA is all over that house and Clements' body," Blake said. "Help us out here. I never had you down as a killer but right now, it looks like you're responsible for the murders of Clements *and* Harry Thorpe. I know you've been cautioned and charged with public order offences connected with protests but have you ever been in prison, banged up for a long time?"

Noonan bit his lip and glanced at his solicitor who shook her head. "No comment."

Blake sighed. "Right now, everything we have on you is circumstantial, but the CSI team are going to come back with solid forensic evidence that you killed Clements. There'll be fibres from your clothes, fingerprints, footprints. Neighbours saw you fleeing from the house. This is your chance to tell us what really happened. People are only going to think the worst."

"I didn't kill him," Noonan said. "I didn't kill anyone."

"Okay," Blake said gently. "What happened?"

"Mr Noonan, I must advise you that..." the solicitor began to say but Noonan shook his head and she fell silent.

"I did go round to talk to Clements, and I did leave that threatening message but I swear, I found him like that. I panicked and started looking for the phone. I knew it would be incriminating, so I turned the place upside down but I couldn't find it."

"What was it you wanted to talk to Clements about?"

Noonan sighed and stared at the table. "I was conning him. It started off as a joke really but somehow it snowballed."

"What did?" Kath said, making Blake wince. Being so abrasive and straight-talking, Kath Cryer could be an asset in an interview just from the fact that she could irritate the truth out of the most resilient suspect. Now and then, though, she could cause interviewees to clam up. Fortunately, Noonan was in full confession mode and wasn't phased by her interruption.

"Clements came round to my house one night a few months ago. He was asking questions about Thorpe's qualities as a landlord, seeing if he could get tenants to make complaints against him. I had no love for Thorpe either and we kind of bonded over that for a while."

"You were friends, then?" Blake said.

"Yeah, we went for a pint every now and then,

did a couple of pub quizzes. Clements was a funny fish, always coming back to the fact that Thorpe had got him sacked. He was bitter. Anyway, one night, we got very drunk and Clements said he wanted Thorpe dead. I said I'd do it for him."

"You offered to kill Thorpe for Clements," Blake said. Kath was busy scribbling notes.

"I wasn't serious but, anyway, I kept the joke going and gave Clements a 'burner phone' with my number on it. I suppose in the stark light of day, he didn't find it very funny and, on reflection, I shouldn't have kept it going for as long as I did. I told him how much it would cost and that I'd be back in touch when the deed was done."

"It doesn't sound like much of a joke to me," Blake said.

"I know," Noonan agreed. "I went too far. Clements didn't think much of it either. He stopped calling round. To be honest, I was quite glad. His hatred of Thorpe was getting to me. I'd come to dread him turning up at the house and ranting on about how he'd lost his pension and his family. I mean, Thorpe was a bastard, don't get me wrong but I got weary of Clements' hatred of him. It was exhausting."

"So what changed?" Kath said.

"Clements rang me on the dodgy phone I'd given him, congratulating me and I realised that someone had done my job for me. So I played along."

"So you didn't tell him he'd got it wrong?" Kath said.

"Of course not. From my point of view, Clements was well-off. He had his own house, he bragged about doing some private investigating, watching middle-aged business execs getting their leg over before he served them their divorce papers. He had it cushy as far as I could see. So I thought, 'why not screw him over for a couple of grand?'"

"So where did it go wrong?" Blake said, giving Kath a warning glance.

"You lot made me nervous and I got anxious. I thought I was going to have to run away, so I told him I needed more money. He was stalling and I wanted to get away. So I left that ridiculous message. When he didn't answer, I went round. That's when I found him. I was in shock, fell over and got covered in his blood. I never killed him. I swear. You see, in reality, I've done nothing wrong..."

"I'm not sure I'd call extortion, fraud and conspiracy to murder 'nothing wrong,' Doug but then maybe we've got different moral compasses," Blake said, sitting back.

Noonan looked as though he'd been slapped in the face. He moistened his lips again. "That's not what I heard, Inspector Blake. Clements told me about what happened on Hilbre Island, that poor young lad drowning. At least I don't *really* have someone's life on my conscience."

"I think we're finished here," Blake said, standing up. "You know nothing about that incident, Noonan and neither did Clements. So forget whatever salacious story he cooked up for you, it's nothing like what really happened." He glanced over at the solicitor. "Your client has identified himself as a flight risk. I'm going to apply to keep him for the full time, pending further investigations. Can you finish up here Kath?" Without waiting for a reply, Blake took himself out of the interview room and away from Noonan and his accusations from the past. One thing Blake was sure of; despite all the evidence, Noonan didn't kill Thorpe. And if he didn't, then who did? That question still needed answering.

*****

Although Laura shared a bed with Kyle Quinlan, she also had her own room in the big house. Quinlan had managed to have most of the rooms downstairs decorated but getting the bedrooms just right was taking a bit longer. So Laura's 'private room' was a nightmare of striped Laura Ashley wallpaper from the 1980s and pine furniture which was kind of growing on her.

Since talking to Nick the day before, she had become unsettled. She was pretty sure she could trust Nick. He was a straight-talking kind of bloke and would probably be open with Kyle about his concerns. But telling her to get ready to take over or run for her life was alarming.

In the back of her mind, she also wondered if it was some kind of test of her loyalty. Nick was Kyle's man, after all and would do whatever he asked. What if Kyle had put Nick up to it? She wouldn't put it past Kyle; he was insecure enough.

But Nick was right, Kyle's behaviour was erratic from the start and was getting worse. She didn't mind the other women particularly; she saw this as a business arrangement that would end sooner or later. Jealousy wouldn't serve her well. It wasn't as if she didn't intend on abandoning Kyle when things got too hot, anyway. She'd said as much to Will Blake last time she'd seen him. Give Kyle enough rope and he'd hang himself, that was certain. The secret was not to get tangled up in the mess yourself. So, from that point of view, Nick was only echoing her own thoughts anyway. It all came down to whether or not she could trust Nick and she was pretty sure she could.

A gentle tap on the door brought her back from her thoughts. Kyle stood outside, smiling smugly at her. "Can I come in?"

"I suppose so," Laura said, pulling the door back to let him in.

"I need to get that lazy decorator back here to finish off the bedrooms," Kyle said, looking around the room. He glanced slyly at Laura. "I saw your old boyfriend, Blakey, yesterday."

"Really?" Laura said, trying not to sound too interested. "What the hell were you doing talking to him?"

"Just helping the boys in blue with their enquiries like an upstanding citizen, that's all. He didn't seem to think much of my big plans for the Wirral. But I put him straight on the Harry Thorpe case."

Laura closed her eyes and breathed slowly out through her nose. "What have you done now, Kyle?"

"Nothing," Kyle said, all faux outrage. "They just invited me in and I went to have a chat. I suggested they might want to look a bit closer to home with the Harry Thorpe murder."

"Closer to home?"

"Yeah, they'll be sniffing around that old witch Shirley, now. She never liked me. Serves her right." He grinned and narrowed his eyes. "Women eh? Can't live with 'em can't live without 'em."

"Shirley Thorpe? You told them she killed her

husband?"

"Why not? Happens all the time, doesn't it? Anyway, it'll make her life a misery for a bit. Or maybe they'll start looking at that head-the-ball Thor or Fabian or whatever his name is."

"Jeez, Kyle, why can't you just leave well alone? You should be focusing on the business, not getting mixed up with the Thorpes. What if they decide it was you who killed Harry after all? Did you think of that?"

"Relax. They won't."

"How can I relax if you won't tell me what's going on, Kyle Quinlan? How can I help you?"

Quinlan held her by the shoulders. "You don't need to. I'm doing just fine..."

"That's not what I've heard. You need to stop spending money and start generating some or we're in trouble."

"You been talking to Nick?" Kyle snorted. "Honestly, you two are like my mum and dad or something."

Laura hugged Kyle. "I'm serious, Kyle. I know you borrowed heavily from some dodgy people. They're going to want some kind of return on their investment before long, aren't they? So you better start acting like a businessman instead of an idiot or we're sunk."

CHAPTER 28

The smell of the day clung to Blake as he sat in the car and enjoyed the growing iciness of the air-conditioning. Sweat, a trace of Kath's body spray, the disinfectant tang of the Custody Suite and even the imagined undertone of Clements' blood all mingled, blown about by the car fan. It was so hot outside now that it seemed like Blake was melting. For a moment, he closed his eyes and let the air chill his face.

It was inevitable that the past business at Hilbre Island would rear its ugly head, given the location of the current murder and the personalities involved. It was a long time ago now and Blake had been a young man. If Blake had a time machine, he'd go back and have a word with his younger, less experienced self. In that instant, Manikas came to mind. He'd been so busy, he hadn't had chance to consider what the young detective constable was going through now, but he had a good idea. He took his phone out of his pocket.

"Sir?" Manikas said, his voice slightly slurred.

"You okay?"

"S-sure. I'm fine... I was just..."

"I'm on my way round. I need to talk to you,"

Blake said, ending the call before Manikas could object.

He drove through Liverpool, away from the tunnel and towards Alex Manikas' house. Even though it was late, the sky wasn't truly dark and Liverpool's thrill seekers were out in force, moving from pub to club to bar to eatery. Lads perfectly groomed and immaculately dressed, despite the sultry night, laughed and joked as they rolled along the street. Girls in short dresses and tottered on skyscraper heels holding each other up and shrieking. Nobody could say that scousers didn't make an effort when they went out and they certainly knew how to enjoy themselves. The party flowed through the streets on a summer's night like this. Blake had become used to the late-night sights in town. He'd been part of that flow of young humanity once and, sometimes, he envied them their youth.

As he drove further out, he saw fewer people. Here, small houses and low blocks of flats replaced the high buildings of the city centre. Lights glowed in the windows, showing that families were settling to evening telly. Blake felt a little jealous of them, too. Being a copper didn't exclude him from having a loving family or a busy social life; it was something in his personality. Maybe it was his past that held him back. For years, he'd thought he didn't deserve to have a happy life but Laura had turned him around.

She'd shown him that he could enjoy life and then delivered a gut punch by leaving him for Quinlan. Blake sighed as he sat at traffic lights. Maybe her last lesson was that he shouldn't rely on anyone. He didn't believe that, though. He wasn't the man Talen Doyle, the knot expert, had described; a man who always needed a way out of any relationship. Blake was loyal. That was his downfall, really. He devoted himself to his work, his partner, his pets. But he let the past hold him back. "No more," Blake muttered. Nothing should hold him back, not his past, not Laura, not Hilbre Island.

He turned into Manikas' road, a new development off Edge Lane, a major arterial road leading in and out of Liverpool. The houses looked modern but small and Blake imagined they were inhabited by single professionals like Manikas. He pulled up outside the house and turned off his engine, steeling himself to step out into the heat and wondering what he was going to say to Alex.

Alex Manikas looked sheepish and tired. He was clearly wondering what Blake was doing at his door. "Sir, good of you to call and see me," Alex said, ignoring the fact that it was close to eleven at night. "Come in."

"Thanks, Alex," Blake said. He could smell wine on Manikas' breath and as he was led into the living room, he saw a plate of congealed meatballs. Clearly Alex didn't have much appetite. Blake sat down. "I-I thought you might need some moral support."

"Right, sir," Manikas said, sitting in the armchair opposite Blake. The room was nicely furnished, with a laminate floor, painted walls and subtle lighting. It was clearly a single man's house, but it felt homely. A fan tracked back and forth fighting against the humid night.

"Have Personnel been in touch?"

Manikas nodded. "And I've spoken to my Federation Rep, too, sir."

"Good," Blake said. "Look, I'm sorry, Alex, but I had to report it once I knew. I'd be neglecting my responsibilities if I didn't..."

"I know that, sir," Alex said, flatly.

An awkward silence fell between them and, finally, Blake drew a breath. "I know what you're going through, Alex."

"Do you, sir?" Manikas didn't sound convinced.

"You mentioned my experience at Hilbre Island when you told me about Thor's party," Blake said, launching in before he could stop himself. "And I said it was totally different but, in truth, you were right. It was like that and it nearly finished me."

"Really, sir?"

"It was after my time with Searchlight and all

that celebrity nonsense, my daughter had just died and I'd split from my wife…"

"Sir, I'm sorry. I knew you'd lost your daughter, I'd never really thought how those events all happened so quickly."

"In the space of twelve months, I was back living with my parents, but I was a driven man. It was my way of coping. I'd be the first in the office and the last to leave. If a dirty job needed doing, I'd be the one who volunteered. I'd take work from other people if they needed time off. I had no life of my own."

Alex nodded. "I can see how that could happen, sir."

"I was a robot," Blake said, laughing ruefully. "Robocop… that was me. Dispassionate, delivering justice regardless of whose life it destroyed. I swear, if I'd caught my mum or dad committing some minor infraction of the law, I'd have slapped the cuffs on them."

"You took things too far, then?"

"Don't forget, having been on the Searchlight programme, I'd spent three years rubbing shoulders with media types and celebrities. As far as my fellow officers were concerned, I was just another 'luvvie' with no clue about real police work. So I was eager to prove myself."

"But weren't you effectively ordered to go on

Searchlight, sir?"

"It was suggested that it would be 'a good idea' and even good for my career. I think if I had turned it down, it would have been seen as a snub and anyway, I was young and swept up in the glamour of it all. Either way, it meant that after my stint with Searchlight was over, I had to work twice as hard and be twice as good to get any respect. And that's where Carl Harris came in."

"Carl Harris, sir?"

"Harris was eighteen years old but had lived a hundred lifetimes already; each one of them more unpleasant than the last. He was a rangy, whippet of a lad but dangerous. We were searching for him in connection with a number of sexual assaults on small children around the Wirral."

"Sounds like a charmer, sir."

Blake nodded. "In many ways, he was a victim himself; a drug-addicted mother, abusive father and relatives. He didn't really stand a chance but what he did to those kids was truly terrible. He had to be stopped. For some reason, he decided to hide out on Hilbre Island…"

"A bit of a random decision, sir. I mean, he'd be trapped there by the tide for what, twelve hours?"

"Something like that, Alex, yes. I think he thought it was the last place anyone would search for him and in one sense, he was right, but a member of the public spotted him as they were leaving the island and rang the police. I happened to be nearby, interviewing a witness, so I said I'd investigate."

"Let me guess, sir, the instructions were not to approach him..."

"Exactly. So of course, I headed over to the island, even though the tide was coming in. Harris wasn't going anywhere. I could have waited and made sure every avenue of escape was blocked but no. I wanted my moment of glory. In all likelihood, I'd be trapped on the Island with Harris which was a dangerous prospect."

"You could have handled him, though, sir, surely."

"I could but Harris had a fondness for sharp implements and it doesn't matter how big you are, if someone sticks a knife in you, you're stuffed. Anyway, over the sands I went and I only just made it. Carl Harris was there, sure enough and he was waiting for me."

"He'd spotted you running across the sand to the island, I suppose, sir."

"I managed to get the knife off him but he was high as a kite on something and his rage turned to paranoia. Then I was trying to stop him from running off the island. I managed to cuff him but he head butted me, hard. When I came to, he'd vanished. Hilbre is a tiny island, and I searched every inch of it. Of course, his body was washed up later, cuffed. Clements was on the team investigating his death. In the end, they only had my account of events which was corroborated by what evidence was left. His family accused me of executing him; binding his hands and throwing him into the sea. The force tried to suppress it, but I had such a public profile. They didn't know whether to make an example of me or what."

"I presume they decided not to, sir."

"Obviously, Alex but it was touch and go. So, I guess what I'm saying is, I understand how easy it is to get carried away in the excitement of a case. And I know what you're going through and that I didn't make any decisions lightly..."

Alex looked thoughtfully at his wine glass. "Thanks, sir. Can I ask, when you thought your career was over, what did you consider doing?"

"I don't know," Blake said, nonplussed by the question. "I was determined to stay in the force. I was happy to take any disciplinary action that was deemed appropriate but fought the suggestion of dismissal tooth and nail. Just as you should."

"I just wish I'd never gone to that party..."

"And I wish I'd never run across that sand to

beat the tide but we make the decisions and have to face the consequences, Alex. But don't give up on the force, Alex, you're a good detective. I mean that. Anyway," Blake said, standing up, "I'd better get going. Let me know if you need anything."

But Alex Manikas was no longer looking at Blake. Instead, he was staring over Blake's shoulder in horror. Turning, Blake saw Thor Magnussen, axe in hand, looming outside the patio door. Then that whole end of the room exploded in a shower of glass.

CHAPTER 29

Thor Magnussen looked deranged, his eyes wide, his teeth bared; he reminded Blake of a wild animal. There were dark circles under the man's eyes too and he looked as though he hadn't slept properly in days.

"Two birds with one stone," Thor said, his voice was a hoarse rumble. "I shouldn't be surprised. What were you up to, planning the cover-up of my father's murder?"

"Thor, you've got to listen to me. You need to calm down. We are close to finding your father's killer and..."

"Ha!" Thor barked, slipping the axe from hand to hand. "Close to finding someone to pin it on, you mean. I know you've had it in for my family since Clements tried to frame my father and he stood up to you."

"Clements lost his job because of what he did and he's more than paid for his actions now, but I suspect you know that, already, don't you?"

Thor gave an unsettling grin. "No comment, Inspector. Now, who's first?"

"Stop and think!" Blake snapped. "Why would we kill your father so publicly? Why would anyone? It's bizarre. Honestly, Thor, if I was going to do away with your father, I'd have done it much more quietly and you'd never have found the body..."

"Showing your true colours, at last, Blake? I don't know what you mean but I'm going to put your heads on pikes and leave them on show in Sefton Park. Is that public enough for you?"

"Use your brain, lad. We would have nothing to gain from killing your father. Nothing at all. He was retiring..."

"You might think he was slipping off the hook; getting away from you before you could stitch him up..."

"If we were going to do that, we'd have done it years ago. You know I'm right, Thor. Stop now before any more lives are lost."

Thor's steady glare faltered. "But you bribed Bjorn and Terry Ford. They were meant to protect him..."

"You think that, Thor but it's not true. You killed Ford for no reason. He was loyal to your father and you killed him."

"Who did kill my father then?" Thor said, blinking rapidly. Blake wondered just how wired and edgy he was. They were walking a tightrope with him.

"What can you tell me about Rio Pecina?"

"Rio? He's my mother's personal trainer. Has been for a couple of years. Why would he want to kill my father?" Thor said, licking his lips. His eyes widened as the implications of the revelation sank in. "No. If he did it, then you're saying my mother was involved in some way and that they..."

"It's just a theory, Thor but there's a girl we're trying to track down. She was Spanish, too. And she was in a relationship with your father."

"You're sick," Thor snarled. "Not happy with just killing my father, you want to trash my mum's reputation too. Well it's not going to happen."

Thor lunged at Blake and they both fell back. Stars exploded before Blake's eyes as he cracked his head on the coffee table. Thor's fist filled his vision and then pain burnt across his face and the world turned red. He pushed the heel of his hand against the big man's bearded chin, but another punch caught the side of his head. The room vanished for a second, replaced by total darkness. Things slowed down and Blake felt as though he was staring at Thor through dark, swirling seawater.

Then Thor's weight vanished from on top of him. Blake dragged himself onto the sofa and stared around, blinking and trying to make sense of what was happening. Manikas was dancing, spinning round and round. For a second, Blake almost laughed, it looked so absurd. But Manikas had Thor in a headlock and the giant was whirling around, trying to break away. Manikas' free hand smacked repeated into Thor's head, hard and fast. A few teeth fell onto the carpet. Then Manikas swept a leg against Thor's ankles.

"I should have done this in the first place," Manikas growled as Thor fell to the ground with a shout of pain. For a horrible moment, Blake thought Manikas was going to beat Thor to death. The young man's face was bloody and swollen. Alex jumped up from him and rummaged in his jacket, pulling something from the pocket. Thor staggered to his feet and roared but Manikas turned butting his forehead into Thor's face and sending the big man down again. Manikas jumped on him again, dragging his hands behind his back. "Thor Magnussen, I'm making a citizen's arrest. DCI Blake might caution you if he's in any fit state." Blake heard the click of the cuffs above Thor's frustrated, gargling moans.

"I think, by rights, you should have handed them in, Alex," Blake panted, grinning.

Alex smiled back, blood streaming down his face. "Just add it to the list of my sins, sir," he said, trying to wink. "Anyway, they're for personal use." Alex fell back onto the sofa next to Blake, laughter shaking both their bodies.

*****

Blake lay in the bottom of a rowing boat in Laura's lap as she stroked his brow. The sky was dark, filled with brooding black and purple clouds.

"You're awake," she said. "I was worried you'd never come round."

"If I'd known you were here, I'd have woken up sooner," he said, trying to sit up. His legs wouldn't move. Looking down, he saw they were bound with coils and coils of rope. "What are you doing? Laura untie me."

"Talen Doyle says I'm an expert knots-woman. You'll never get out of that. It's a work of art."

Blake stared at the rope tightening around his legs. It slithered and twisted around him like a snake. The boat bobbed on the waves and Blake was suddenly aware of a huge figure rowing the boat.

"We're here," Kyle Quinlan said, grinning down at Blake. "Throw him over the side."

"No, Laura. What are you doing? I thought you loved me, once. Why would you want to kill me?"

"Why does anyone ever want to take a life, Will?" Laura said, picking him up as though he was a weightless child. "Revenge? Money? Self-preservation?"

"But I would never harm you..."

"Goodbye, Will," Laura said, swinging Blake in her arms. Suddenly, he was weightless, the sea racing towards him as he fell.

"No!" Blake yelled and sat up in bed. He felt cold, drenched in sweat. Something stung his arm and it felt stiff. He looked down to see a cannula and a tube. The bed was metal and the disinfectant smell of a hospital filled his nostrils. Somewhere close-by, a machine beeped. A young nurse stood beside his bed. She was pretty, Blake thought, blinking, with dark hair and brown eyes. Laura's caress still warmed his brow.

"Inspector Blake, you were having a bad dream," the nurse said. "I'm Jenny Fields, I'm on duty…"

"Where am I?"

"The Royal Liverpool…"

"Hospital?"

"Well, yeah," Jenny said. "You had a nasty bang on the head and lost consciousness apparently. You're in the assessment ward now. How are you feeling?"

Blake tried to piece together the events at Manikas' house. They'd cuffed Thor and were laughing and joking. Then Blake's vision had faded and he'd passed out. "Like someone has stamped on my head. My detective constable, Alex Manikas, is he okay?"

"I think so, yes. I don't think he was kept in. He rang the emergency services. I can find out for you. The doctor will be around soon, to see how you are..."

"I can't stay here," Blake said, lurching forward and the ward swam around him. Jenny pushed him back into the pillow firmly.

"You aren't going anywhere until the doctor has seen you. You had quite a mauling and you need to lie still and rest. Besides, by the look of you, if I let you get off this bed, I'd only have to call the porters to pick you up off the ground and put you back."

Blake grunted but didn't try to move. She was right, he was weak and needed rest. He would play the good patient. For now.

CHAPTER 30

West Kirby Concourse Leisure Centre was busy and Detective Sergeant Vikki Chinn gave a silent prayer of thanks that she wasn't a punter today. Harassed mums and dads shepherded their children through the foyer to get to swimming lessons while a crowd of adults headed for the dance studio and the gym. Others were coming out, making the whole reception point feel chaotic. Everyone was sweaty and irritable in the crushing heat.

Vikki slipped through the crowd and headed for the dance studio, too. Rio Pecina stood at the front talking to a small group of women as the previous class wandered out. His grin faded as he saw Vikki walking across the studio towards him. Muttering his apologies to the women, he straightened his back and reinstated his white smile as they filed away.

"Detective Sergeant Chinn, what a pleasant surprise," he said in an overly cheerful voice. "To what do I owe the pleasure?"

It struck Vikki that when she had met him on the beach, and he was merely a member of the public helping them, she had been taken by his looks and positive demeanour. Now, viewing him as a suspect, those same qualities struck her as false and shallow. "I just needed to ask you a few quick questions, if I may..."

Rio looked at his watch and grimaced. "I have another class coming in any minute. They have paid and expect their full time." He looked up at her and beamed once again. "But if it's quick, fire away!"

Vikki gave a tight smile and pulled out her notebook. "Can you tell me what you know about Shirley Thorpe?"

"Who?" Rio said and then put a hand to his temple. "Ah, si! I know who you mean. Forgive me. Yes she is a client of mine. I am personal trainer to her."

"Right and how often do you meet her?"

"Once, maybe twice a week. Sometimes more if she requests it." He shrugged. "It is hard to say, 'no,' when a client is as keen as Mrs Thorpe."

"I see," Vikki said. "How would you describe your relationship with her, then?"

Rio pouted his lip and scratched his head. "I do not know. Business-like? Friendly?" His eyes narrowed. "What are you suggesting? I am totally professional in my dealings with clients. I can assure you there was nothing else between us..."

"Just building up a picture, that's all," Vikki said, giving a brief smile again. "On the night

Harry Thorpe died, Mrs Thorpe told us she went to a Pilates session at her local health club. You confirmed that as the person in charge of the session."

"That is right."

"Was it a group session or a one-to-one?"

Rio's face darkened. "I can't remember. It might have been a group..."

"It was less than a week ago," Vikki said. "Try a bit harder, Rio."

"All right, yes. It was an individual session..."

"At the health club? Or at Mrs Thorpe's home studio?"

"It was at her studio."

"Then why did you go through the charade of pretending that she was at the health club when her husband was being murdered?"

"I didn't say anything that was untrue. I just confirmed that she had been with me. If she told you she was at the health club, then you should take that up with her. I'm worried about what you are getting at, here. Do you think *I* killed Mr Thorpe?"

"Why would I think that, Rio?" Vikki said, raising her eyebrows.

Rio's face hardened. "You people like to put words in people's mouths. It is the same in Spain.

The police will pin the blame on an innocent man when they can't find the true culprit. Talk to Mrs Thorpe. I have a class to take."

*****

Shirley Thorpe flung open every door of the white fitted wardrobes in her bedroom and stared up at the suitcases on the top shelf. When they went on holiday, it was one of Harry's jobs to get them down from there. She'd need something to stand on if she was going to do it. Pulling up a stool that normally stood by her dressing table, she climbed up and pulled at the topmost case.

She had looked high and low, turning out drawers and emptying boxes to find anything that told her where this 'other woman' lived. DS Chinn had suggested that Harry was having an affair and Shirley's rejection of the idea had been a reflex denial. Of course, Chinn was right. Harry had been unfaithful before, but they never really meant anything. She realised that sometimes, to him, it was like getting a side order of chips with his beer. It was his idea of a good night out; a few drinks with the lads, pick up some slapper and book into a hotel. She'd accepted it a long time ago, taking slim satisfaction in the knowledge that she meant more to him than any of these one-night stands.

Something had been different recently, though.

Harry had been distracted all the time, as though he wasn't really there at all but somewhere else. He'd lost all interest in home improvement plans or the little things they used to do as a couple to keep the spark going. Not sex, she wasn't talking about that but places they'd visit, the little rituals and sayings that made life as a couple whole. They'd all fallen by the wayside in the last few months. Shirley sniffed loudly and gulped down a sob. Someone had taken her place in his affections. She knew it and it hurt more than she cared to admit.

She pulled the first case down and threw it on the bed. Some of the cases were empty, others held old clothes that, for various reasons, either she or Harry were reluctant to throw away. Another couple held family heirlooms, photographs and baubles worn by long-dead relatives.

Of course, she had realised that Harry's unfaithfulness had been going on for some time. It had taken her a while to cotton on to it. When he started talking about liquidising assets, alarm bells rang in her mind. She knew she'd lost him, but she'd be damned if she would lose everything else. Shirley stopped and frowned.

Right at the back of the wardrobe, it seemed like a section of the rear panelling had come away. She stood on tiptoe and squinted into the darkness. A section of wood had been cut out and then replaced. She had dislodged it with her rummaging around. It was far to the rear and she almost had to haul herself up onto the top shelf to reach. At one point, she slipped and almost fell back onto the pile of cases and tat that covered the bed. She reached again, wincing at the way the wardrobe creaked under her weight. Look well if the whole lot fell on top of her.

After the fifth attempt, and just as she was about to give up, her finger snagged a leather handle and something heavy slid towards her. It was a small case made of brown leather with stitching up the sides and corners. It reminded her of a school satchel she used to have when she was a little girl. The handle was nearer now, so she dragged the case towards her, aware of the heaviness. Something about it made her shiver. Carefully, she held it to her chest and stepped down, laying the case on the bed.

She opened the lid and bit her lip. Inside, there was a fair bit of money; rolls of fifty-pound notes. There was a plain, brown cardboard box, too. But what made Shirley Thorpe pause was the handgun that lay amongst these objects. It was a revolver, she knew that much. This must have been some kind of emergency escape stash kept by Harry, just in case. A gun to fight his way out of the house if need be and money to pay his way wherever he went. She wondered where she appeared in his escape equations and the ember of anger that glowed in the pit of her stomach began to flare into flames of rage. Would he have just left her to fend for herself if the house had been attacked? She picked up the gun. It couldn't be that hard to use, surely. The box contained bullets. She'd keep looking. And God help this other woman when Shirley found what she was looking for.

*****

Blake fully intended to slip out of bed the moment the nurse turned her back. There was too much at stake; the case was at a critical stage and he didn't know if Ian Youde, his neighbour knew what had happened and would look in on Charlie, the Jack Russell terrier. At the very least, he needed to get a message home. On top of that, he had no idea if Serafina had returned in the night or if she was still with the Leekies. When the nurse had left, though, a drowsiness overcame him. Blake remembered wondering if he'd been sedated and then nothing.

It was light when he came round and DI Kath Cryer sat at the end of his bed. Blake winced as he sat up, steeling himself for Kath's hacksaw voice. "You okay, sir?" she said, leaning forward. "Alex Manikas said you took a proper bang to the head."

"I'm fine, thanks, Kath," Blake said, sounding anything but 'fine,' even to himself. "Is Alex okay?"

"A few bumps and bruises but yeah, he'll survive. We've got Thor Magnussen in custody and have charged him with the murders of Terry Ford and Nigel Clements. He didn't deny either but didn't say much. Looks like Doug Noonan is off the hook..."

Blake poured himself a cup of water and sipped at it, letting it soothe his sore throat and gummed up mouth. "What about Shirley Thorpe and Rio Pecina?"

"Vikki saw Pecina earlier but didn't get very far with him. He denies any kind of relationship with Mrs Thorpe or any collusion. I can't raise Mrs Thorpe at all. I was thinking of calling round there after I'd visited you..."

Blake leaned forward. "Great idea, Kath, find my clothes, will you? We can both go..."

"Is that wise, sir? I mean, no disrespect but you look like crap, and you've got all kinds of drips sticking out of you."

"I told you, I'm fine," Blake said. He looked down at the cannula in his arm and pulled it out, wincing a little. Then he took the monitor off his finger. "Get my clothes."

"Sir, shouldn't you at least speak to the doctor?"

"Can you see one anywhere? It's Saturday, Kath, they'll line me up for all kinds of tests, all of which will have to be done on Monday. I'll be stuck in here all weekend. Let's go. I'll be fine." He smiled at her and tried not to sway.

Kath pursed her lips and rummaged in the bedside cabinet, pulling out his crumpled trousers, jacket and shirt. "I'll draw the curtains round you, sir," she said, throwing the clothes on the bed. "Nobody needs to see through the crack in the back of your gown."

"Cheers, Kath," Blake said, grinning. The curtains swished around him and he dropped the bravado, taking a deep breath before beginning the ordeal of getting dressed. The clothes didn't have too much blood on them thankfully, but he knew he would look a sight. He gritted his teeth as he slid his aching legs into his trousers. His head swam and for a moment, it seemed like the sleeve of his shirt was trying to wriggle away from his hand. "Jeez. That hurts." Finally he pulled his jacket on. "Ouch."

The curtain swished back and Jenny Field, the nurse glared at him. "Inspector Blake, what do you think you're doing? Get back into bed at once."

"Sorry, Jenny, I've got too much to do. I can't lie around here all weekend…"

"But you can't leave."

"Unless I'm being detained under the Mental Health Act 1983, I'm entitled to walk out of here right now. Which is what I intend to do."

"But you had a serious head injury. There could be internal bleeding and all kinds of other complications we don't know about..."

"Thanks, that makes me feel better, Jenny."

"I'm just trying to be honest with you. You're better off staying here until we know the full extent of your injuries."

"Jenny, I'm very grateful for all you and your colleagues have done for me, but right now I have a murder to solve. I've got a thick skull. I'll be fine. Let's go, Kath."

CHAPTER 31

Kath was quiet for a while as they drove through the tunnel. In the end, Blake broke the silence. "Did you get any feedback from the Spanish authorities, Kath?"

"Not yet, sir," Kath said. "These things take time, I guess. I'm still not convinced by that line of the investigation, to be honest."

Blake's head throbbed and he gritted his teeth. "Well, it's good to be sceptical, Kath. Is your money still on Quinlan?"

"I think so, sir. Should we swing by your house and get you a change of clothes?"

Blake nodded. "And some painkillers, Kath."

They emerged from the tunnel into Birkenhead but it didn't seem any lighter. A heavy shroud of black cloud pressed down on them, trapping the heat and sweat and car fumes.

"There has to be a storm, soon, Kath," Blake muttered. "I think we'll all melt otherwise."

Ian Youde was waiting for them at the front door, but he wasn't alone. Peter and Heather Leeky stood beside him, their arms folded, their mouths tight. Blake groaned.

"Looks like you've got a welcome party waiting

for you, sir," Kath said, smirking.

"Just what I need," Blake muttered, clambering out of the car.

"Ian, I'm sorry I..."

"We've got Smokey and we're keeping him, Mr Blake. I don't care what your hired thug, here says or does," Heather Leeky snapped, marching forward. As soon as she got close enough to Blake to smell the sweat and blood on him, she stopped dead. "Eww, what happened to you?"

"Hired thug? What are you talking about?" Blake said, deliberately ignoring her question.

"Mr Youde here decided to try and steal Smokey back from us. Came banging on our door and shouting the odds," Peter Leeky called from the doorstep.

"She's trapped in the house, Will," Youde said. "I couldn't bear to see her pawing at the window..."

"We don't want any trouble, Mr Blake but we'll call the police in if you or Mr Youde come near our house."

Blake scowled at her. "But you can't imprison Serafina. She needs to go outside. She's a free spirit."

"It's not safe," Heather Leeky said. "If she strayed onto the dual carriageway, she wouldn't stand a chance. She's got her food and her litter tray."

"Look, this has gone far enough. I'm really busy right now, so I'm telling you this: Give me Serafina back or I'll come round there and get her myself."

"Are you threatening us?" Peter said, folding his arms, sweat trickled down his forehead.

Blake sighed. "Serafina isn't yours or mine. She isn't anyone's and she can't be imprisoned like that..."

"We're keeping Smokey safe," Heather said. "If you come near us, I'll call the police. What will your bosses think of that eh? The famous DCI Blake bullying neighbours and stealing family pets? That won't go down very well, will it?"

"Get away from my house," Blake growled, "and don't come back unless you've got Serafina with you. Rest assured, I'll have a solicitor onto this and the RSPCA if I think you've harmed her in any way."

He pulled his house keys out of his pocket and rattled them into the lock. Kath and Ian Youde followed him in. Charlie yapped and jumped up, almost bouncing to head height with joy at seeing Will.

"I'm sorry, Will. I didn't mean to make things worse. She's right, though, you look terrible. What happened?"

"Just a run-in with a critic, that's all. Don't

worry Ian, it's not your fault. I've just about had it up to here with the Leekies. That cat needs to be free."

They're right, though, sir," Kath said. "You don't want to get accused of intimidating them, that won't help matters at all."

*****

It was an email receipt that gave Shirley Thorpe the lead she wanted. After turning the house upside down, she threw herself into the nearest chair in frustration only to find herself staring into the blank screen of Harry's PC. She switched it on, praying that Harry hadn't succumbed to her regular nagging about creating an access password or PIN to make it more secure. For someone involved in clandestine and underworld business, Harry could be quite laid-back about certain types of security. He was more old-school and never really got used to technology.

He had been quite careful to delete any incriminating emails, though and most of them were dull messages from some of his even more dull golf club friends about when and where to meet up. The fact that Harry still used email rather than text to arrange his social life spoke volumes. There were a lot of them. Others were Amazon receipts, spammy sales emails for Viagra. Shirley pursed her lips. A lot of spammy emails for Viagra, actually. And other 'performance-enhancing' products.

And there, in the middle of them all was a single email for a scented candle. Harry hated them. He always went on about the smell of them making him feel sick. He hadn't bought her a scented candle in years and this email was quite recent. Unless he'd undergone some massive change of heart, then this was for someone else. It was called 'Pink Jasmine' which to Shirley's old-fashioned mind, seemed very feminine. She clicked on the link on the email and it took her to Harry's orders page. And there it was; a different delivery address: Ginebra Garcia, Savrin House, Sarn, North Wales, LL19 7ZY

Shirley printed the page off and folded it with trembling hands. Just a few more loose ends to tie up and it would all be over.

*****

By the time Blake had had a quick wash and pulled on another crumpled, but unbloodied, shirt and suit, his stomach was growling. The urge to go down the road and kick Heather Leeky's door down was almost overwhelming but he knew that Kath was right. If he got caught up in a dispute in that manner, he'd come off the worse for it. He could imagine the local headlines: Celebrity Cop in Bullying Row over Cat. No, he'd have to find another way to get her back; maybe by using a solicitor.

"Much better, sir," Kath said, handing him a stale-looking cheese sandwich and a black banana. "I hope you don't mind but I made you something to eat. There wasn't much in your fridge, but I did my best."

"Thanks, Kath, you're a star. I'll eat them as we go." With a grunt, he kneeled down to stroke Charlie and waited for the rest of the world to follow him. He still felt like he was in an elevator and his head throbbed despite the painkillers he'd taken earlier.

"Don't worry about him," Ian Youde said. "I'll take him out for a run later on."

"Thanks Ian," Blake said, scratching Charlie's ear. "I will spend a bit more time with you soon, buddy, I promise."

"Very kind, Will, but I'm not pining for you, yet," Ian said, smirking.

"I was talking to the dog," Blake muttered. "Listen, Ian, I know you mean well, but stay away from the Leekies. I'll work out a way of getting Serafina back but we have to be beyond reproach. The last thing I need is accusations of intimidation or harassment..."

Ian's face hardened. "Sorry, Will, they just drive me mad, Will. They've no idea about how to look after an animal of any kind. If your mum did take Serafina from them, there may well have been a very good reason."

"All the same, mate, don't do anything stupid, okay?"

"Okay, Will, I'm sorry for causing you all this trouble."

"It's not you, mate, it's the Leekies but we'll work it out." Blake climbed into Kath's car and they drove off. Stale or not, the sandwich and banana made him feel almost human again, although his head still throbbed.

"You okay, sir?" Kath said glancing over at him.

"Feeling a bit better, Kath. The world isn't swimming around but my head feels like it's in a vice."

"We can go back to the hospital if you…"

"No," Blake said. "Let's get to Shirley Thorpe. Her story is full of holes now and I want to know why she moved all the money from her husband's accounts so suddenly. You know, we ignored the simplest question when it came to Harry Thorpe's murder: who gains the most from his death?"

"So you think she had her husband killed when she found out he was going to leave her for this Ginebra Garcia woman?"

"It hurts to think right now, Kath but it seems the most obvious explanation. Maybe Rio Pecina was an accomplice, paid to do the job. Killing Harry Thorpe wouldn't be easy, though. He was a wily old fox and knew his own tricks best. He was guarded, too."

"But he trusted Shirley Thorpe. She could have tricked him easily. Or maybe Shirley and Rio were romantically involved, and they hired Ginebra Garcia to lure Harry into a trap."

"Either way, Shirley Thorpe has a lot of explaining to do." They fell into silence as they skirted the edge of Birkenhead, heading across the Wirral to Thorpe's farm. The rows of red-brick terraced houses gave way to larger semi-detached properties and then they were into the country lanes that criss-crossed the middle of the peninsula. The indicator plinked as Kath turned into the pristine, gravelled farmyard. Blake looked suspiciously at the black BMW that sat next to Shirley Thorpe's car.

"Looks like she has visitors, sir," Kath said.

"Judging by the number plate, they might be unwelcome," Blake replied. "KQ2, Kath ring any bells?"

"Bloody hell, it's Kyle Quinlan, sir."

CHAPTER 32

The knock on the door had startled Shirley Thorpe and snapped her out of her vengeful daydream. She hadn't heard a car pull up and wasn't expecting anyone and besides, she'd been so preoccupied with familiarising herself with the revolver that she probably wouldn't have noticed a brass band marching past.

Stuffing the weapon in her handbag, she hurried to the front door and pulled it open, fully intending to give whoever had disturbed her a mouthful. The words stuck in her throat as she stared at Laura Vexley, who stood on the doorstep, looking concerned.

"Shirley," she said. "Can I come in?"

"Well, I didn't expect you," Shirley Thorpe said, stepping back and only remembering what a mess the place was as Laura headed towards the living room. "Come in. I've been sorting out Harry's old stuff, if you're wondering why the place is upside down."

"None of my business, Shirley" Laura said, pushing aside a pile of old photographs and sitting on the sofa. "You look well." It wasn't true. Despite the carefully applied make-up and designer loungewear, Shirley Thorpe looked haggard from too little sleep and too much thinking, and she knew it.

"I look like shite warmed-up, love," Shirley said, taking an armchair opposite Laura. "You, on the other hand, look fabulous." Laura had always been slim and tall but now she looked toned from regular workouts at the gym. Her short hair was cut beautifully, and her tight jeans and skinny leather jacket set off her figure perfectly. Shirley envied her poise and self-confidence. "D'you wanna drink?"

"No thanks. I just came to offer my condolences. It can't be easy for you at the moment," Laura said. A hint of unease entered her voice. "I just wanted to make sure that you knew Kyle wasn't involved in Harry's death in any way."

"Okay," Shirley said. She looked at Laura Vexley. "Why did you need to tell me that?"

Laura shrugged. "There are rumours flying round, that's all and Harry did sell most of his assets to Kyle. I just didn't want you to get the wrong idea and maybe come after him..."

"Come after him?" Shirley laughed. "D'you think I'm capable of that?"

Laura looked levelly at Shirley Thorpe. "I've known you a long time, Shirley. You took me under your wing when Kyle first started working for Harry. You're capable of a lot of things."

"As are you, Laura. Harry never really got over you two betraying him and stealing his money."

"How about you? Did you get over it?"

Shirley Thorpe shrugged. "It was only money. To be honest, it was a bit of a slap in the face after all I'd done for you. The nights I let you stay here after Kyle had knocked you about, but I don't blame you. We fend for ourselves, don't we? No-one else is gonna help us."

"I suppose not..."

"What puzzles me is why you went back to Quinlan after getting away from him. Has he changed that much?"

Laura chewed the question over for a while. "In some ways. But I've changed. He knows he can't push me around anymore..."

"You know, I envied you when I found out you'd escaped from him, from this lifestyle. I wondered if I had the strength to get away from Harry. There's a part of me that's glad he's dead and I feel so guilty about that. But I'm free. For the first time in my life, I can do what I want, go where I want without having to consult with anyone or have some musclebound dope at my shoulder..."

"That's only natural," Laura said, keeping a poker face. "You shouldn't beat yourself up about it."

"You still haven't told me why you went back

to Kyle. What do you think you're going to do? Change him? Control him? Believe me, Laura, I thought Harry would change or that I could keep clear of his shenanigans somehow, but you can't."

"I came to offer some sympathy, Shirley. I don't need a life coach, thanks very much."

Shirley Thorpe shrugged. "Really? What's Kyle been up to then? Taking silly risks? Keeping business news to himself?"

"Nothing gets past me," Laura said, with a steely look.

"That's what you tell yourself, Laura. I think you came here because a little bit of you worries that Kyle did actually kill Harry, but he hasn't told you. You're worried that you haven't got the control you want over him and I'm telling you, you never will have."

"I'm not so naïve as to think I can control Kyle Quinlan. I know that sooner or later, he'll bring himself crashing down and I aim to be clear when that happens."

"Don't you realise, Laura? You're in too deep already. You think you've got it made but you're riding a tiger; too afraid to get down. I know because I was the same with Harry. The only difference is that Harry was a rational man while your Kyle..." She left the implication hanging between them.

Laura stood up suddenly. "Well, I just wanted to be sure that there was no bad blood between us. You were always good to me, and I'd hate for you to think that we would harm either you or Harry like this. I mean stealing money is one thing, but the way Harry died, that was just plain wrong."

More car tyres scrunched on the gravel and this time, Shirley heard them clearly. She hurried over to the window. "God, why am I so bloody popular today? It's an old friend of yours by the looks of things, Laura."

Laura jumped up and joined Shirley at the window. A black Volvo had pulled up alongside her car and she saw Blake and Kath Cryer climbing out. "Brilliant," she muttered.

"What's up? Don't you want to meet your old flame? You missed a trick, there, Laura. Will Blake would have kept you safe from Kyle..."

"I don't need keeping safe from Kyle; I can look after myself," Laura said. "Do you want me to stay? It'll put him off his line of questioning for sure."

Shirley laughed, partly amused by the joke but also by Laura's obvious discomfort despite the bravado. "No, I'll be fine. I don't know what they're after now but, knowing plod, it'll be Harry's inside leg measurement or something equally useful."

She went into the hall and opened the door before Blake could knock, Laura hot on her heels.

*****

The White Star pub in Liverpool was as busy as expected for a hot, humid Saturday afternoon. The air felt thick and close. A couple of stag parties were clogging up the pub's beautiful semi-circular bar but they'd be moving on to somewhere noisier soon enough. That would leave the regulars and a few shoppers seeking refuge from the bustle of Beatles tourists and sightseers that thronged Matthew Street just around the corner. Not that The White Star didn't have a Beatles heritage of its own, DC Alex Manikas mused as he sipped his pint and watched the punters come and go. Blakey had told him that this was a favourite meeting place for the Fab Four and where their manager used to meet up to pay them. Maybe, on some subconscious level, that was why he'd told Kinnear to meet him here.

DC Andrew Kinnear came shuffling across the tiled floor from the bar, carrying a pint of cola and a bag of crisps. "Don't look like that," he said when he caught Manikas wincing at the cola. "I'm still on duty and I'm looking after Niamh tonight while Chris goes to his mother's. Anyway, how's Blakey?"

"He'll live," Manikas said morosely. "The nurse said he might have a mild concussion but they needed to run further tests. God, it was insane,

Andy. Thor Magnussen burst into my house and attacked us."

"What was Blakey doing round at yours so late?" Kinnear said, ripping open the crisps and offering Alex some.

"I dunno. Apologising? Trying to make himself feel better? He told me about the Hilbre Island business. It was a kind of 'we've all been there' kind of talk…"

"Maybe he was trying to give you some hope. Telling you that you'll get through this with just a reprimand, and you'll be able to move on. Blakey's done all right, hasn't he?"

Manikas nodded. "I suppose so. What's the score with Magnussen?"

"He's raving still. They've taken blood samples for a drug test but it's clear he's high as a kite and totally paranoid with it. Forensics have come through pinning the Terry Ford murder and enough witnesses saw him put Bjorn Iveson in hospital, that's before CSI have finished with Clements' house. I bet he'll crop up there. He won't be coming out of custody any time soon, I wouldn't have thought."

"That's a relief," Manikas said, taking a deep swig of his beer. "Can't help feeling sorry for the poor bastard, though. I mean, he's lost his dad and it sounds as though his mum might be a prime suspect, now. Imagine having to cope with all that."

"He's got bigger problems, now, Alex. He's going to be in prison for a good while. Anyway, I wouldn't shed any tears for him. He's the bloody man-child who tried to bury you alive, remember?"

"I suppose so," Manikas said.

"Look," Kinnear said, leaning forward and lowering his voice. "You made a mistake and you're going to have to own the consequences. But I reckon with Thor Magnussen being such an unstable character and you basically saving the boss' life, you've a good chance of getting off lightly. So what are you beating yourself up for?"

"I dunno. I fucked up, didn't I?"

"So, do better next time. We all fuck up. That's what Blakey was trying to tell you. Just don't do it again."

"Yeah," Manikas muttered, staring into the golden liquid in his beer glass. "Never again."

CHAPTER 33

The sight of Laura Vexley standing behind Shirley Thorpe completely wrong-footed Blake. He stared at her and felt himself blushing like a teenager. "Mrs… I… can we…?" he stammered.

"Hello, Will, you look bloody awful," Laura said.

Blake couldn't help smiling sheepishly. "You should have seen the other guy."

"Hello Laura, fancy meeting you here," DI Kath Cryer said. It was a question rather than a statement.

"Just visiting my old friend, Shirley, here. She's had a rough time of it, lately and needs some companionship. Especially with you lot trampling all over her house and rights. No law against that is there?"

"We haven't been trampling over anything but no, there's no law against visiting a *friend*," Kath said, her emphasis suggesting something else; a different connection between Laura and Shirley, that they were both criminals' partners. *Birds of a feather flock together*.

"How are you?" Will said, quietly.

"I'm fine. Never been better. You, on the other hand, Will, need to start looking after yourself,"

Laura said. "Anyway, I'm on my way." She gave Shirley a peck on the cheek. "Call me if you need anything, okay?"

Shirley nodded and Laura pushed between Will and Kath to get to her car.

"So what do you want?" Shirley Thorpe said, folding her arms and snapping Blake's attention back to the task on hand. Laura's car started and all he could hear was the crunch of her tyres on the gravel as she drove away.

"We just need a quick word, if you don't mind, Mrs Thorpe," Kath said, filling the awkward silence left by Blake.

"I do mind. I'm busy."

"It's very important," Blake said, coming back to his senses and letting his anger at himself give his voice an edge. "To be honest, we can talk right now, or we can go down to the station. It's up to you but I just want to get to the bottom of things."

Shirley Thorpe looked him up and down as if assessing his resolve and then stepped back. "Come in then, you'll have to forgive the mess, I'm sorting stuff out."

"Looks more like you were searching for something, Mrs Thorpe," Blake said, bluntly. He watched the blood drain from her cheeks.

"What do you want to know?"

Blake sat down on the sofa without being invited. He was tired of pussyfooting around and it seemed to him that Mrs Thorpe owed them an explanation. "You told us that you didn't have any interest in your husband's businesses."

"I don't. I get an allowance and I have a couple of side-businesses of my own but they're mainly property rentals..."

"So, how come you had access to your husband's accounts and managed to syphon virtually all his money into your own account on the day he was killed?"

Shirley Thorpe looked at her fingernails. "Just because I had access to his accounts, doesn't mean I was involved in his businesses."

"You haven't answered the question, though, have you?"

"Harry told me to. He made me do it. I didn't know why. We had a row about it and he stormed off. I never saw him again."

"Have you *any* idea why he wanted you to put all your money into one account? Into *your* account? I mean, that must have seemed very odd to you. He must have trusted you completely."

"Of course he did. Look, every now and then, things got ropey with the tax man or a creditor or whatever and he'd shift some funds into my account. Fair enough, that amount of money was a bit of an eye-opener but I reckon he had his reasons."

Blake nodded. "I see. Does the name Rio Pecina mean anything to you?"

"Yes, he's my personal trainer..."

"And what's the nature of your relationship with him?"

Thunder grumbled distantly and Blake felt sweat trickling down his back.

"I told you, he's my personal trainer. He takes me out for runs, helps me work out in the gym or my studio..."

"Your personal studio, not the health club?"

"Yeah, my personal studio."

"Only when you were first asked where you were on the night your husband was murdered, you said you went to the local private health club for a Pilates class. Something Mr Pecina confirmed."

Kath chimed in. "But when it came to double check this alibi, it appears that your session with Mr Pecina was a one-to-one, and it wasn't at the health club. So we can only assume it was here." Another peal of thunder grumbled at them from somewhere high up; a threat of more violence later, perhaps.

"Why did you lie to us, Mrs Thorpe?" Blake said.

"Were you covering something up? Were you and Rio going to sail off into the sunset with your husband's cash?"

Shirley Thorpe went pale. "No. How dare you. I loved my husband and Rio is a friend. A good friend. The best kind but you wouldn't understand that with your filthy minds and bad opinion of everyone you meet."

"Your husband was having an affair with Ginebra Garcia and you found out. Admit it. You were furious. You wanted revenge on your husband, so you plotted with Rio Pecina to kill him and take his money."

"No," Shirley Thorpe shook her head. "It was nothing like that. You've got it wrong."

The next boom above them was closer and louder. Rain would fall soon, washing the heat and grime away. It was so dark inside the house, it felt like night.

Blake looked over at Kath Cryer, she gave a nod as though reading his thoughts. "Shirley Thorpe, I'm arresting you on suspicion of conspiracy to murder your husband, Harry Thorpe. You do not have to..." Blake broke off because Shirley Thorpe had picked up her handbag and produced a gun.

"Stand up," Shirley said, glancing around, as though looking for some sort of way out. "I won't let you take me away. There's too much to do. Follow me, slowly." She backed out of the living room into the hallway and, with her free hand, opened a door to a cupboard under the stairs.

Blake glanced at Kath again. She was pale and shaking. It was barely a year ago that she'd been caught in a shotgun blast that had hospitalised her. The physical injuries had healed but Blake couldn't guess what this experience might do to her mental recovery. "Shirley, this is a big mistake..."

"Get in the cupboard," Shirley Thorpe snapped, waggling the barrel of the gun.

Hands held high, Blake edged in front of Kath, to shield her should anything go wrong. Shirley Thorpe didn't strike Blake as a markswoman, but she didn't have to be in this small space.

The cupboard was dark and smelt of mothballs, old shoes and polish. Blake squashed himself in and Kath, breathing heavily, squeezed in with him. He felt ridiculous, doubled up against the slope of the staircase, leaning over Kath as though he was bowing. But he was more worried about Kath, her eyes sparkled with tears and she was gasping. "Shirley, we promise we won't follow, just don't shut us in here. My DI is having a panic attack..." The door slammed shut, leaving them in a dim twilight. Blake reached out and put a hand on Kath's shoulder as a bolt slid home outside. "It's okay, Kath, we're safe."

The front door slammed and Blake heard a car

engine grumble into life outside. Shirley Thorpe was getting away.

CHAPTER 34

Cursing as he banged his head and elbows, Blake swivelled around to face the cupboard door. “You okay, Kath?”

“I-I don’t know, sir,” Kath said, faintly. Her breathing was ragged and she sounded weak. Clearly the situation had taken her back to the last time she looked down the barrel of a gun. “I-I can’t breathe… I….”

“Listen to me, I’m going to try and kick the door down. It’s going to be loud…”

“J-just get on with it, sir,” Kath panted. “Don’t worry about me.”

Blake patted her arm. “Don’t worry. We’re safe.” He raised his foot and kicked against the edge of the door, feeling it give a little. His head swirled and his whole body complained, painfully. This was an old house and the door wasn’t made of plywood and chipboard it was solid wood, held to an oak frame by iron hinges and bolts. Blake kicked again and again in the confined space, skinning the side of his leg on the frame as the door gave. His leg ached, so he turned his shoulder against the door. The world swam and a dull pain leeched through him. He felt like he was going to throw up. A sliver of light shone in as Blake gritted his teeth and rammed himself against the door. Something cracked loudly and suddenly the top of the door leaned out, drunkenly. With one last heave, the big man hurled himself at the woodwork. Everything gave way at once sending Blake sprawling headlong onto the hard floor. The wind was punched from his body and he lay there gasping for a moment.

Kath staggered out and slumped onto the bottom step of the stairs. "Kath?" Blake said, scrambling to his feet. She had regained her breath but sat with her head in her hands, sobbing.

"I'm sorry, sir. I just couldn't…"

"Hey! I understand. Anyone would have found that traumatic, but you've got an extra reason to be freaked out. You've nothing to be sorry about. We've got to go after her…"

Kath looked up at Blake ashen faced. "I'm not sure I can, sir…"

"Don't worry, you stay here and call for backup. I'll drive out and see if I can catch-up with her."

"She's long gone, sir. We'd be better off figuring out where she's heading," Kath muttered. She still trembled and her voice still sounded thin. More thunder roared, right overhead this time and lightning dazzled him for a second.

Blake turned his head to shield his eyes and

found himself staring through the open door at the other end of the hall, where a monitor winked at him. On stand-by. Striding into Harry Thorpe's office, he jabbed the keyboard and the computer whirred into life. One click and Blake found himself staring at an email from Amazon. One scented candle to go to: Ginebra Garcia, Savrin House, Sarn, North Wales, LL19 7ZY.

"Bingo," Blake muttered. He turned and looked at Kath. She was in no fit state to jump in the car and head for this address and even if they caught up with Shirley Thorpe, there was no telling how Kath would cope. Blake steadied himself on the computer desk. He wasn't in great shape himself but the woman was armed and there was no telling what she had planned for Ginebra Garcia.

He scribbled down the address and strode back into the hall and knelt down beside Kath. "I think I know where she's going. You stay here and call for back-up. Here's the address. If the local force can be alerted all the better..."

"I can do that in the car, sir, you can't go alone. Sh- she's armed..."

"I won't take any silly risks Kath but we can't lose her. If she did kill Harry Thorpe, then she might well be going for Ginebra now and I can't stand by and let that happen."

"Then I'll come with you, sir..." Kath said but she didn't sound very convincing.

"No disrespect, Kath but you're shaking at the thought of it. It's no reflection on you but I have to get going and I don't want to put you in any more danger."

"But..."

"Call HQ. I'm going, now. Car keys, please." Kath reluctantly handed him the keys. He jumped up and hurried out into the courtyard where Kath's vehicle stood. Taking a breath, he pulled open the car door and slid in. Shirley Thorpe had a head start but Blake had the advantage of lights and sirens to clear his path. He punched the postcode into the car's satnav and accelerated across the farmyard, sending gravel spraying in all directions.

Blake was almost oblivious to the traffic and the increasingly heavy rain as he screamed down the road. Seeing Laura had totally phased him and thinking about it now, he wondered what she was doing there. Comforting an old friend seemed unlikely, although Laura would have known Shirley Thorpe, Blake supposed. In all likelihood, he thought she was there to make sure everything was square between them. There would be plenty of people convinced that Kyle Quinlan had buried Harry Thorpe alive and if Shirley believed that rumour, maybe it would make waves for Laura. That made more sense. Quinlan had sent her to make sure nothing was going to rock the boat. He grinned ruefully. How thoughtful.

Another thought struck him. Laura was just like Shirley Thorpe in many ways. Would he end up arresting her for Quinlan's death one day? Is that what the future held for them both? He shook himself, slowing as he wove through the traffic squeezing itself through the bottleneck of Heswall. His wipers slapped back and forth and thunder rumbled above him, loud and angry.

There was something Shirley Thorpe had said when he questioned her about Rio Pecina that made him think things weren't quite so straight forward. He slammed on the brakes as a tractor and trailer struggled to get out of his way. As it rolled to the side of the road, he swerved around it and accelerated towards the dual carriageway ahead. Pretty soon, he'd be on the road out to North Wales.

The phone rang and Blake put it on speaker-phone. "Sir?" DS Vikki Chinn said. "I thought you were in hospital… is Kath with you?"

"Long story Vikki, Kath should have let you know by now. I'm after Shirley Thorpe. She pulled a gun on us…"

"Oh my God, are you okay, sir?"

"Fine," Blake lied. He'd slowed right down and his head pulsed. "Did you have some news?"

"The Spanish Authorities finally got back to us.

Ginebra Garcia is certainly a person of interest in the murders of the four men in Spain. They all had their bank accounts cleared out before they died and they all had romantic attachments to Garcia. They were all drowned too. She's also the niece of a Galician Clan leader. Went missing a couple of years back. There's a warrant out for her arrest. They described her as dangerous and suggested she might even have some of her clan with her."

"Galician? Didn't our friend Rio say he was Galician?"

"He did, sir. He wasn't known to the Spanish Police at all. He might be working under an assumed name, or just hasn't been caught by them before. Want me to pull him in?"

"Worth a try but something tells me that he will have jumped ship by now. These clans, know much about them?"

"Only a brief bit of internet research, sir. Seems like they're families of fishermen who switched to smuggling tobacco at first but then their range contraband widened. They're highly organised and focus mainly on drug trafficking now with close links to Columbia. There's a fierce rivalry between these clans and they fight amongst themselves too. It might be that Harry Thorpe rubbed shoulders with them at some point and Ginebra Garcia thought he was worth shaking down."

"If she has her own mob with her, things could be tricky. Kath should have sent for back-up but can you just check? She wasn't in a good place when I left her."

"I will, sir."

Blake hung up and looked ahead. If Shirley Thorpe thought she was just tying up loose ends by hunting down Ms Garcia, then she could be walking blindly into a hornets' nest. A deadly one.

*****

Savrin House was a large building perched up in the hills above Prestatyn. A long, hedge lined lane ran up to it from the main road. It was a dark and forbidding block of grey stones with eight large square windows scowling out across the Irish Sea. It was an old house, Shirley Thorpe could tell that much from the style of the window frames, the carved, stone lintels above each one and the steps leading up to the front door. Against the black, furious sky, it looked bleak and threatening.

Nobody had ever taken pleasure in this house, of that she was sure. The land around it was contained by a bleached drystone wall and looked like it had never been cultivated or cared for. A few stray sheep nibbled at the scrubby, windswept grass.

Parked at the main gateway, she shivered, wondering what kind of woman lived in a place like this. If someone had asked her to imagine a dwelling for the kind of woman Harry would go after, it would be a modern and sleek flat in the city. Or maybe a small house full of pottery dogs and lacy curtains. Some of his 'conquests' had been girls, still living with their parents. This place spoke of a different kind of person, completely and, being honest, Shirley felt afraid. She slid her hand inside her handbag and felt the cold handle of the revolver. It was solid and gave her some kind of courage. She was going to finish this once and for all.

Thunder growled across the sea and hillside, making her flinch. Doubts assailed her once again. How did she do this? Did she just walk up to the front door and shoot the first woman she met? Or did she hold her at gunpoint and demand answers? Harry's voice echoed in her head, 'sometimes you've just got to take the bull by the horns.'

"Or the tiger by the tail," she muttered, climbing out of the car.

The concrete path up to the house was cracked and rough with stones breaking the surface. Twice, Shirley nearly went over on her heels and cursed Blake and Cryer for interrupting her when she was going to prepare for this. Had she thought about it, she would have worn some flat trainers or even walking boots instead of slipping her feet into the nearest pair of shoes which happened to be high heeled.

Her heart thumping against her ribs, she rapped on the door, slipping her hand into the handbag and feeling the gun once more. The man who opened it looked almost as surprised as she did. She had been expecting some slight bit of fluff in a negligee and slippers rather than a burly, dark stranger dressed in jeans and a leather jacket. He could easily have been one of Harry's bodyguards; he had that look about him. His Mediterranean looks also reminded Shirley of Rio Pecina except, there was a rougher edge around this man and a scar down his right cheek. She hadn't expected this woman to have a man with her. For a split second, Shirley's mind went blank. She wanted to turn and run from the house and the man. But years of managing panic situations kicked in; sudden police raids, volatile customers of Harry's turning up at the house and Harry's sudden moods had trained her well for this moment.

"Sí?" the man said, looking suspiciously at Shirley.

"I'm here to see Ms Garcia," Shirley said, gripping the handle of the gun in her bag.

The man blinked at her. "Garcia?" he said, latching onto the only word he thought he recognised.

"Wait here."

A jolt of panic shot through Shirley. If he left her on the doorstep, any advantage of surprise would be lost. She knew she was outnumbered now so she had to play the one advantage she had. "No," she said, pulling the gun from her bag and levelling it at the man. "You take me to her. Now."

The man's eyes widened, and he raised his hands. Shirley stepped into the hall and the man backed away, eyeing the gun nervously. Shirley scanned the hall. It was large with a central staircase leading up to the second storey. Like the outside of the house, the inside looked faded and bare. Several large cracks snaked their way through the plaster on the walls which had fallen away from parts of the ceiling. What little furniture there was, looked as though it had stood there for a hundred years. A grandfather clock stood silently and a coat stand looked as though it would crumble to dust if the lightest jacket was placed on it.

"Where is she?" Shirley said.

The man's eyes hardened, and Shirley could see she was going to have trouble. She raised the gun with both hands and tried to hold it firm without shaking. The man's eyes widened again and he nodded towards a side door. "After you," Shirley said. "Go."

He pushed the door open and stumbled forward.

Whilst still past its best, this room looked more homely. It had a carpet and thick curtains. Armchairs and sofas offered a comfortable retreat around a large fireplace. Shirley could imagine it would be quite snug in the winter. For one, heartbroken second, she wondered if Harry had lain on one of these sofas and watched the flames. Then she saw Ginebra Garcia.

From her sleek, black hair to her lithe, firm figure, down to her shapely legs, Ginebra was exquisitely beautiful. Shirley could see that Harry would have stood little chance resisting her. She wore a short black dress and black stilettos and sat as though she'd been waiting for Shirley.

"Ah, Mrs Thorpe," she said, in heavily accented English. "I was wondering how I was going to get to you, but it seems you have saved me the trouble. Put your gun down and I may let you live."

CHAPTER 35

The white Range Rover told Blake all he needed to know as he pulled up the lane from the main road to the grim house. Shirley Thorpe was inside and he could be too late. Ideally, he would wait until an armed response unit came but he didn't know how long that would be. He hadn't heard from Kath Cryer at all.

Leaving his car further down the lane, he crept back to the Range Rover and peered from behind it at the house. Lightning flashed and rain fell heavily now, soaking Blake by the time he reached the car. There was no cover once he ran from the gateway; if someone was looking out, they would see him. Shirley Thorpe could take pot-shots at him as he scuttled across the grass to the door.

Blake thought about all his advice to Manikas about going by the rules and using your head. But he couldn't just sit here and let Shirley Thorpe kill someone. That's if Shirley was doing the killing. In all likelihood, she'd bitten off more than she could chew and was in terrible danger. Either way, Blake wouldn't allow himself to sit huddled behind the Range Rover hoping someone would come and sort this mess out. He had to act.

Keeping low, he crept around the edge of the car and then dashed across to the wall of the house, squatting beneath one of the windows. He sat there for a few seconds, listening over his gasping breath and thumping heart to see if he had been spotted. He heard nothing apart from the occasional bleat of a sheep and the distant rumble of the A55, the main arterial road along the North Wales coast.

Taking a breath, he eased his head up and peered through the window. The glass was old and the frames rotten, allowing sound to travel as though Blake was inside. Shirley Thorpe stood, the gun shaking in her hand. A man in a leather jacket glanced between Shirley and a slender, beautiful woman whom Blake took to be Ginebra Garcia. Despite having the gun pointing at her, Ginebra acted as though she had the upper hand.

"You took all of your husband's money before I could, Mrs Thorpe," Ginebra said, folding her arms. "This is very clever of you, but now I need you to transfer the funds to *my* account as Harry promised he would..."

"Like you're in any position to tell me what to do," Shirley Thorpe sneered. "The only thing I'm going to do is make you beg for mercy, then I'm going to put a bullet in your pretty little head. Nobody screws the Thorpes over and gets away with it."

"I think Harry quite enjoyed the screwing," Ginebra said, with a cruel smile. "I made him a man again."

Shirley's hand shook even more but Blake saw rage in her face, as well as fear. "If you'd seen the number of orders for Viagra on his email account, love, I wouldn't brag too much about putting lead in his pencil."

Blake froze, uncertain what to do. At the moment, Shirley had the advantage and if he came bursting in, he might cause a bloodbath. On the other hand, he could see that Ginebra was taunting Shirley to distract her enough so that her henchman could make a grab for the gun. He looked around for some kind of weapon and his eyes rested on a large rock. It had been painted white at sometime in the last fifty years but most of it had flaked off or been coated in moss.

He looked back in time to see the door behind Shirley creak open a crack and Rio Pecina's head peep out.

"Ah, fuck it," Blake muttered, standing up. He hurled the rock through the window, taking the glass and rotten frame into the room, and then jumped in after it.

The next few moments were chaos and confusion. Shirley Thorpe fired the gun, filling the room with noise and smoke. Blake saw her hand fly up with the recoil and Ginebra fall to the ground. Rio leapt forward but the other henchman was quicker and landed a heavy punch on the side of Shirley's head. The gun flew up into the air and Blake watched in horror as the man reached out to grab it.

With a roar, Blake threw himself at the man, grabbing him around the waist and bringing him down with a crunch. Every muscle in Blake's body pulsed with pain as he rolled over and tried to get up. The henchman had landed heavily, banging his head and he was on his hands and knees blinking and groaning. The gun lay just under the window.

Blake crawled towards the gun but a shapely leg appeared between him and his goal. He looked up at Ginebra, just in time to see her other foot flash towards him. Fire and pain exploded inside Blake's head and he fell back. His last sight was Ginebra Garcia picking up the gun and giving him a perfect, white smile.

*****

The dark world lurched up and down, bringing bile to the back of Blake's throat. He opened his eyes and found himself in a small room. At first he thought he was in a caravan but the pitch and roll told him he was on a boat. He was slumped next to Shirley Thorpe, and they were linked at the wrist by Blake's own handcuffs. They sat on a cushioned bench that ran along one side of the cabin. There was a table in front of them and Blake could see a small galley area with a fridge and cooker. Oval portholes dotted the wood-panelled walls. Sitting across the table was Ginebra Garcia. A heavily-set Spaniard in jeans and a T-shirt that revealed sinew and muscle stood silent and grim, leaning against the cabin door so he didn't have to compensate for the constant movement of the boat. Thunder still bounced around outside above their heads and the shifting of the boat made Blake's stomach lurch.

This was the first chance Blake had got to really see Ginebra Garcia and, on a purely physical level, he could understand how Harry Thorpe's head had been turned. She looked as though she'd just stepped off the cover of a magazine. Her shining black hair spilled onto her shoulders, framing her perfect features, almond-shaped eyes, snub nose and full, ruby lips. Shirley Thorpe's revolver lay on the table, barrel pointed at Blake. A laptop sat next to that. Even scowling at Blake, she looked beautiful.

"You've complicated things for me, Mr Blake," she said. "Just as they were getting easier, too."

"It's Detective Chief Inspector Blake to you. You're in enough trouble already. Let us go now."

"I intend to let you go soon enough," Ginebra said, with a fleeting smile, "but first, I need Mrs Thorpe to transfer my money out of her account."

Blake raised his free hand to massage his brow and instinctively, the woman took hold of the gun. Blake noticed it was in her left hand. "I'm hardly going to try and snatch the gun in this position, am I?" Blake murmured raising the wrist that was tethered to Shirley Thorpe.

"Just in case you *are* thinking of trying to get the upper hand, somehow, I have three men on board with me and we are miles out at sea. There's no point in trying to escape."

"It was you who tied Harry Thorpe up before he died then," Blake said.

Ginebra looked confused and suspicious. "What makes you think that?"

"You're left-handed. Whoever tied the knots on poor Harry was too. You killed him and tried to take his money."

Ginebra shrugged. "Very clever, Inspector. I can see you are a good detective. I was partly successful in getting some of his wealth. He bought this yacht for me. It will get me to where I want to go." Her eyes narrowed at Shirley Thorpe. "*She* beat me to the main prize, though."

"I wasn't going to let you take everything from me, you bitch," Shirley hissed. "I was too late to stop you from killing my husband, but I could make damn sure you didn't benefit from it."

Blake looked from Ginebra back to Shirley. "You mean, you knew she was planning to kill your husband?"

"Yes, Mrs Thorpe, how *did* you know what I was planning?" Ginebra said, waving the gun in Shirley's direction.

Shirley Thorpe wasn't easily cowed, though Blake could tell she was hiding something. "I didn't know you were going to kill Harry, that's why I couldn't stop you…"

"Is that what you do?" Blake interrupted, largely to save Shirley from further interrogation. He suddenly knew what the phrase 'all at sea' really meant. If Shirley knew something or had an ace up her sleeve that might help them, he would do anything to buy her time. "Kill rich old men for money?"

"You make it sound so… crass and pedestrian, Mr Blake. It's just business. All of my victims are criminals of some kind. They are usually enemies of my family. Or rivals. Harry Thorpe is a good case; an old man who has carved out a small local business but would be a thorn in the side of anyone wanting to expand into his area."

"Your family for example…"

"Not us directly. Harry had always bought a small amount of cocaine and heroin from us to sell on the streets for many years, but he resisted requests to grow the market. My family were once simple fishermen, Mr Blake, so we sympathised with Harry's position to a degree. But our Columbian partners always want more, and they lost patience with him. They have bigger plans and have sent the right man to replace him."

"Kyle Quinlan," Blake muttered. Blake had known that Quinlan had been in the United States, but it seems his travels took him further afield. "So he's bank-rolled by Columbians."

"It's Globalisation, Mr Blake. Just like the grocer's shop in the village loses out to the big supermarket which in turn loses out to the global corporations, our world is just the same. The Galicians are merely the transporters, though, and drugs will always need smuggling."

"But you could have killed Harry Thorpe much more discreetly. Why tie him up and bury him?"

Ginebra gave a nasty smile. "What can I say, Inspector? I am an artist. I like my knots and I like to be creative when I finish off my victims."

Blake looked at her, appalled. "So you drugged Harry and then tied him up, leaving him to drown..."

"My men helped me of course, but what great artist doesn't have apprentices?"

"You're sick," Shirley Thorpe snarled. "When I get free, I'm going to make you sorry you were born."

"I doubt either you or Mr Blake will be interfering with my plans." Ginebra looked thoughtful. "Anyway, you haven't told me how you came to suspect that I was going to kill your husband, Mrs Thorpe. No doubt Rio let something slip. He's a pretty boy, isn't he? Lacking in brains, though, I would say. No matter, I will speak to him about that when we reach my uncle's boat…"

"We're being picked up?" Blake said, trying to tease as much information out of the woman as possible. Out here on the sea, he felt completely vulnerable.

Ginebra Garcia gave a sad shake of the head. "We are meeting my uncle but you, my friends, are going to have an 'unfortunate accident.' This boat will sink to the bottom of the sea and you two with it. I doubt you will ever be found. Why else did you think you were still here?"

"You could have killed us on land and carried our bodies out," Blake said, suspiciously. His head thumped and the constant movement of the boat was making him feel sick.

"What a wicked mind you have, Mr Blake," Ginebra said. "However, I need Mrs Thorpe here to move the money to my account. Besides, a death at sea is so much… cleaner… forensically speaking, don't you agree?"

A muffled grunt and a thud on the deck above them cut Blake's reply dead. Something flashed past the porthole, sending water splashing against the hull as it landed in the sea. "Don't move," Ginebra muttered, levelling the gun at Blake. "I can just as easily finish you now. Maybe I should..."

The silent bodyguard at the door, opened it and shouted out something in Spanish. A muffled reply made his eyes widen. Blake picked out the name Rio as the man relayed a message to Ginebra. She snapped an order back in Spanish and he vanished out onto the deck.

"It seems Rio has fallen overboard," Ginebra Garcia said. "My men will fish him out. Don't get any silly ideas..."

"Should we even be out in this storm?"

"My family are men of the sea, Inspector," Ginebra said. "We know what we are doing."

A crack of thunder and lightning made Blake flinch and a heavy wave thudded against the hull of the boat. More urgent shouting came through from the deck above. The words seemed indistinct, but Blake didn't speak the language. Ginebra seemed to be straining to hear what was going on. She backed away towards the door, still pointing the gun at them and opened the door a crack. Then she glanced back at them. "Wait here, while I see what's going on."

"We're hardly going to go anywhere, are we?" Blake muttered but he knew this would be their only chance.

CHAPTER 36

As soon as Ginebra Garcia left the cabin, Blake began searching around for something, anything, that might help them get free. He stood up, yanking Shirley Thorpe's handcuffed wrist into the air. "Ow! Watch it, Blake."

"We can't just sit here, we need to get free. Can you see Ginebra's bag anywhere? She might have the keys to the cuffs."

Shirley Thorpe seemed remarkably calm. "Rio has them, just sit down; it'll all be over in a moment."

"Rio has just gone overboard, Shirley."

"He's on board."

"Even if that's true, he's not on your side, you must know that now; we wouldn't be here now if it wasn't for him, would we?"

"We wouldn't be here now if you hadn't decided to launch yourself through the window back at the house and play the hero."

"What are you talking about? Rio was about to sneak up behind you and..."

Gunshots rang out on the deck above their heads, cutting Blake's words dead. Another splash followed and then hurried footsteps clattered along the side of the boat towards them. Rio Pecina burst into the cabin and turned slamming the door shut. He fumbled with the lock and it clicked into place.

Outside, Ginebra hammered on the door with the handle of the gun, whatever she was shouting in Spanish, it didn't sound friendly.

"Rio, are you okay?" Shirley said, staring at the spreading red stain on Rio's t-shirt.

Rio winced, pulling the shirt up. His side was a gory mess. "It hurts like a bitch, but I think she only winged me." He fumbled in his jeans pocket and hurried over to unfasten the cuffs.

"No," Shirley said as Rio went to free Blake. "Keep him cuffed."

"What?" Blake said, as Rio snapped the cuffs smartly down on Blake's other wrist. "Shirley what are you playing at?"

"She's right. You might try and stop us," Rio said, pushing Blake back in his seat. "Just stay there."

"Seriously? You've got an armed madwoman and two thugs out there, you're wounded, and you want to keep me cuffed?"

"I have dealt with the two 'thugs' Inspector," Rio said, through gritted teeth. "And we will see what happens to Ginebra…"

"It's what happens to us when she gets in here

that I'm concerned about," Blake snapped. "She's got a gun or did that slip your notice? And who's controlling the boat in this storm?"

"She has Harry Thorpe's revolver and has fired four of the six shots," Rio said, steadying himself against the sink in the kitchen area. He pulled a drawer open. "She cannot kill us all…"

The thumping against the door stopped, leaving a brief, eerie silence. "You can't escape," Ginebra shouted. "We are fifteen minutes away from my uncle's boat. He has many men and many guns."

"I turned the boat around, Ginebra," Rio said, trying to keep his voice even. It was clear that he was struggling with the pain and blood still oozed from his wound. Shirley was rummaging around for a first aid kit. "You are going to have to go to the cockpit and change course or stay here and guard us. You can't do both."

Ginebra didn't reply but Blake could hear her moving around the boat. "She's looking for something to break the door down. Uncuff me, Rio. You're in no fit state to stop her if she gets in here."

Shirley had found some gauze padding and a bandage and was busy binding Rio's wound. "Here, take these," she said, handing him some pain killers. "I don't know how effective they'll be."

"Thank you, Shirley," Rio said. He looked up at Blake. "I can't free you, Inspector. You would stop me from doing what I must do..."

"What? Kill Ginebra Garcia? What for?"

"My real name is Rio Ortega. My father was a man very much like Harry Thorpe and he met the same fate..."

"Ginebra."

"Si," Rio said. "We didn't find out about her until it was too late. I was living over in Columbia, attending to my father's business so I never met Miss Garcia and she never met me. It was a whirlwind romance which resulted in my father's drowning and Ginebra walking off with a huge chunk of our family's wealth. It wasn't the money, though. She destroyed my family and shamed my mother..."

"Some might say your father had a hand in that, Rio," Blake said.

"He wasn't a wide-eyed innocent, I agree but he didn't deserve to die like that. I've hunted her ever since and when she moved in on Harry Thorpe, I made contact with Shirley..."

"Why didn't you just tell Harry what was going on?"

"You knew my husband, Inspector," Shirley said. "He was a proud man. By the time Rio reached me, that woman had her claws into

Harry and he wouldn't have listened to reason."

"Besides, I had infiltrated Ginebra's little gang by then and I couldn't risk Harry Thorpe blowing my cover," Rio said.

"I tried to reason with him on the night he died," Shirley said, clenching her fists. "I tried to stop him from going out and we had a big row. He told me I was just jealous and that he was leaving me."

"But if you were in Ginebra's little gang, you would have known the plan to kill him, Rio," Blake said. "Why didn't you just stop them? Or call the police?"

"They didn't trust me enough to reveal the full plan," Rio said. "By the time I'd found out it was too late. I cannot stop the tides, Inspector. As for the police" he gave a pained look. "Let's just say that my background in the clans would not endear me to them."

"So you see, Blake," Shirley said, folding her arms, "there was nothing *going on* between us and I was only trying to protect my husband."

"I believe you, Shirley," Blake said. "Really, I do. But I don't trust him one bit. He's a criminal..."

"So am I, then," Shirley said.

"You never organised Harry's drug smuggling deals, did you, Shirley?" Blake said. "This lad spent months over in Columbia doing just that.

He's no white knight. What if he engineered this whole situation just to get to Ginebra Garcia?"

"Well that went well for him, didn't it, Blakey?" Shirley snapped. "In case you haven't noticed, we're trapped on Ginebra's boat and she's holding the gun."

"And I'm wounded," Rio said, pointing to the red stain on his shirt and jeans.

"Your plan hasn't exactly gone swimmingly, Rio but I suspect you sacrificed Harry Thorpe to worm your way into Ginebra's gang..."

"No. Why would I want to see another man die in the same way as my own father?"

"Wait," Shirley said. "Listen."

Waves hammered against the hull and the boat shook. "The engines have stopped," Rio said. "We are drifting."

Ginebra's footsteps clattered across the deck above and came to the cabin door. "I have called my uncle. He is coming to us. His boats are fast. All we have to do is wait and he will find us. It is all over."

CHAPTER 37

The whole house creaked as Heather Leeky lay in bed shivering. She hated storms at the best of times but this was a wild one. Besides, she'd heard noises and was certain that they weren't alone in the house. Her husband, Peter, lay on his back like a human hill, snoring despite the rumblings and flashes outside.

If he did a bit more around the house then maybe she wouldn't worry whenever she heard a noise at night. The window frames were rotten and anyone could break in with little effort. They'd complained to the landlord a number of times but he always fobbed them off. She'd had a go at Peter to sort out the rotten bits but he was always too busy.

"I'm too busy, right now," he'd say, not taking his eyes off the screen as he played some 'shoot 'em up' nonsense on his PlayStation. At the very least he could get dressed before he started playing in the morning.

"Peter," Heather hissed at him, digging a bony elbow into his ample backside. "Peter!"

Peter snorted and twitched awake. "Uh? What?"

"I think there's someone downstairs. It could be

that Blake come to get Smokey back or that sour little man, Youde…"

"Go back to sleep, it's just the storm," Peter mumbled, sleepily and rolled onto his side.

"I can tell the difference, Peter," Heather snapped. "Go and have a look."

"Why don't you, if you're so bothered?"

"Are you a man or what? You going to send your wife to get killed by burglars?"

"And it's okay if I get murdered? You're just after the life insurance…"

"We don't have life insurance, idiot. Just go and see, will you?"

Grumbling, Peter Leeky heaved himself out of bed, dragging the duvet away from Heather and making her squeak with indignation. "Not that scared then, eh?" he jeered.

A bump downstairs wiped the smile off his face and he nearly jumped back into the bed but Heather pushed him away. "Phone the police," she whispered.

"Oh, yeah, that'll look good if it's just the wind, won't it? Maybe I should just stay here until they've taken what they want…"

"We haven't got anything apart from that bloody cat. That's worth a fortune. If they nick that then we won't be able to sell it and all the trouble we went to will be wasted, won't it?"

"What if it *is* Blake?"

"He won't harm you and if you get a picture of him, we'll have evidence of him breaking in. Imagine what we could do with that?"

"B-but what if he's found out that we sold Smokey years ago and we're just trying it on? He might be angry..."

Heather pursed her lips and slapped him. "Just go and see. Take your phone, in case..."

"All right for you to say," Peter grumbled as he slid his sweaty feet into his shapeless slippers. Pulling on a dressing gown, he shuffled over to the bedroom door and opened it a crack.

It was pitch black apart from a little streetlight that managed to penetrate through the grimy windows and thin curtains. Something crashed to the floor down in the back room, making Peter push the door shut for a second.

"What is it?" Heather whispered.

"They're smashing the place up, I think," Peter said in a low, trembling voice. "I heard something break."

"You've got to stop them," Heather said. "We can't afford to have anything broken. Just make a noise, it'll frighten them away."

"A noise?"

"You know, talk in a deep voice as though you're a copper calling for back up and they'll leg it. It's probably kids..." Heather didn't sound very convinced by her own idea, but Peter could see that she wasn't going to just let him sit up in the bedroom.

Taking a breath, he stepped onto the landing. "Okay, whoever you are," he yelled in a gruff voice, that cracked into a falsetto squeak once too often, "I've called for backup and they'll be here in a few seconds. Don't make me use this gun..." He winced. The gun was probably a step too far but he didn't know what else to say.

Silence.

"I'm coming down. The best thing for you is to leg it before I get there..."

His heavy tread made every stair creak but, apart from the grumbling storm outside, there was no noise.

Peter's foot crunched on something, and he stopped, looking down. Shards of pottery littered the hall floor and he realised it was heather's favourite vase. He hadn't even heard that smash.

He held the phone to his ear, faking a phone call as he flicked the light on. "That's right DCI Blake, intruders. They might have run away but... you'll be here in a few seconds... right..." Peter stopped and stared at the rest of the hall in disbelief.

It looked as though the chaos outside had come roaring through the house. Wallpaper hung in tatters behind shredded curtains. Coats had been dragged from their pile on the banister and torn. A pungent smell told Peter that the dark smears on them was probably some kind of crap.

"C-cat poo," Peter muttered.

Everything that had once sat on a surface now lay on the floor in the copious puddles of what must be urine. Given that the Leekies had a lot of piles of rubbish in their house, the floor looked like a landfill site.

The back room was their living room and Peter dreaded pushing the door open to see inside. Something else crashed in there and Peter whimpered. The door creaked and he flicked on the light. The sound of movement stopped instantly and he poked his head inside.

The faux-leather armchairs looked as though someone had taken a knife to them and again the curtains hung in strips. Every item had been wiped off the shelves, tabletops and arms of the chairs. Including the ashtrays. Peter squeaked again as he smelt smouldering paper.

In the middle of this carnage crouched Serafina, her orange eyes fixed on him. Behind her, a pile of months-old pizza boxes was cheerfully giving off a spiral of grey smoke. Any moment the glowing cigarette butts would ignite the dry paper linings and old card and the place would become an inferno.

Peter stepped forward to stamp on the pizza boxes but Serafina gave a long, threatening growl and he inched back, whimpering. "Come on, Smokey... good girl... "

Her growl became a hiss and she crouched, preparing to leap. Peter gave a yelp and backed out of the room, bumping into Heather who had heard the commotion and couldn't bear the suspense.

"What's going on?" she snapped.

"It's that cat," Peter stammered, "it's burning our house down..."

"What? How can a cat burn a house down?" she said, pushing past him. "It's only a cat..."

Peter watched her enter the room. "Bloody hell!" she yelled. "Shoo! Get out of it!"

"I wouldn't..." Peter began to say but Heather's shrill scream cut him short.

Heather staggered back out of the room, with Serafina firmly clinging onto her head and biting down. Its yowl of anger chilled Peter to the bone. Still screaming, Heather bashed into him, and they both fell to the floor. Serafina kept scratching at her. Heather leapt up and managed to dislodge the cat, staggering back upstairs. With a meow of fury, Serafina charged after her.

The flames grew, sending an orange flicker

into the hall. Peter scooped up one of the coats, pulling a face as something sloppy and smelly splashed against his cheek. He supposed he should be thankful that the coat was damp but he wasn't feeling it as he threw it over the flaming cardboard and then patted it down, smothering the blaze.

Above him, the screams had stopped and for a horrible second, Peter wondered what had become of his wife. Swallowing his fear, he edged to the bottom of the stairs. "H-Heather? Are you okay, love?"

His question was replied with a rumble of thunder from outside, but no human voice called out to him. "Heather?"

Peter crept halfway up the stairs. "Heather?"

Another rumble of thunder and the lights went out. At the same time a flash of lightning illuminated the hall and Peter stared in horror at the image of Serafina, face twisted in a snarl, her muzzle bloodied, leaping from the banister rail above him.

The big cat hit him straight in the face, her rear paws paddling at his face and shredding his cheek. He reached up to grab the cat and suddenly, he felt weightless as he fell back down the stairs. His head cracked on the hall floor. His last sight was the growing snake of smoke crawling across the ceiling from the back room. He hadn't put the fire out properly.

CHAPTER 38

Rio moved close to the door and called through to Ginebra Garcia. "The storm has worsened. We can't drift, we'll be swamped."

"Give yourselves up then and I can steer the boat. My uncle will be here in a while. We might survive until then."

"No! You better call your uncle off, Ginebra," he said, his voice ragged with pain. "Or I'll kill the Thorpe woman and then you'll have no way of getting at her money."

"I'm sure she's happy about that idea, Rio," Ginebra said but she sounded uncertain. "Besides, I doubt that Inspector Blake would let you." The boat shook under another wave.

"Blake is handcuffed. He can't stop me. Believe me, I will do anything to stop you. I'm bleeding out. Nothing to lose."

"You're bluffing."

"You killed my father, Uxio Ortega. I swore I would avenge him. If I can't do that then I will do the next best thing."

"Uxio? Y-you are Uxio's son?"

"Ginebra, please, help me," Shirley said. Blake wasn't sure if she was genuinely scared but it sounded convincing. “We can do some kind of deal. Just don’t let him hurt me…”

“Very well,” Ginebra said. The gun went off again and Rio staggered back. Blake could see a neat hole punch in the thin wall where Rio had stood. The bullet had missed him but had sent splinters of panelling flying into his face. He staggered back, holding his eye. At the same time, the door crashed open and Ginebra appeared brandishing a fire extinguisher that she had used as a ram. She hurled it at Shirley Thorpe who screamed and threw herself over the table, landing on top of Blake.

Rio lurched towards her, a knife from the kitchen drawer in his hand. She fired straight into him and he fell forward, slamming the blade deep into her swan-like neck. Blood streamed through her fingers as she struggled to staunch it. The gun fell from her hand and she fell back, staring at Blake and Shirley with dying eyes. She slumped down the side of the cabin, the knife poking out obscenely.

“Quickly, get the first aid kit,” Blake snapped, bringing Shirley Thorpe to her senses. She jumped up and grabbed it, kneeling at Ginebra’s side.

“I think she’s dead,” Shirley whispered, her hands hovering gingerly over the knife. “I don’t know what to do…”

"What about Rio?"

Shirley Thorpe twisted round and laid a hand on Rio's outstretched arm. He stared at her, eyes vacant and his t-shirt completely soaked in blood from a second wound. She bit her lip. "He's dead too." Tears glistened in her eyes. "He wouldn't have killed me really, would he? We were working together."

"I don't know, Shirley it seems to me like he was hell-bent on revenge and would have pushed you under a bus to get it. Either way, you have to get the keys from his pocket and unlock me."

Shirley Thorpe scowled at Blake. "So you can arrest me for all of this? No chance."

The boat shuddered again and thunder rumbled outside.

"We don't have time to argue," Blake said. "We need to figure out how to get this boat moving before it gets torn apart by the storm or before Ginebra's uncle arrives. If you think you can do that on your own, fine, get us away from here. Otherwise get these cuffs off me and we can work together."

Shirley glanced at the bodies. "But I'm in trouble, aren't I? I pulled a gun on you, ran away, resisted arrest, that's what you call it, isn't it?"

"Yeah, you did. You had a firearm, too but I don't think anyone's going to throw the book at you under the circumstances. Ginebra's uncle, on the other hand, will more than likely just kill us when he sees this mess. We need to get away."

Seawater splashed down through the door and the boat tilted, sending Shirley, staggering towards Blake. Grimacing, she fell to her knees and slid her hand into Rio's jeans pocket, pulling out the keys. A moment later, Blake was free.

"Come with me," Blake muttered, leading Shirley out of the bloody cabin and up on deck. Blake had only experienced storms from the relative safety of dry land. He used to love watching waves crash against New Brighton Prom, but this was like nothing he'd ever experienced. For a moment, he thought they were on a hillside that towered above them before he realised it was a wave. The boat seemed to ride up the slope and Blake only just managed to roll back into the cabin, dragging Shirley with him as the wave hit.

Cold water rained down on them as they fell. Blake's body burned with pain as he landed on the floor of the cabin. The two bodies had slid to the side and been forced up onto the seats. They lay there as though dozing.

"We've got to get to the wheel and take control of this boat," Blake panted and dragged himself back out of the cabin. Shirley gripped his jacket as he dragged himself along the deck towards an upper cabin on the deck. The deck twisted and bucked and Blake lost his footing, slithering towards the edge and banging up against the side. He was dressed for the office, not to keep upright on a sodden, slippery deck. The craft threw them the other way and Blake found himself staggering towards the cockpit of the boat. They both fell inside, soaked and freezing. Even then, the bow of the boat rose up, making Blake's stomach lurch. A bang like a gunshot rattled his teeth as the craft hit the water again.

Blake stared at the controls. The wheel looked much like that of a car but it was surrounded by a confusing array of dials and switches. "Jeez," he muttered. They were being thrown around like a cork. Lightning flashed, making Blake feel small and insignificant. Shirley Thorpe pushed him out of the way and jumped behind the wheel.

"That's the throttle," Shirley Thorpe shouted over the roar of the storm. She pointed at a handle to the side of the wheel. "I've been on a few of these with Harry in my time. The keys are in the ignition. We just start it like a car and ease the throttle forward."

"I see," Blake muttered. It was twilight now and he was sure he could see a faint light on the horizon. Ginebra's uncle was coming. If he caught them, he would show them no mercy, he was certain.

"Is that land over there?" Shirley shouted,

pointing to Blake's right. He glimpsed a row of distant lights briefly before they were masked by another mountainous wave.

"Let's find out," Blake yelled back. "At least we'll be away here. Wherever here is." He felt totally lost. In an alien element. He knew nothing about boats or the sea. Shirley pushed the throttle hard and the engine roared only to sputter and die. "You stalled it!"

"Okay! Just calm yourself," Shirley yelled back. She turned the key again and eased the throttle forward more gently. The boat throbbed with power but trying to turn her towards the coast seemed impossible. The craft had a mind of its own. Another wave hit them side-on and Blake was flung against the side of the cockpit, Shirley thrown out her seat and falling heavily against him. Blake groaned. It felt like a giant was shaking the boat back and forth. Waves punched the hull and deck.

The whole world flipped over, and, for a moment, Blake was convinced they'd capsized. Shirley groaned, a smudge of blood on her temple. Dragging the wheel down, Blake pulled himself into the seat and, slowly they turned around. Lightning lit up the sea again and Blake's mouth went dry at the sight of the mountainous waves and, not far away, another boat ploughing through the water as though there wasn't a storm.

"Oh my God," Shirley muttered, pulling herself up from the deck. "They're coming straight for us."

Pushing the throttle forward, Blake wrestled with the wheel, sending the boat back towards the row of lights in the distance and what Blake assumed was land. There was nothing else he could do but run.

Wincing at every thump and crash, Blake pushed the boat on but their pursuers were closing on them, bouncing over the water like a dolphin. Blake looked back and couldn't help admiring their skill. Then he was climbing a hill of water, skidding off to the side as he struggled to keep any semblance of control. Suddenly they were airborne.

"Hold on!" Blake managed to shout before they smacked back onto water as hard as concrete. Shirley screamed and gripped onto a handrail. Something cracked below them, and Blake prayed they hadn't been holed. He risked a backwards glance and saw that the Galicians had fallen back. Blake's triumphant grin faded as he turned back and saw another wall of seawater rising up in front of him.

Water crashed down onto the bow of the boat, sending some kind of hatch cover frisbeeing into the cockpit window. Glass and seawater filled the small cabin and Blake clung onto the wheel.

Shirley Thorpe gave a gargling screech and disappeared.

"Shirley!" Blake yelled, twisting in his seat. More water roared through the shattered window and Blake suddenly found himself hurtling to the back of the small cabin and out. His head clipped the doorframe, and the world became a maelstrom of boiling blackness.

CHAPTER 39

Gulls screamed and somewhere in the distance, sirens joined in. Blake opened his eyes a crack, the blinding sunlight making his head pulse. Somewhere the tide beat a steady, calming rhythm. His mouth felt salty and gritty and something poked painfully into his back. Slowly the world swam into focus and Blake remembered what had happened.

He lay in the cockpit of the boat, only it was on its side. Groaning he pulled himself upright, struggling like an overturned turtle. After the third attempt, he managed to pull himself into a sitting position. The windows of the cockpit had lost their glass and there was a huge hole in the forward deck. Rope, cushions, paper and various plastic packets lay scattered all over the small space, half buried in wet sand.

"Here! Over here!" Shirley Thorpe yelled outside.

"Shirley!" Blake yelled scrambling out of the cabin and nearly falling down the almost vertical deck. He couldn't see her at first. Above him, she perched on the port side of the hull and waved to someone. Coated in sand, she looked like some kind of wild animal, her hair an explosion of curls. She stared at Blake, wide-eyed and excited.

"It's a hover craft! They've come for us!" she yelled.

"Where are we?" Blake said, dragging himself up beside her. Shirley didn't have to say anything as he stared at the white finger of New Brighton Lighthouse pointed skyward before him, the high stone walls of Fort Perch Rock behind it. "Jeez," he muttered, looking around. "We must have been washed up on the sandbanks..."

"I don't remember much about it," Shirley said, watching the RNLI hovercraft drift towards them. "There was that big wave and all that glass and then wave after wave. I just clung on as best as I could."

"Same here," Blake said, quietly. "I don't know what happened to Ginebra's uncle."

Shirley shrugged. "No. Don't care, either. We're safe." She looked round at Blake. "Are you going to arrest me?"

"Not right away," Blake said, wincing. "I think we both need some first aid and a shower at the very least."

"Cos I don't care," she said. "I know I threatened you with a gun and I'm happy to pay the price. I'm just glad to be alive."

Blake looked at her and wondered what she'd think when she found out that in all probability, her son was going to prison for a double murder. "Let's get off this boat before we make any decisions, Shirley."

*****

A succession of visitors sat by Blake's hospital bed during his brief stay. The medics had insisted that he stay in for observation once he'd described what had happened and, this time, Blake didn't object.

DI Kath Cryer had looked sheepish and pale when she appeared at the foot of his bed. "God, boss, what were you thinking of? If I'd known you were going sailing, I wouldn't have let you leave that cupboard under the stairs."

"You okay, Kath?" Blake said, smiling; he could see bravado a mile off.

"Yeah, I think so. I've been fine for months. I thought I'd got over it but when I saw that gun, I just froze..."

"Probably a wise thing to do. Shirley Thorpe wasn't used to handling guns which, in some ways, made her more dangerous. That thing could have gone off without her meaning it to. It'll be fine. What about some counselling? Do you think that'll help?"

"I think it will, sir, yeah. But maybe I need to think further ahead. I dunno. The job doesn't get any easier and I'm wondering if a change of role might help…"

"Jeez, Kath, I'd hate to see you leave. You're one of the best. What would you do instead?"

Kath shrugged. "Dunno, teaching, maybe…"

"Teaching?" Blake said, staring at her. "What were you thinking of teaching?"

"Kids, probably," Kath said, smirking.

"Right. Nobody would mess about in your class, that's for sure," Blake said. "Don't do anything rash. Let's have a proper talk about this, Kath. Seriously, you're a great inspector. You could go far and we'd be all the worse for not having you on the team."

"Cheers, boss. I'll think on it for now. So, Shirley Thorpe didn't kill her husband, after all."

"No," Blake said, with a sigh. "It looks like she and Rio Pecina were trying to stop Ginebra Garcia and her gang from doing it but they were too late. They managed to keep Harry's wealth out of Ginebra's grasp but that's about it. Rio's father had been a previous victim and he was trying to get back at Ginebra. Look at the mess it made, though; two people dead and a young man in prison. Lives ruined." He shook his head. "I suppose at the very least, we know that Kyle Quinlan's backers are Columbian. Perhaps that might open up some way of stopping him."

"Yeah. Listen I'm sorry I kept banging on about

Quinlan when it was plain to you that he wasn't involved, boss..."

"You could have been right. In a sense, he was on the side-lines. He must have known what was going on to some extent. Anyway, no time for sorrow, as my namesake once said."

"Sir?"

"William Blake. The busy bee has no time for sorrow. If we aren't busy bees, then I don't know who is, Kath."

"I can't argue with that," Kath said, pulling her bag onto her shoulder as she stood up to go. "You take care, boss. I'll see you soon, yeah?"

Blake had watched her leave and wondered to himself whether she wasn't right. The job veered between mind-numbingly dull and positively life-threatening. That couldn't be healthy for anyone. Maybe he should consider giving it all up, too. And do what? Grow roses and play snooker like Ian Youde? He couldn't see himself doing that. He couldn't see himself doing anything other than what he did now.

*****

A small picket line awaited Blake at his gateway. Ian Youde stood, looking grim next to Mr and Mrs Leeky who stared, equally stony-faced as Blake pulled up in his car. For a moment, he wondered just how long they had been standing there. Ian had been looking after Charlie and had popped into hospital with fresh clothes, so Blake had been kept up to date with any progress on the Seraphina story. There hadn't been any news, so Blake was surprised to see the Leekies at his gate.

They stepped aside as he pulled into his drive and Blake got out of the car. He frowned as he looked at his front room window or rather the large Persian cat glaring at him through it.

"What's going on? Serafina decided she didn't want to stay locked up?" he said, climbing out of the car.

"W-we just came round to say you can keep her," Peter Leeky said, taking a step forward. "She's psychopathic, that cat…"

Blake squinted at Peter's face. "You seem to have scratches on your forehead and cheeks…"

"Cat trouble," Peter said, simply. He looked pale and a neck brace kept his chin high. Blake sniffed. There was a smell of smoke about him, too.

"But I thought she was your long-lost Smokey," Blake said, allowing himself an amused grin.

"That cat isn't our Smokey," Heather Leeky said, a haunted look on her face, "she's a bloody demon…" Blake noticed tell-tale crisscross lines across her face too. "She smashed and tore all our best stuff. She even set fire to the house…"

"Really?" Blake said, staring incredulously at Heather Leeky. "You must have really pissed her off."

"We tried our best to make her feel welcome, Mr Blake," Peter said. "We didn't mistreat her, but she went wild on us." His voice dropped. "I honestly thought we were going to die."

"She does know her mind, Mr Leeky," Blake said, glancing over at the cat narrowing her eyes at Leeky from the front room window. "I did warn you that she didn't belong to anyone. She won't be owned, that one."

"Well I hope we can draw a line under all this... nonsense," Ian Youde said. "And you two can bugger off and let Inspector Blake get into his house. He's been in hospital, you know."

"No, it's fine, Ian," Blake said, turning to Heather Leeky with a wicked grin. "Maybe we could do a cat share. You know, I have her half the week and you..."

"No!" Heather yelped, backing away. "You can have her and... and ... if we ever see her round our house again, we'll call the police..."

"And I'll be round right away," Blake said, smiling.

"If both of you just stay away, that'll suit us fine," Peter Leeky said, grabbing his wife's elbow. "Come on, let's get away from here before that cat gets out again."

Blake and Ian watched the couple stagger down the road.

"Well that ended better than I expected," Ian muttered, scratching his head.

"Do you really think she managed to set fire to their house?" Blake said. "I mean, how does a cat do that?"

"Nothing you could tell me about Serafina would surprise me, Will."

"Cup of tea, Ian?" Blake said.

"Yeah, but you can go in first. I don't know what kind of mood that cat of yours is in."

"She's not my cat, Ian, she's her own cat."

The End

About the Author

Jon Mayhew lives on the Wirral with his family and has done all his life. A teacher for many years, he enjoys traditional music and plays regularly in ceilidh bands and sessions. Jon is also an award-winning author. His dark children's books are published by Bloomsbury.

Find out more at www.jemayhew.blogspot.com

Find JE Mayhew on Facebook and twitter.

To keep in touch with Jon and get news about upcoming publications, what he had for dinner last night, and how his dogs and chickens are faring go to https://dl.bookfunnel.com/gs5oc6n68k There is a free prequel novella waiting for you there, too…

Printed in Great Britain
by Amazon

17165617R00201